THE SHAKA REED SERIES

BOOK ONE

JENNIFER SCHULTZ

Hearts of Prey
Second Edition

For more information contact jenniferschultzbooks@yahoo.com.

Cover design by 100Covers.com
Formatting by 100Covers.com

First Printing 2020.
Second Printing 2023

For more information on the author and other upcoming books visit www.jenniferschultzbooks.com

ACKNOWLEDGMENTS

Thank you to Brook and Sue McPherson for being excited to be part of this from the start. Your feedback was priceless!

Thank you to my mom for going through my original manuscript with a fine-tooth comb and correcting my many spelling and grammatical errors.

Thank you to my dad for being one of my first readers and for giving me realistic advice. As with all things, I may not heed every piece of advice I receive, but I do appreciate them all.

If it hadn't been for joining a writers' group, I don't know that I would have taken myself seriously enough to finish this novel or felt capable of publishing it. As much as I like to think of writing as a solitary endeavor, it took hearing the processes and success stories of others to complete this book. As this is the second edition of Hearts of Prey, I'd like to thank those who offered me constructive reviews after the novels release. My decision to rewrite this novel two years after its publication came after finding myself excited to promote my second book, House of Stars, yet hesitant to promote Hearts of Prey. Being my first novel, I was so excited to release Hearts of Prey that I rushed through the editing phase. Because of this, it still contained some very noticeable grammatical errors and a bit of awkward dialogue. Now that it has received some overdue TLC, I hope it is a more fluid and enjoyable read. Through this experience I learned a valuable lesson for a first-time novelist: don't skimp on any part of the writing process, even the tedious editing part!

And finally, as always, thank you to the reader for sharing this experience with me.

Hearts of Prey

CHAPTER ONE

SHAKA WOKE UP. IT WAS LIGHT OUT, AND SHE WAS ALONE. HER clothes were gone. She remembered where she'd left them. She remembered everything.

The evening had started at an art show for her friend Rena, who unlike Shaka, thrived in the spotlight. Rena had always drawn her light from others, and Shaka had admired her ability to engage with anyone she met since they were children. Now they were both twenty-two years old and becoming very different people, but despite their differences, they had always fit together like two pieces of a puzzle.

Rena was more than just a social butterfly though, and it showed in her art, which Shaka had always found quietly stunning. The event had been held in a new gallery in their home city of Duluth, Minnesota. It was a small space, but stylish. There was a tiny stage in the corner of the room, where a woman in a soft pink dress played the violin, swaying back and forth as her bow slid across the strings. Waiters in black jackets circulated through the room, offering champagne flutes and hors d'oeuvres to the guests. Shaka sipped from one as she examined Rena's work. A painting of an old oak tree muted by rain hung next to a Flamenco dancer in a dress of cascading red waves. On another wall, a painting of a smiling child holding a balloon in a forest hung next to a portrait of a fat king wearing a crown of broken glass and teeth.

Rena silently snuck up behind Shaka.

"What do you think?"

Shaka jumped, almost spilling her champagne. She looked over her shoulder at Rena and smiled. "I think they're great!" she said. "I really like this one." She pointed to the painting of the child in the forest.

"I figured you would, as woodsy as you are."

"Lots of people here. You must be a big deal!"

"Please. Half of them are Salem's employees. He forced them to come."

"You're being modest. That's unlike you," Shaka teased. Rena shrugged and gave her a smile.

From across the room, they could hear Rena's boyfriend, Salem. His voice carried above the others.

"This piece was in *Minnesota Monthly Magazine* in

April," he said proudly. "Take a closer look. Notice the detail in the cityscape."

Rena and Shaka turned toward each other and giggled. If there was anyone more outgoing than Rena, it was Salem. Though he was tall and wide, and she was short and petite, they shared the same dark hair and eyes. They almost looked like they could be related, though they came from very different places. Salem had moved to Duluth from Chicago with his family as a child. His father was a lawyer in the mining industry, and Salem had followed closely in his footsteps.

As he was ten years Rena's senior, about the time he'd starting his undergrad at UMD, Rena had found herself being ushered into the foster care system.

She had been born on the Fond du Lac reservation west of Duluth. She grew up living with her mother and father and an ever-changing assortment of her parents' friends in a single-wide trailer in the woods. She remembered her mother fawning over her when she was very young, but as time passed, she became more of an afterthought, an inconvenience. Her mother was preoccupied with trying to curb her father's violent temper, which got notably worse in proportion to the amount of whiskey he'd drunk that day.

The winter Rena had turned seven, her father died. He had passed out in a snowbank, a bottle of whiskey still in his hand,

and froze to death. Rena was always a little ashamed that she wasn't more upset by it, but the truth was, he had been a mean drunk, and his absence was a relief.

Her mother, finally free from the terror of her father's drunken rampages, quickly took up with another man and spent less and less time at home. Rena fended for herself, sometimes for weeks at a time, living off dry cereal and peanut butter sandwiches, until the lady from social services showed up and took her away. That was the last time she'd been to the reservation. She was placed in foster care when she was just eight years old. That was how she came to live in Duluth, and she was frightened and angry as her new life began. Shaka was the first friend she'd made, and they had been nearly inseparable ever since.

Now their lives were very different. Since Rena had started dating Salem, she'd lost interest in shooting pool on the west side of town like they used to, but she still always made time for Shaka.

Salem's salary allowed Rena to follow her dream of becoming a full-time artist. Shaka was sometimes jealous of her friend's open schedule, but then, she didn't really have a dream of her own to fulfill. Her deepest desire was to always be near the wilderness, if not within it, and she did that. She paid her own way by cooking at a local grille, and she enjoyed it. Her life wasn't extravagant, but it was comfortable, and it was hers alone.

The gallery party lasted for two hours, and as the last of the guests were filtering out the door, Shaka squeezed Rena's hand. "I really am thrilled for you, Rena. These are your people. This is happening."

Rena's eyes wandered around the room and finally settled on Shaka's face.

"Maybe it is," she said, smiling, "but you are my people."

Shaka leaned in and hugged her before turning to the door and filtering out with the others. She felt a pang of guilt as she left. There were things about her that even Rena didn't know.

CHAPTER TWO

SHAKA HAD GROWN UP SURROUNDED BY ADULTS, AND THIS made her a serious child. She had few friends, and it never occurred to her that there was anything wrong with that. She was only interested in one person anyway: her grandfather Arnold. He was her father's father, but the two men couldn't have been more different. Her father always looked at her with fear in his eyes. She didn't see it until she was older, but once she noticed, she couldn't stop seeing it. Yet every time her father pushed her away, her grandfather was there to pull her in. Whether he was teaching her the names of the plants and animals of the forest or letting her win at checkers, it was he who single-handedly taught her what a family was.

Her grandmother had died before she was born, and her mother had left when Shaka was eleven. Shaka always knew there was a separate code of behavior for women, but with no one to teach it to her, she concluded that it couldn't have been that important anyway. By the time she was a teenager, it was too late for anyone to convince her that things like flirting, styling your hair, or keeping up with fashion trends mattered. While those things were second nature to Rena, Shaka rarely took any interest in them. It was too much work to bother with every day, and she never really understood what the payoff was.

The only time they had ever come close to talking about it was in tenth-grade math class. Rena was braiding Shaka's hair, and when Shaka reached back to feel the braid, Rena grabbed her wrist. A breeze blew through the room, shuffling papers across the desks. The other students looked around the room and murmured, excited by the mysterious disruption. Shaka turned and looked quietly at Rena, whose eyes were closed. Her face twisted for a moment, then calmed as the breeze died. She opened her eyes and whispered one word to Shaka: "Wolf." Shaka pulled her hand away and looked at her friend with both bewilderment and anger.

"I'm sorry," Rena said quickly.

Shaka didn't say anything but rubbed her wrist where Rena had touched her. She felt like someone had pulled back a curtain inside of her. It felt like a violation.

"I'm sorry," Rena repeated.

Shaka didn't quite understand what had happened. It was like Rena had looked inside her mind. She wondered what she had seen. Was it just a flash? Was it more than that? She was afraid to ask her. Once it was spoken, there would be no taking it back. She turned from Rena and glared straight ahead at the chalkboard.

"I'm sorry, Shaka. I didn't see anything," Rena added.

Shaka didn't hear her though. Her mind raced with questions. Instilled in her was the rule that the family secret was more important than any relationship. That included her friendship with Rena. Whether or not Rena had some kind of psychic power was an afterthought, something Shaka would wonder about later.

"Shaka," Rena whispered again.

"Girls!" their teacher yelled. "Attention up here!"

Rena fell quiet, and not another word was spoken between them that day. When class ended, Shaka hurried out of the room and didn't look back. The next day, she feigned an upset stomach and asked her father to let her stay home. His response was, "What ever you want to do is fine," and he left for work. She was used to his detachment by then. She simply went back to her room and read a book in bed, as if she really were sick. She wanted to tell her grandfather. Maybe he knew about people like Rena; maybe he had some way of finding out what she knew. He would know if they had to be worried. He always had a plan.

As she reached for the phone to call him, she remembered it was Wednesday morning, and he volunteered at the library on Wednesdays. As she pulled her hand back, it occurred to her that maybe his plan would be for her to stop spending time with Rena. If that happened, she wouldn't have any friends. She laced her fingers together as she thought about that. If she didn't have Rena, she would only have her grandfather. She treasured him, but she couldn't make fun of the cute attendant at the movie theater with him, or dance to her favorite songs with him. If she lost Rena, who would make her laugh during gym class, or help her cheat on her biology exam? There would be no one.

She realized in that moment that she couldn't afford to lose Rena's friendship— not over this. She knew that meant she couldn't risk telling her grandfather. For the first time, she would keep something from him. It scared her a little, but she knew that some secrets were made to protect people, and with this one, she was protecting herself. She wouldn't speak about it to anyone. She told herself Rena would forget whatever she had seen, and she would forget that Rena had ever touched her, and it would all go back to the way it was before.

When she returned to school the following day, Rena was waiting for her by her locker.

"Hi," Shaka said.

Rena looked at her apprehensively. "Are you mad at me?"

"Nope," Shaka replied simply.

"I don't know anything anyway," Rena added.

"I know you don't know anything," Shaka said with a grin— and just like that, the tension between them was broken. They instantly fell into their old patterns of chatter and suspicious glances at their peers. Shaka knew she had made the right choice in letting the whole thing blow over, and from that day on, they both had an unspoken agreement not to ask about, or steal, each other's secrets.

Despite having so few people in her life, Shaka was usually happy. The people she did have, she cherished, and she cherished her solitude too. It was only in recent years that she'd come to know the slow burn of loneliness. After her grandfather had vanished into the woods, Shaka found a painfully silent hole in her life. For months she searched for him, sometimes as a girl and sometimes as a wolf, but she never found a trace. Eventually, she'd accepted that maybe he didn't want to be found. He was getting on in years, and like her, he'd always valued solitude.

She had dulled the pang of abandonment by leaning on Rena. She told herself that was enough. But as Rena's life filled up more and more with long days in the art studio and cocktail parties with Salem, Shaka wondered if it had been wise to only ever trust two people.

CHAPTER THREE

OUTSIDE IT WAS DARK, AND SHAKA WANTED TO WASH THE party off her skin. She'd only had two flutes of champagne, but her head was already throbbing. She walked a calm, straight line down 9th Street and turned right, then followed Connor Avenue nearly three miles until it dead ended in the park. The park soon gave way to a forest, which grew wild all the way to Canada. She always felt a thrill when she walked through the gates. She stood for a moment and took a deep breath of the cool night air, then kicked off her shoes and ran barefoot down the trail. A wayward branch caught her dress and ripped it along one side, but she didn't slow down. Another branch whipped her skin, and a welt quickly rose on her arm, but she didn't stop until she reached the small lake in the woods.

When she arrived, she found it quiet and deserted, as it

usually was. She slipped out of her ruined dress and stood naked in the moonlight, letting the pale rays turn her skin marble white for a moment, then she walked into the lake until the dark water encircled her waist. She dove under and swam to the bottom. It was a shallow lake, but still cold down there. That didn't bother her. Her body was changing, and this was the best place for it: under the soft pressure of the water. Her joints grew loose as her bones shifted and changed shape. Her skin thickened and sprouted coarse hair. Her face narrowed, and her teeth grew into a fierce grin of white daggers. Finally, her mind changed. That was when she knew the transformation was complete: when longing was replaced by instinct, and the business of survival grew bigger than the business of happiness.

She kicked back up to the surface with four thin legs and swam to shore, where she shook the water from her coat and walked purposefully into the woods. In the trees, her only audience was a lone owl who curiously turned his head from side to side as he watched the gray wolf disappear into the dark forest.

CHAPTER FOUR

WHEN SHE WOKE UP, SHE WAS AGAIN A WOMAN.

She found herself lying on a soft bed of moss on an island in a state forest, and she remembered everything. She used to have trouble remembering, but her ability had evolved over the years. She had run north for many miles, then slowed to a trot when the moon was high. She'd heard some campers and stopped to watch them: a group of men telling hunting stories around the fire. They didn't interest her for long. She silently snuck away from them and swam to the familiar island with the rock jutting up on the west end. This was one of her favorite places, a spot her grandfather had shown her. She trotted along the zigzag path that took her over the back of the island, and when she reached the rock on the west end, she paused to sniff the air. She could still smell their campfire, hot dogs, and beer, as well as the water that surrounded her, the pine needles and dirt. Deep inside of her, the urge to howl swelled. She longed to join her call with the brisk night air, and to give the hunters pause.

She threw her head back and let her howl ring out across the water. The hunters stopped talking and listened.

Sometimes, such hunters would grab their guns and try to find her. Of course, she was always gone by the time they reached her howling perch. She missed the days when her grandfather would howl with her. They would sometimes play games with the campers: one would lure them from camp, while the other would steal their food. But these hunters just stayed close to the fire and listened. She gave them another howl and roamed back down the zigzag trail.

Whenever she changed into a wolf, she missed her grandfather terribly. He was the only one like her that she had ever known, and when they were wolves together, they could understand each other with only a look. She had always hated to return to the human world, but he wouldn't let her stay a wolf for long. He reminded her that she was as much a human being as she was a wolf, and she couldn't deny either part of herself. She knew he was right and that arguing was useless—though as he'd aged, he had changed back to a man less and less. Eventually, Shaka would only find him when she was a wolf ... and then one day, she couldn't find him at all. That summer, when she'd searched for him every night, she lived with the fear that she'd come across his body, or a sign that he'd been killed by a hunter. But she never did. He had just vanished. Wherever he was, she didn't begrudge him his absence; she just missed him. There was no one else in the world who understood her so completely.

After she woke that morning on the island, she stayed hunkered down in case the campers were still close by, or a fisherman was out on the lake. She scanned the shores, but saw no one. The lake was perfectly still, and the only sounds were those of lapping water and the occasional loon. She stood up and let the sunlight cascade over her body, just as the moonlight had done the night before. It warmed her. Around her, almost everything was either blue or green, and she thought of the way the Earth looks from space. Sometimes after coming back, she still thought in images and acted on impulses. She took a deep breath and ran toward the cliff.

When she reached the edge, she leapt far and high, then closed her arms and legs, making her body into an arrow that pointed to the water. She felt like a white swan as she dove into the crystal water, shattering it into a thousand tiny beads. She went down, down, down under the surface, and started to change. She began paddling back up midway through the transition, her body both beautiful and monstrous. Then, she emerged some fifty feet from where she had plunged into the water, snout first, kicking her way to the south shore and beginning her journey back to the city.

CHAPTER FIVE

SHE SLEPT ALL DAY, WOKE UP TO EAT DINNER, THEN SLEPT ALL night. Though she was a woman again, her body still needed to rest from the things she had done as a wolf.

The next morning, her alarm woke her at 7:00 a.m. Her shift at the grille started in an hour. She sipped black coffee and watched the traffic from her living room window for most of that hour, then had to rush to get to work on time.

She twisted her long brown hair up and stuffed it under a baseball cap as she walked into the grille's kitchen. Her boss, Jim, had been on the line since six, and he was happy to have some help.

"Morning, sunshine!" he said.

"I don't know about the sunshine bit, but good morning to you too," Shaka replied. She reached for the ticket hanging in front of her, quickly scanned it, and fell into action. She and

Jim worked together rhythmically, and one table after another was fed without any mistakes.

Shaka enjoyed the fluidity of her job, even over the lunch hour, when tensions ran high. The busier she was, the quicker the time went by, and before she knew it, it was two o'clock, and Jim was getting ready to leave. Soon the dinner crew would be coming in. Afternoons were usually slow, and Shaka used this time to do prep work for the dinner rush.

"Shaka!" a voice rang out from behind her. "You look lovely today."

She didn't need to turn around to know that it was Jason, one of the evening cooks. She glanced at him over her shoulder and gave a quick shrug. "Thanks."

Shortly after he came in, he was joined by the other evening cook, Ken. The two of them couldn't have been more different. Where Jason was thin, outgoing, and friendly, Ken was big, quiet, and mean. He never greeted anyone, and he rarely smiled. His forearms were covered in tattoos in Old English lettering that was so ornate Shaka couldn't even tell what they said. She didn't want to get caught trying to figure it out either. He frightened her, and she spent as little time around him as possible. She usually only saw him at shift change, and she was grateful for that. She was also grateful that somehow, he and Jason got along, and even seemed to enjoy each other's company. She didn't ask how; she was just happy that they did.

Ken stood next to Shaka behind the line. He didn't look at her, but she knew this was her cue to tell him what the specials were. She started with the soups, then went on to the nightly specials.

"Why the hell is it chicken fried rice?" he interrupted.

"Because we had to use up the leftover chicken from last night's chicken fry."

"Stupid idea," he said as he turned toward the cooler.

Shaka didn't wait for him to come back, she'd done her part. She walked back to the time clock, punched out, and pushed through the back door without saying a word to anyone.

As she walked down the street, wandering in the direction of the lake, she dug into her pocket and pulled out a pack of cigarettes. She opened it and glanced inside. It was still there: the joint Rena had given her last week. She only wanted a hit or two— just enough to relax and allow her mind to wander to places that didn't matter.

When she reached the lake, she looked around to make sure no one was near, then climbed down on the rocks where she was hidden from the boardwalk and lit the joint.

She watched the water as she smoked. The waves were rocking all the way to the horizon. About a mile out, a ship idled. She closed her eyes and took a deep inhale through her nose. Scent was always her strongest sense, whether she was wolf or human. It painted a picture of what was happening around her. She smelled the lake, the popcorn stand on the boardwalk, grease from the restaurants along the shore, the suntan lotion of a jogger, fuel from a boat near the pier, a dog that was running along the rocks, and then something she couldn't name... It smelled like her own scent: human, but wild. She opened her eyes and sniffed at the air again, but the odor was gone. She must have been imagining things. She reminded herself that she was a little high, after all.

Still, she got up from the rocks and walked back to the boardwalk. Looking around, she saw two joggers, a family at the popcorn stand, and a man and his son sitting and watching the ship in the distance. Her gaze came to rest on them. The father was tall and thin, with oil-black hair that framed his face and fell over his shoulders. He wore big glasses that covered half of his face and looked like they had gone out of style about twenty years ago. He pointed out at the ship and the boy listened to him quietly. The boy was about ten years old, with the same black hair and dark complexion as his father.

As Shaka watched them, suddenly the man's gaze shot over to her, and for a moment their eyes locked. She froze. She got the sensation that he was looking *inside* her. For a second, she thought of Rena grabbing her wrist that day in math class. She wondered if this man was doing the same thing right now, and whether he had been talking to the boy about her. Who were they? She'd never seen either of them before.

Without warning, the man stood up and put a hand on the boy's shoulder, and the two of them crossed the boardwalk and disappeared between two tall buildings.

Shaka stood staring after them, wondering. Then she shook her head and mumbled to herself "I must be high," and walked back the way she'd come.

"Hey, Shaka!" someone called from behind her. She jumped and spun around. It was Salem. He was walking down the boardwalk holding a bag of caramel corn, Rena's favorite. "Whoa, didn't mean to scare you," he said. "A little jumpy today?"

"Yeah, I guess. It's your girlfriend's fault. She gave me the pot I just smoked."

"I won't tell her you said that. Don't want to hurt her feelings!"

Shaka couldn't tell if he was joking or serious; he gave no indication either way. "No," she replied. "Wouldn't want to do that."

He tipped the brim of his dark cap to her and said, "Enjoy your afternoon, my dear."

"You too." She smiled and watched him go, shaking her head as if to clear it. It was something she'd learned to do as a wolf, but it worked just as well for her in human form. She quickly forgot about the stranger and his son and made her way through town to her apartment.

CHAPTER SIX

IT WAS A TUESDAY AFTERNOON, AND RENA LAY ON SHAKA'S couch chatting about art while Shaka cooked lunch. Meeting for a late lunch was an easy way for them to spend time together. Shaka was usually done working at the grille by two, and Rena didn't start painting until after dark.

Shaka's apartment was modest, her kitchen was really just one end of her living room. The smell of simmering fish and potatoes filled the entire apartment, and probably the buildings hallway too.

"Do you know what Salem says about art?" Rena asked. "He says it's a telltale sign of privilege. Hasn't he heard of the starving artist?"

"Yeah, but the starving artist still sells to the rich."

"The *starving* artist doesn't sell to anyone."

"Well, maybe they suck," Shaka joked as she placed a steaming plate in front of Rena.

"Yum, this looks great!" Rena said as she sat up and grabbed her fork. "And don't let me forget to tell you about Adrian Davidson."

"Is that someone you want to set me up with? Because if it is, I'd rather you did forget."

"He's just a friend of Salem's. He's new to the area. You might like him." Rena glanced up at Shaka, who was staring at her squarely.

"Am I *that* pathetic?" she asked.

"Of course not! But you never know when love will strike. And I think you'd like him. He's cute, and he works downtown."

Shaka knew this was Rena's way of saying he had a good job. "I'm flattered that you and Salem would think of me as a match for this affluent businessman, but I think I'll pass. No offense, but your setups haven't worked out so great in the past."

"That's not my fault. I didn't know Bobby Ridel was still married. And besides, Adrian isn't a businessman, he's a lawyer."

"In that case, I'll definitely pass. And Rena, it is noteworthy that you never used to suggest these blind dates before you met Salem."

"I just want to see you happy," she said, then stared off for a moment, lost in her own thoughts. "Do you think he's changed me?" she finally asked.

"Of course he has. It would be weird if he hadn't. That's what happens in relationships."

"For better, or for worse?"

"For better, of course. You're always happy now, or at least you always seem that way, and you've been able to do so much with your art now that you're not stuck working the front desk in that hotel all night. I think it's great—but your happily ever after isn't my happily ever after."

"No one ever said happily ever after. It doesn't exist, and you know it."

"I know. It's just an expression, like 'Let's eat,'" Shaka said.

Shaka didn't want to offend her friend, but it was true that Rena had changed, and Shaka feared it wasn't all for the better. Rena seemed to be losing sight of what life had been like before she moved in with Salem. Now she lived in a gated condo on the shore of Lake Superior and spent her weekends hobnobbing at fundraisers. Shaka sometimes worried that her friend's world was shrinking.

Rena said she was networking to get her art out to a bigger market, but Shaka was the only person who'd known Rena before Salem that she still spoke to, and even their time together was shrinking. Sometimes Rena couldn't even make their weekly lunch date. Shaka didn't want to worry about losing touch with her friend, so she tried to push the thought out of her head. Still, she knew that Rena's world was changing into one where she didn't quite fit.

CHAPTER SEVEN

IT WAS ANOTHER MORNING BEHIND THE GRILL, AND SHAKA was in a bad mood. It had been four days since she'd last talked with Rena. She hadn't been returning Shaka's calls since they'd had lunch at her apartment. Shaka was worried that she had offended her somehow. She had noticed in recent months that Rena was becoming increasingly sensitive. Shaka hated the idea of having to tip-toe around her in conversation, but she also hated the idea of pushing her away. She knew that she was more disposable to Rena now than she had ever been before. Sometimes she wondered if Rena was looking for an excuse to end their friendship, thereby ending her obligation to drive her Audi down the streets of West Duluth once a week. But it was a dumb idea born of anger, and Shaka knew it wasn't true. They had been friends since they were in second grade. That was fifteen years ago now, and they'd scarcely fought in all that time. Shaka was confident that it would take more than a man with money to come between them. She was considering just apologizing, even though she didn't know exactly what she'd done wrong.

When her shift ended, she was the first one out the door. She didn't even look over her shoulder when Jason yelled, "*Adios, amiga!*" She just wanted to get out of the kitchen, away from everyone. She knew she'd feel better if she could shift, if she could run through the forest, but it was the middle of the day, and there were people everywhere. She was safe in the darkness, where vision was more of a suggestion than a rule, but daylight left little to interpretation, and she knew better than to take a risk like that. So, she just started walking.

She walked to the end of the street and felt like turning right, so she did. And at the end of that street, she felt like going straight, so she did. Then she turned left, then straight, straight, and right, and so on as she wandered around the city with no particular destination. It was calming in a way, to have no purpose. An hour passed, then two, and she found herself halfway up Thompson Hill, which overlooked the city. She sat down, closed her eyes, and inhaled deeply. The smell of the city was washed out by the wind. Now she could smell the leaves on the trees, and the tall grass. Behind her, the sun was getting lower. Its rays reached around her in an embrace, and when it sank below the treetops, she felt like leaving, so stood up and walked back down the hill.

She was halfway back to her apartment when she saw him: the boy from the waterfront. He stood on the opposite street corner, waiting for the light to change. He was wearing a red T-shirt that was too big for him. His hands were stuffed in his pockets, and he was looking down at his shoes. Then the light changed, and they walked toward one another. Shaka didn't take her eyes off him. Suddenly, there was that scent again, strange but familiar, wild like her own.

When she reached the boy, she held her hand out and touched his arm. He looked up at her instantly, and his eyes widened in surprise and fear. They both felt it: a thousand tiny sparks shot between them, and she knew he was like her.

The crowd of pedestrians pushed them apart, and then they were each on opposite sides of the street again. They both stopped there and looked at one another cautiously. Shaka hit the button to cross the street again, but the boy ran. She stayed where she was, she wasn't going to chase him. She had a feeling she would see him again.

CHAPTER EIGHT

When Rena finally returned Shaka's calls, it wasn't to explain her silence, but to tell her that Salem had arranged for her to join them for dinner, and she could meet them downtown at seven. Shaka was relieved. She must have just overreacted again. Maybe Rena hadn't been upset with her, but just busy. Either way, she was sure that once they were together again, it wouldn't matter. She couldn't wait to tell Rena about her week, dull as it had been, and to hear about what Rena had been doing that was so important that she couldn't call her back.

She was meeting them at a restaurant where suit coats were required and the waiters were forbidden to write down your order. Shaka always felt like an imposter in places with such specific social rules, but she could play along well enough. She knew that a casual sundress wouldn't do. She went to the back of her closet and pulled out a long sleeveless blue dress with tiny buttons down the back. The buttons made Shaka think of vertebrae, like a tiny delicate spine on the outside of her body. That was why she'd bought the dress in the first place, but she rarely had a reason to wear it. She knew that if she decided to stop by the park and shift on her way home, this dress wasn't one she could just leave crumpled on the forest floor. It was the most expensive piece of clothing she owned, and she had to take care of it. Still, the thought of running thrilled her, almost as much as the thought of seeing Rena.

Shaka matched white heels to her dress and found a white clutch purse in her closet. She put her wallet, phone, and a pack of cigarettes in it, then walked to the bus stop.

When she got off of the buss, she had to walk a few blocks to the restaurant. There weren't many bus lines in that neighborhood, and by the time she reached the door, her feet ached. But as she entered the restaurant in her long dress and white heels, with her hair hanging loosely over her shoulders, accented with tiny braids, she knew she had pulled it off: she looked like she belonged.

She gave the hostess Rena's name and was led to an empty table with five chairs. Shaka sat down. Behind her, a man was playing gentle, unassuming piano. When the waiter came, she ordered a glass of pinot noir instead of her usual whiskey sour and sat up straight like her neighbors. She thought about the irony of feeling like a fraud based on the size of her apartment and her salary, not her ability to shape-shift. *If they only knew* ... she thought, and smiled.

When her wine arrived, she swirled it around in her glass—one of the few things she'd learned from her father—then she took a deep sniff of it and finally a sip. She felt like a fool, but she also enjoyed acting the part of the upper classist.

Just then, the waiter led a tall man with dark blond hair to her table. Shaka shifted in her seat uncomfortably. He sat down across from her and ordered a whiskey.

"Hello. Shaka, I presume?" he asked.

"Yes. And you are?"

"Adrian. Salem's friend? Did Rena mention me?"

"Oh. Well, I haven't seen much of her this week, but she did mention wanting me to meet a friend of Salem's."

"You two have been friends a long time, I hear."

"Since second grade. I was awkwardly available, and Rena needed someone to long-jump off the swings with her," she said with a little grin.

"Really? Rena doesn't strike me as a jump-off-the-swings kind of girl."

"No, not now. But she used to be a thrill seeker, and I always loved her adventures."

"Sounds like a balanced relationship." He smiled at her. His gaze made her nervous, but she tried not to show it. When his whiskey came, he swirled the glass in his hand, making the ice cubes clink.

"Adrian," she said. "That's a pretty name. It makes me think of water, for some reason."

He watched her for a moment and took another sip of whiskey. "You're right on the money," he said. "It actually means 'water.'"

"Huh. Interesting."

"And Shaka? I've never heard that name before. What does it mean?"

"Depends on where you're from. It's both the name of a South African war chief and a Hawaiian greeting." She made a fist and stuck her thumb and pinky finger out to demonstrate.

"And I can see those traits in you: laid back, yet not to be underestimated," he said, smiling.

Shaka blushed and grabbed her wineglass. She was glad to see Salem and Rena approaching the table. Shaka stood as Rena pulled out a chair beside her.

"Hi, friend," Shaka said to her. "I see what you did here." She nodded toward Adrian.

"Somebody has to get you back in the game," Rena said as she sat, then gave a quick half smile and looked away. Shaka sat down and took a sip of her wine. Salem greeted Adrian with a handshake, and the two fell into an exclusive conversation about their work.

"Who is he?" Shaka ventured to ask while Adrian's attention was away from her.

"He's a lawyer, remember? He works somewhere downtown. Salem met him in college, I think."

"So, is this like a double date, or is it just 'bring a friend to dinner' night?" She grinned at Rena, who remained straight-faced.

"I told Salem you didn't want to meet him, but he insisted. I know you're not interested in all this." She waved her arm at their surroundings. "But all you have to do is sit here, drink some free wine, eat some prawns, and then you can go."

"Prawns? Are there no snails?" Shaka joked, trying to lighten the mood.

"Look, Shaka, I know what you think of me. I know you think I sold out. It gets more and more obvious each time we hang out. It doesn't make me feel great to be around you. But this is my life now, and I'm not ashamed of it."

"Rena, I do not think that! It's true that our lives are different, and you're right, I don't love 'all this,'" she said, waving her arm around, "but I love you, and I want to be your friend no matter which neighborhood you live in."

Rena sealed her lips. Shaka had seen her do this many times before—sometimes with her foster parents, or her old boyfriends, and even Salem—but she rarely did it with her. It meant that she was keeping herself composed under pressure. Shaka knew not to say anything. She just took a sip of her wine and tried to appear as though they were having a normal conversation.

"How can you say that to me as you sit here judging me?" Rena began. "I'm sorry for giving you a chance to stop picking up guys at the pool hall, or maybe stop buying dresses at the Goodwill." She motioned to Shaka's dress. "And I say I'm sorry only because I know you think you're owed an apology. You don't even appreciate what I do for you."

"Are you kidding me, Rena? Now who's being judgy? And believe it or not, I *like* my dress, and I like meeting men in shitty bars. At least I can be myself with them."

They looked away from each other, both fuming, as Salem and Adrian chatted away obliviously. Shaka swallowed what was left of her wine in a single swig and raised her hand for the waiter. If she was going to make it through this dinner, she would need something stronger.

"Whiskey sour," she said when he noticed her.

"Real classy, Shaka," Rena muttered. "I should have known you could only go about ten minutes before turning back into a lumberjack."

Shaka couldn't help but laugh, and this made Rena's face turn red.

"So, by 'classy,' do you mean inviting me to dinner, then insulting me over and over again?"

"Oh, stop it. You aren't innocent. You detest my life, and you know it, but I bet you don't know why. It's because you're jealous. It's because I have something that you don't: a healthy relationship. And to be honest, I doubt you ever will, since you've never been good at putting yourself second."

"Wow. First off, I think you're projecting, and second, assholes fall in love too. It doesn't make you a good person."

The table was quiet for a moment. Salem and Adrian had stopped talking and were looking at them. Rena and Shaka noticed at the same time. Rena sealed her lips and looked down at the table, while Shaka stood up.

"Well," she said as the waiter placed the whiskey sour in front of her. She picked it up and drank the whole glass in three long swallows, then set it back on the table and looked down at Rena. "Thank you for a lovely evening." And without another word or even a glance, she turned around and walked out the door.

CHAPTER NINE

OUTSIDE THE RESTAURANT, SHAKA FOUND THE VALET SMOKING and borrowed his lighter, she had forgotten hers. She smoked her cigarette slowly as she walked down the street. She wondered if that dinner would mean the end of their years-long friendship. She didn't know how either of them could come back from some of the things they had just said to each other. They weren't children anymore; they were adults now and standing on opposite sides of an invisible class line. Shaka never would have thought something so silly could divide them, but then, she hadn't known how powerful those differences could be.

"Goodbye, Rena," she whispered as she finished her cigarette. She decided that tonight, she would run after all. What use would her expensive dress be to her now?

She came to a little bar and ducked inside. It was grimy,

the floor covered in peanut shells, and it smelled like stale beer and bleach. She felt more comfortable here than she had all evening. She ordered another whiskey sour and sat down. When it came, she just stared into the glass. Her life really was changing. It was hard to resist the urge to just abandon everything and go live in the woods. Who did she have left? Her grandfather was gone, and now Rena too. Why shouldn't she just leave? She could build a cabin, like her grandfather had done, and change into a wolf whenever she wanted. Maybe she could move further north. She had always liked visiting the little towns that bordered the Boundary Waters Canoe Area, which was a protected wilderness that spanned most of northeastern Minnesota.

Her fantasy was just starting to take off when someone tapped her on the shoulder and pulled her out of it. It was Adrian.

"May I?" he asked, pulling out the stool next to her.

She smiled and shrugged.

"Things broke up pretty quickly after you left. I never got a real chance to talk to you."

"Yeah, sorry. I just had to get out of there," she mumbled.

"I'm sorry about your night. I thought you two were thick as thieves."

"Me too... But I don't know that I really want to talk about it right now."

"Okay. Do you want to talk about something else?"

She looked at him squarely for the first time. His eyes were blue, like the ocean, and warm. His lips were perfectly symmetrical, and they revealed a glimpse of what was assuredly a set of straight white teeth. He was a bit more clean-cut than Shaka preferred, and part of her wondered what a man from an affluent background and obviously good genes was doing following her into a dive bar. But then she just gave a little shrug as she finished her whiskey. If he was Rena's last gift to her, she might as well accept it. She ordered two more whiskeys and sat one down in front of him.

"Do you have something in mind?" she asked.

"Yes. Why do you drink whiskey?"

"Because it burns, and then I know I'm drinking."

"No wine coolers for you, huh?" He smiled at her.

"Wine coolers? Do they even make those anymore? ... Okay, now it's my turn. Did you always dream of being a lawyer?"

Adrian laughed awkwardly. "Does any boy dream of wearing suits and filing papers all day? I dreamed of being an artist, but settled for the complete opposite."

"What kind of artist?"

"Nope. My turn now," he said. "What dream do you chase?"

The word "chase" stirred something in her. If she kept drinking, she would not be able to change tonight, it never worked when she was tipsy. She looked at him and smiled. He was watching her patiently. "I want to be a wild animal," she finally said.

"Oh." He laughed quietly. "I can assure you that your dream will come true before mine."

"Who knows?"

When the bartender walked past, Adrian ordered a second round. She decided she wouldn't be running through the woods that night after all. At least her dress wouldn't be ruined. Instead, they ordered greasy hamburgers and ate them with cocktail napkins protecting their evening attire. The conversation flowed lightly as they ate, and when they finished, they strolled down the street, following the sound of a blues guitar. It led them to a small bar one block over with a big dance floor. They sat at a high-top table and watched the band as they sipped light beers, until finally Adrian asked her to dance. Shaka looked out at the empty dance floor, and the seating area packed with customers. She was a horrible dancer, but thanks to the whiskey, her inhibitions were all but gone.

"I'd love to," she answered, and he took her arm and led her to the floor.

He placed one hand on the small of her back and the other held her hand in the air. When the music began, he whirled her around the floor. She tried to stumble along with him as he led her through the steps.

"Wow, you really know how to do this!" she laughed.

"Consolation prize from my liberal arts degree," he answered. He danced well enough that he made her look like she knew what she was doing too.

When that song ended, they danced to the next, then the next, then they ordered more beers and fell into conversation again. Before they knew it, it was twelve thirty, and the bartender was taking last call. The room was nearly empty.

"One more dance?" he asked.

The musician was packing up his things. "Show's over," Shaka said.

"Not necessarily," he replied and led her over to the jukebox. "Don't watch," he told her as he put a dollar in. She turned around and shut her eyes.

She felt him move in front of her and put a hand on the small of her back again, waiting for the song to start. A few seconds passed, and she heard the opening beats of Stevie Wonder's "Isn't She Lovely" as he whisked her onto the floor. She opened her eyes and laughed as they spun around the room.

"I thought this song was about a baby," she said.

"Don't over think it."

Everyone else in the bar stopped what they were doing and watched them. She tripped twice, but each time, he pulled her to her feet so quickly that it looked like it was part of the dance.

When the music ended, they were standing in the middle of the floor. The few members of the band applauded, and when they did, he tipped her back and kissed her—and the applause was accented with cheers and a whistle. The kiss made her feel warm in her belly, and chills of excitement ran through her body. He pulled back, still holding her over the dance floor.

"A man of many talents," she said.

He smiled at her, his eyes sparkling.

When she stood up, she felt a little spin and squeezed his shoulder. His arm tightened around her back. She looked into his eyes; they were so blue, and he was warm and kind. *What do you know? Rena was right about him,* she thought.

"You're warm and smell like rain," she said.

"Oh, and she's a poet!" he joked.

"Yep. That's why I drank so much whiskey."

"Whiskey is the poet's water," he said. "Should we get some air?"

"Please," she answered, and they walked out into the street. The air was warm, and the night was half over. At its center, it was the darkest, and she suddenly longed to be alone in it. If the night had gone differently, she would have been howling deep in the forest instead of standing drunk beside a man she barely knew. He watched her curiously. She glanced at him and felt a pang of pity for him. There were so many things he would never know about her.

"Adrian, I think I'd better go home. Thank you for turning my night around," she said.

"I can't let you walk home alone at this hour. Let me walk with you. You can tell me where you learned to dance."

She smiled and started walking. He looped his arm through hers, and they turned toward her apartment. After the first block, she took off her heels and walked in her stockinged feet. She was relieved that he didn't try to talk the whole way. She was getting tired, and she just wanted to smell the air and feel the damp of the night on her skin.

It was almost thirty minutes before they reached her building. When they did, she turned to face him. His eyes were red from the whiskey. She leaned in and rested her head on his chest.

"Thank you," she said.

He hesitated for a moment, then wrapped his arms around her and rested his chin on her head.

"I want to see you again," he said.

She squeezed him and let go. "Now you know where I live. Just don't start stalking me."

He smiled at her. "No promises."

She leaned forward, and he kissed her one more time. This time it was short and sweet. Then she turned around and walked up the steps to her apartment building, leaving him alone and centered in the night.

CHAPTER TEN

SHAKA WOKE AT NOON WITH A POUNDING HEADACHE. She squinted as she limped to the bathroom to find the Tylenol. She'd had a fun night, even if she had over done it. And she had a feeling that she'd be seeing Adrian again. She'd felt at ease around him, and that didn't happen on just any date. As she swallowed the Tylenol, she sighed at her reflection in the mirror. It was almost worse when she actually liked the guy; her relationships were all doomed from the start, either way. She never knew how long to wait before breaking it off. She wanted the comfort of companionship, but she couldn't trust anyone with her secret. It was just easier to end things before they started asking questions—questions like where did she disappear to at odd hours of the night? Or why did she always come home covered in dirt and with torn clothing?

Shaka turned from the mirror and went back into the living room. She would worry about that when the time came. For now, she wanted to see Adrian again. She just needed to shift first. It always helped her clear her head. She would just have to wait out the sun.

When the afternoon sun touched the treetops, she put on dark pants, a sweater, and her running shoes, then started toward Connor Avenue. The air smelled like wood-smoke. She had imagined she would be running off to the woods, but she just strolled, enjoying the moments as they passed. The night was clear and crisp, and she didn't want to rush through it. There were kids on bikes riding up and down the street, shouting and laughing at each other. She thought of Rena and forgot about their fight. Instead, she remembered all the nights they'd spent biking around the city themselves. She blew the thought off before she could start feeling lonely. Her heart felt full and happy at that moment, and she didn't want to ruin it.

She reached the woods at twilight, dark enough to see a shadow, but not a face. She cut into the forest and followed the familiar trail north, planning to walk at least a mile or two before she shifted. She wanted to shift at the lake, but when she got there, there were people there. She slipped past them unnoticed and walked another mile to the river. Here, she was alone. She heard an owl hoot high in a tree above her, and another answered from across the river. She stripped and waded in. The water was icy cold and deep. She slipped under the surface and felt the electricity run through her body as she shifted. She felt stronger, and her thoughts were clearer as she climbed out of the river, shook off, and sniffed the air. It smelled clean and damp, like the forest and nothing else.

Knowing she was safe, she started to run. She ran north — always north. It had always been that way with her grandfather. When she was deep in the woods, she looked for a high spot to howl. She found a rocky ledge near a lake and climbed to the top. Then she threw her head back and let her call ring out over the still water.

A moment later, her call was answered by another. She whined in excitement, then howled again. It was quiet for a minute, but she waited, and it came again. She wondered if it was her grandfather; it had been so long since she'd heard him, she'd forgotten the sound of his howl. She returned the call and waited. This time there was no answer. She howled again and again, partially because it felt good—it was cleansing—but also because there was someone out there listening to her.

Behind her, she heard another owl hoot. Sniffing the wind, she caught the faint scent of campfire, probably from a fire that had been extinguished hours before. She looked out at the lake, and the moonlight rippling on the water was hypnotic.

She was growing tired, and her bed was in a different world. She gave one last howl across the lake, then turned around and trotted south.

She reached the river and waded back in, letting the water wash through her thick coat. If felt good, but as she stuck her nose up in the air, she smelled people again. She didn't see anyone though, so she ducked below the surface and shifted back. She climbed out of the river cautiously, making sure no one was nearby. She found her clothes and shoes and put them on quickly, then started running down the trail. Soon she was back to the lake where she usually shifted, where now there were five people drinking around a fire. She slipped by them unseen and continued down the trail. When she was out of earshot, she started running again. She heard the owl behind her, then another further ahead. She must have intrigued them. It made her smile. It was cooling down now, and she could see her breath.

When she reached Connor Avenue, her legs ached, and her heart was pounding. She felt both exhausted and refreshed. When she finally turned down her street and saw her building, there was a man standing in front of it. She paused and sighed. Inside her were the warring hopes that it was and was not Adrian. She was excited at the thought of seeing him again, but at this point she just wanted to shower and go to bed, and she didn't want to have to come up with an explanation as to why she was dressed in black and out running in the dark.

She approached guardedly, and when she was close enough, she saw that this man had black hair and wasn't Adrian. It was some stranger who had nothing to do with her at all. She felt relieved, but also a little disappointed. As she approached her door, she heard the owls again. She smiled because at least *they* knew her secret.

CHAPTER ELEVEN

THE DAYS PASSED SLOWLY WITHOUT HAVING RENA TO TALK TO. Shaka even found herself looking forward to her shifts at the grille: the mindless rhythm she fell into, and the easy humor of her coworkers. After her shifts, she would often sit by the lake and listen to the water slap against the rocks, and watch it pool between them then funnel back out. Her life had slowly become a routine. She felt empty, and despite her grandfather's advice not to overindulge in one world and neglect the other, she felt that soon she might change and not change back. There was nothing holding her here.

Then one day, as she sat on the shore and stared out at a ship stalled miles out in the water, something happened that changed her mind.

She heard them before they even decided to approach her. She heard the voice of a boy asking his father, "Is that her?" And the father responded, "Yes."

She waited for them to approach her, but seconds turned into minutes. Finally, she heard their hesitant footfalls coming close, and the boy reached out and touched her shoulder. Again, she felt that wild electric current. She looked over her shoulder, and there was the dark-haired man and his son whom she'd seen at the boardwalk before. They looked down at her with nearly identical impassive expressions.

"Excuse us," the man said, "may we speak with you?"

She eyed them suspiciously.

"I'm sorry to interrupt. I won't take too much of your time. I just wanted to tell you that I've seen you before, and I think we have something in common."

"What's that?" she asked.

"We share a great gift."

"What gift?" she said flatly, her voice growing defensive.

The man looked around. There were people nearby, walking on the boardwalk and sitting on the rocks.

"We shouldn't talk here. Will you meet us up the shore? If you cross the bridge and walk for two miles, you'll find an abandoned stone house. We'll be there in one hour."

He looked steadily into her eyes, and she could feel his desperation. She gave a small nod, and immediately he took his son by the hand and walked away. She watched them go, feeling as though she was about to get pulled into something she didn't want to be a part of. She didn't know what this man wanted. It crossed her mind that maybe he was trying to tell her that he too was a shape-shifter, though that seemed impossible; she had never met another one, other than her grandfather. Yet something urged her to find out what he had to say. If it turned out he was just trying to lure her out to a desolate place to rob her or hurt her, then she looked forward to making him regret his choice. Either way, her afternoon was going to be interesting.

Forty-five minutes later, she stood alone in the abandoned stone house. It smelled like woodsmoke and moisture inside. As she ran her fingers along the crumbling water-stained walls, she felt an uneasiness start to swell in her. This was a house of ghosts. She didn't belong there.

Then a new scent drifted to her, and she knew that she wasn't alone. She looked up and saw an owl perched on the stairway railing. It spread its wings and flew down toward her, its wingspan growing as it neared. She had to crouch to the ground or it would have flown into her. Then she heard feet hit the floor behind her and she spun around to face the man from the boardwalk standing nude before her. He was tall and unashamed. Shaka saw that he had a tattoo on each arm: on his left was a band of feathers, and on his right, a ring of fine print in Ojibwe. His face remained calm—friendly even, despite having just shifted in front of her and now standing before her naked.

Her lack of shock at what had just happened immediately exposed her as a shifter herself. She realized this too late.

"You're a wolf," he said simply.

At first her mind raced with responses that would evade the truth, but she knew that was pointless. He had seen her. This man was the owl in the woods.

"Yes," she said.

"Are there others like you?" he asked.

"I don't know. I've never met any others, until now." For some reason, she didn't want to reveal that her grandfather also shared their ability. "Where is your son?"

He pointed up to the rafters. Her gaze followed to find a small owl perched quietly on a beam above. "Come down now, Michal. It's safe."

The little owl wove back and forth on the beam, then sprang forward into a wobbly, graceless flight. Again, Shaka watched as the wingspan lengthened and the owl grew quickly into the familiar shape of the boy.

"Are there others?" she asked.

"Yes," he said, "but no one close. What is your name?"

"Shaka."

He raised an eyebrow but continued, "I'm Winston, and this is Michal, my son."

She'd always felt that if she ever met another person who could shift, she would have so many questions, but now her mind raced in circles and couldn't grasp a single one.

"Dad, she might be dangerous," Michal said. "I don't like wolves."

"Hush, now. We just have to trust her," Winston said to his son, then turning to Shaka he said, "You are dangerous, Shaka, and I don't think you know it. You use your gift to run through the woods, but your gift also makes you a killer, and a skilled one. Have you ever killed?"

"That's a strange thing to ask someone you just met... but no, I haven't. I don't need to kill anything, so why would I?"

"Because you were built for it. The wolf is a creature of action."

"What would you have me do? Go on a killing spree? Because if you're about to ask that of me, I'd like to stop you now."

"No. I don't want to ask anything of you. I only wanted to tell you that if I know what you are, the others could know too. I wanted to warn you to be careful."

"What are you talking about? I thought you said you two were the only ones around here."

"We are, now. But there were three of us. I have a sister."

His expression darkened as he paused for a moment. "She was captured," he continued. "It happened one night when we were flying together, four years ago. She was shot out of the sky, not killed, but wounded. They tried to get me too, but I made it to the cover of the trees, where I watched, unable to help her. There were too many of them. After she lost consciousness, she changed back to her human form. They carried her to a white van and laid her in the back. I followed it as far as I could, but once it reached the interstate, I couldn't keep up. Since then, I have seen these same men several times. They look harmless, ordinary, but they are looking for us. When I saw you change in the woods a few months ago, I knew I needed to warn you. If I were you, I would get comfortable with your inner killer."

She watched him, trying to piece together his story. Were there men watching her in the woods? Had the campers by the lake seen her? And who were they? But the only person she knew who had been following her was Winston.

"How do I know you're telling the truth?"

"You don't. I don't have proof. Just keep an eye out, be discreet. That's all."

"Well, what do these men look like?"

"They look ordinary. There's nothing about them that stands out. It will be in the way they watch you. You will feel them before you see them."

Suddenly, Winston turned his head and listened. Shaka heard nothing at first, then there were voices in the woods—young men laughing.

"Michal, change back. It's time to go," Winston commanded.

In an instant, Michal was an owl again, perched in a window sill and ready or flight.

"I'll see you again, Shaka," Winston said as he spread his arms. In a moment, they were both gone, just dark shadows in the sky and the sound of wings. A minute later, a voice in the woods exclaimed about the two owls overhead.

Shaka turned quietly and walked out of the house.

CHAPTER TWELVE

THAT NIGHT, SHE SHIFTED. IT WAS A MOONLESS NIGHT and she felt safe in the darkness. She knew Winston was right about one thing: she needed to do more than just run and howl when she shifted. She needed to kill. She might not have believed there were people out there stalking her or preparing to capture her, but at least they could agree that she had all the tools to kill, and she should know how to how use them.

She trotted through the woods until she came upon a clearing. Sniffing the air, she knew there was a rabbit warren in the field. She decided she would hunt them. Always best to start small. She kept low, nearly crawling on the ground toward the scent. As she got closer and could hear their movement, she slowed, only taking one step every several minutes.

She saw two small brown rabbits eating clover less than

thirty feet away from her, their ears flicking this way and that. Then the wind shifted, and one of them sat upright to sniff the air, and froze. He smelled her. Knowing she had nothing to lose, she leapt out of the grass and sent them running, darting in a wild zig-zag path. Her long legs moved over wide swaths of earth with each stride, but the rabbits were faster, and they disappeared down a hole and into their warren before she could reach them.

She stopped at the hole and sniffed. The smell of fear was strong. Somewhere beneath her paws, their hearts beat like hummingbird wings, but they didn't need to be afraid; they had escaped. She could try to dig them out, but she was standing over a network of tunnels and dens. By the time she reached the place they were now, they'd be somewhere else. If she'd had all night, she would have waited at the edge of the wood for them to come out again, but she didn't. She would be gone from the woods by morning. She turned her back on the field and trotted off.

It wasn't long before she picked up the scent of a doe. She followed it to a small pond where two deer were drinking. The chances of her taking down a deer on her own were slim, but she needed practice, so she crept around the edge of the pond. The closer she got, the longer she waited between steps. They finished drinking and walked back into the woods, where they began to strip leaves from low-hanging branches. She crept up behind them, gauging them as she went. One was clearly smaller; she would try for that one. She stood behind the small doe silently, ready to charge, when they both stopped chewing and stood still like statues. The scent of fear filled the air again. She took another cautious step closer to the doe, and they both turned to run.

Suddenly, Shaka leapt up from the grass, closing fifteen feet of space in one leap, but the doe was fast and took huge springing steps. Shaka kept tightly behind her. She tried to chase her toward the soft, muddy ground near the pond to slow her down, but the distance between them was growing. Shaka kept pushing, running as fast as she could despite the doe getting further and further away. But then the doe stumbled, and Shaka gained on her a little. She stumbled again, and Shaka closed more distance. The ground had turned wet and soft under their feet. Shaka's wide paws allowed her to easily run over the top while the doe's hooves sank in. She remembered, as if from a dream, a man telling her she was "built to kill."

Again, the doe stumbled, and this was all Shaka needed to reach her. The air was choked with the scent of fear as Shaka leapt and landed just behind the doe, her teeth sinking into her back leg, pulling her down. The doe let out a scream as she fell, and Shaka jumped to her throat and silenced her, crushing her windpipe and opening her carotid. She was gone within a minute.

Filled with the thrill of the hunt for the first time, Shaka stood over the doe's body and howled. The sound rang through the dark forest in a heavy, powerful song. Then she turned back to her kill and tore at the flesh, until her belly was full.

She trotted back to the field where the rabbits had their warren. They had come back out of the ground and were eating clover again. They ran in wild patterns when she entered the field, and soon all had disappeared, though this time they had no reason to fear her. She only wanted some long grass to curl up in and take a nap. When she found a soft patch, she turned several times, then lay down and dozed for an hour.

When she rose, the sky was turning gray. She stretched her front legs out before her, then her back legs out behind her, and then she trotted without slowing until she reached the lake. There she waded in and swam out to the center, where she dipped below the surface and came out on the other side a few moments later as a woman. Her clothes were where she had left them. She slipped on her pants and T-shirt and started jogging out of the woods.

She'd gone less than a mile when she noticed the owl flying above her. She stopped and looked up at it defiantly.

"Are you stalking me?" she demanded.

The owl only hooted and flew ahead of her. She shook her head and started jogging again, but when she rounded the next bend, Winston was standing on the trail. She skidded to a stop.

"How did it feel?" he asked.

"Jesus! A little warning would be nice! Or maybe take a second to put some clothes on?"

Winston stepped off the path. "I'm sorry. I didn't mean to startle you. I just wanted to know how that felt."

"Why?"

"Because if you're a good hunter, you can defend yourself against them, maybe even stop them."

"How? By killing them, whoever 'they' are?"

"Something like that."

"Well, assuming these people even exist, I wouldn't count on me to stop them. I might be able to take down a small deer, but that's not like killing a man. There's a reason wolves are endangered. I mean, I could get shot just running through the woods on a night like this! What makes you think I'm any kind of match for these people who are supposedly trying to catch us?"

"Because they may not know you exist yet. If we worked together, we could set a trap for them. We could free Rachel."

"Rachel?"

"My sister."

"I don't know. I mean, I don't even know if I believe all this. I think I'm going to need more than just your word to go on if I'm going to start conspiring to kill people."

Winston nodded and stood quietly for a minute, his eyes flashing back and forth as he thought. Finally, he said in defeat, "I can't prove it."

Shaka shrugged her shoulders. "Then I'm sorry. That's just not enough for me."

"I understand," he replied. "You don't trust readily; you are a lone wolf. But Shaka, if I find a way to prove this to you, will you help me?"

"If you can prove it to me? Sure."

"Okay. Then I'll find a way."

"Well, good luck with that," she said as she pushed past him and kept running down the trail.

"You never answered: how did it feel?" he yelled after her.

"Natural!" she yelled back.

She ran until she reached the edge of the woods, then walked into the park as dawn began to warm the eastern sky. Halfway through the park, she stopped and leaned up against a tree, feeling weak and queasy—then she doubled over and vomited the contents of her stomach. She was shocked and disgusted by the amount of raw deer meat she had ingested, fur and skin mixed with muscle. She'd had no idea her stomach could hold that much! Just looking at it made her feel dizzy.

She straightened up and looked around. The park was empty. She sighed in relief and started walking again, vowing not to eat any of her kills again.

CHAPTER THIRTEEN

THAT AFTERNOON AT WORK, SHE SEEMED TO BE DOING everything wrong. Two orders were sent back in her first hour. The sight of red meat made her stomach turn. She breathed through her mouth to avoid the smell and ingested nothing but 7 Up all day. After she messed up her third order, her boss sent her home, telling her to get some sleep and come back tomorrow with her head in the game. Embarrassed, she apologized and said she didn't know what was wrong with her. "Just an off day. We all have them," he said, but she saw the concern in his eyes. It wasn't like her to have off days.

The trip home took longer than it had ever taken her before. By the time she opened her front door, she felt like she was crawling. She pulled the curtains closed, fell into her bed, and was asleep in less than a minute.

She woke up hours later to her phone ringing. She

rubbed her eyes until the number came into focus. She didn't recognize it.

"Hello," she mumbled.

"Good morning." It was a man's voice.

She glared up at her clock. It was after 7:00 p.m.

"Who's this?" she said as she pulled herself out of bed.

"Boy, you really know how to make a guy feel special, Shaka."

"Oh, Adrian! Hi. I just haven't been feeling great today." She had made her way into the kitchen and put a kettle on the stove for tea. "Wait—did I give you my number?"

"Busted! No, you didn't, I asked Rena for it. I hope that's okay. I mean, I won't abuse my privileges, I just wanted to know if you'd like to get dinner."

Shaka felt her heart sink a little as he asked. She did want to see him again. He was fun and cute, but it just wasn't the same when you already knew the ending.

"So ... dinner? ... With me? ... Any thoughts?" he asked.

She smiled. "I would love to get dinner with you, but I can't tonight. I'm too tired."

"That's great! I mean, that you want to go out again, not that you're feeling down, of course. How about tomorrow?"

"Tomorrow would be okay. I'm supposed to help with the dinner shift, but I could meet you after, like eight?"

"Eight works! Should we meet at The Hallow?"

The Hallow was one of Shaka's favorite bars. The velvet

furniture and dim lighting from thrift store lamps, along with the undertone of goth music, gave the place a truly unique atmosphere. It usually wasn't a first choice for a second date.

"I do like that spot," Shaka said. "Did Rena tell you to take me there?"

"She may have mentioned it. I can see you liking that Carrie White meets Ichabod Crane type atmosphere. Would you like to dress accordingly?" he asked.

"Absolutely, and no smiling. Get that out of your system tonight," she teased.

"Okay, I can do that."

"So, you talked to Rena? How is she?"

"Yes, just briefly. She seemed stressed out about something. I think she misses you."

"Hmm. That's insightful for a person you just met."

"Well, I'm very intuitive."

"A man who's in touch with his emotions? I better not mess this up!" Shaka said, giggling.

"Just remember, no giggling tomorrow!"

"Yes, sir. See you tomorrow—and don't forget to wear your pentagram!"

"Never do, my dear! See you then."

When she hung up the phone, she felt light and giggly for the first time in days. Her kettle started to whistle behind her, and she spun around and pulled it from the stove. She no longer felt tired and queasy, but happy and energetic. She decided to make her tea in a travel mug and go for a walk. This time, she would just walk in the woods like a normal human being, as it suddenly felt like a good night to stay in her skin and be thankful for it. It was the first time in a while that she'd felt excited to be a young woman, not just passing time until she could become a wolf again.

She traced her steps back to the park, the mug of tea warming her hand. Walking the trail back to the woods, she scanned the ground near the opening to the forest for the deer meat she'd thrown up early that morning. She found the tree she'd leaned against, but that horrible pile of meat and hair was gone. Smaller animals must have gotten it. She felt both relieved and a little disgusted that it was gone.

She started down the trail and passed a smiling couple heading back to the street. The sun was getting low, prompting people to head back to the façade of civilization. She could smell a campfire, pine needles, dead leaves, and dirt. She held her warm mug of tea close to her chest and smelled the Earl Grey too. A middle-aged man jogged past her on his way back to the city. He smiled and nodded to her, and she smiled back. She felt as though all was right with the world. Still reveling in the conversation she'd had with Adrian, she let herself feel flattered that he had gone to Rena for her number. She wondered about their date. Would it lead to her going back to his place? She wondered where he lived, and if he was a clean man. Did he have a record collection? What type of art was on his walls, what kinds of books were on his bookshelves? Did he even have bookshelves? Was he the type to display a baseball someone had signed for him when he was twelve? Did he buy his own furniture, or was his living room full of mismatched hand-me-downs like hers?

She ambled down the trail, her mind conjuring different variations of his apartment, and before she knew it, it was dark, and she was nearly to the lake. She hadn't passed anyone since the jogger, but she knew there were others out there; she could smell them. Even though she didn't plan to change, her habit of wanting to stay hidden was hard to break, and she started to feel unsettled in the pit of her stomach. She quickly forgot about Adrian and paid attention to where she was stepping. Once she could see the lake, she snuck off the trail and into the woods.

As she got closer, she noticed a new scent, one that didn't belong in the woods: sterility. These people didn't have the usual scents of beer, salty skin, and roast meat. Instead, it smelled like soap, chemicals, and electricity. She snuck silently through the woods until she was about fifty feet away from them. The water helped to carry their voices. She crouched down behind a log and waited.

"Almost nine. They should have passed over by now," said a man in a blue baseball cap.

"We'll give them another hour. They might have gotten held up somewhere," another man in a black jacket answered.

"I feel like we should have brought some beer," a woman said, and the man in the baseball cap chuckled, while the other was silent. The three of them stood without speaking for several minutes, their eyes scanning the treetops.

"There!" the woman yelled, and the man in the black jacket lifted a black wand and pointed it up at a bird that was flying out of the woods. The man in the baseball cap quickly raised a tranquilizer gun and fired a dart at the bird, which did a somersault in the air and fell backwards to the ground. The man in the hat ran toward it. The other man was looking at what appeared to be a handheld TV, attached to the wand by a wire. The man in the hat came running back, holding an injured owl upside down by its feet.

"We got him?" he asked excitedly.

The man in the jacket didn't answer, but looked at the screen while passing the wand back and forth over the owl's body. "I can't tell. This thing is giving me a bad reading. The frequency is high, but scattered." He watched the screen for a minute as they all stood and waited. Finally, he said, "Nah, it's just an owl."

"Damnit," the man in the hat muttered as he grabbed the owl by the head and snapped its neck. He tossed its body in the woods and wiped his hands on his pants.

"Was that necessary?" the woman asked.

"It would have died anyway. There was enough sedative in that dart to knock out a man."

"Shut up, you two," the man in black scolded. "There's still something out there." He held the wand up and slowly turned so he was facing the woods. He waved the wand back and forth—until it was pointed right at Shaka.

"They're back there," he said in a hushed tone. "Spread out, and dart anything that flies. We'll flush them out."

Shaka's heart was beating like a snare drum. She saw the three of them spread into a line, flashlights in one hand, tranquilizer guns in the other. She inched backwards. She doubted she could make it to the trail before they found her. They were expecting owls, not a wolf. She knew that if she could just change, she'd be able to escape, but then they would know about her. Winston had been telling the truth after all.

There wasn't time to find another way out. The three of them were coming closer, and fast. She slipped behind a big white pine and tore off her clothes. Then she got down on her hands and knees, and her body silently shifted. As a wolf, she felt the same fear she had as a woman, but something else too: rage. Rage at being cornered, at being hunted.

She stayed poised behind the tree. Let them come to her.

She watched them approach. The woman was nearest to her, the others more than thirty feet off. As the woman walked, leaves crunched and branches broke beneath her clumsy feet. Clearly she was not someone who was used to walking in the woods. "Shit," the woman muttered as a branch caught in her hair, and she lowered her gun and flashlight to free it. Shaka took the opportunity immediately, weaving through the trees until she reached the trail. Then she turned and ran toward the lake, skirting around it when she reached it. She needed to get deeper into the woods.

The three of them, whoever they were, kept walking in a slow line toward where she had just been. She didn't wait to see how far they went, she kept running. She passed the carcass of the deer she'd killed the night before. She didn't slow down. She ran until the ground turned rocky and jagged and gave way only to dark bodies of water. They couldn't find her here, they couldn't make it this far.

Above her, the first stars were piercing the twilight. She paced at the edge of the water, back and forth, her eyes darting into the woods. Her clothes and her tea mug were still back there. Would they find them? She paced the rocky shore for an hour. The moon had moved up to the center of the sky when she decided she would go back. She didn't run this time, she trotted.

When she reached the lake, they were gone. She sniffed the air for the scent of a trap, but their strange and disquieting scent had vanished. She walked into the water and changed, emerging on the other side as a naked woman. When she found her clothes, she saw that they had been tossed around. She slipped them back on and went for her tea mug. It was still there, untouched. Dumping the cool tea out, she headed toward the trail.

She jogged all the way to the park, her eyes scanning the woods for anything out of place. When she reached the forest's edge, she stopped. What if they were waiting for her to come out? But then she remembered, they wouldn't be looking for her, they were looking for Michal and Winston. She took a deep breath and stepped out into the open. The park was empty, and the street was quiet. She kept her pace steady; no need to look suspicious.

When she reached the street, she found it deserted, as it should be after 1:00 a.m. on a Thursday night. At the end of the street, she turned back to look over her shoulder. All was empty, except for a white van parked opposite the park. It wasn't running, but the sight of it sent chills down her spine. They were in there; she knew it.

CHAPTER FOURTEEN

WHEN SHE GOT HOME, SHE PACED HER APARTMENT FLOOR UNTIL there was a path worn in the carpet. She didn't know where Winston lived, he was the one who'd found her. He might not even live in the city. She wondered if he was from the Fond du Lac reservation, which rested quietly in the woods twenty minutes west of the city. Or maybe he lived in the part of the city where she'd seen Michal crossing the street that afternoon. There was no way to know. It was all guesswork, and it was late.

She looked at her watch. It was 2:30 a.m. Even if Winston lived on her street, she wouldn't find him out at this hour. She needed to sleep; the panic of the night made her feel weak. But before she headed to bed, she took out a notebook, taped four pieces of paper together, and drew a big W on it with black marker. Then she taped it up in her window. Though she didn't know where he lived, she knew it wouldn't be long before he checked in on her.

Though the stress that rattled her brain had kept her on edge all night, it was no match for the exhaustion of her body. She slept hard right up until her alarm went off. As soon as she awoke, she remembered what she'd seen the night before, and the urgency to find Winston returned. Then she looked at her clock and realized she didn't have time to search for him, she needed to go to work.

She sat up and glanced at the W in the window. Having it displayed made her feel embarrassed, but she knew Winston would know it was meant for him. She'd gathered that he was a smart man. He wouldn't just stumble into a trap. She had to believe that. She repeated it to herself like a mantra as she got ready for work.

She wanted Winston and Michal to be safe, but that wasn't the only reason she was worried for them. She had realized very quickly that she was going to need them. Winston clearly knew something about these people. The only thing she knew so far was that they were looking for him, and if they were coming for him, they would eventually be coming for her too. It occurred to her that she could still run, and they wouldn't even know she existed. She could just shift and head north like she'd been dreaming of doing for months. But that idea didn't feel like what she was dreaming of anymore. Now it felt like cowardice. She just needed to find Winston.

She quickly got out of bed and taped four more pieces of paper together. This time she drew three pine trees, then she made a big X over the picture. She hung this one in her kitchen window. To anyone else, it might look like the ravings of a crazy person or the ambiguous statement of an artist, but he would understand.

She refused to let herself think about any of that at work. She needed to get back to her old rhythm in the kitchen. She worked with Jim on the grill while Jason worked the fryers. Though Jason talked constantly, Shaka tried not to let herself get irritated with him. He was keeping her mind off Winston and the strangers in the woods. Today he was talking about a nonprofit he'd read about that worked to clean up the ocean. Surfrider Foundation, they were called.

"You can jump on one of their cleanup crews and make a beach beautiful again. I'd love to do that! Cool people working with you, making a difference... A sea turtle population can come back in a year or two after a good cleanup."

"You're in the wrong part of the country, bud," Jim said.

"Just takes a bus ticket to be part of it. And a big part of the problem is these damn plastic cups," he said, lifting his Solo cup full of ice and Dr. Pepper. "I don't know why I'm using one. I should be drinking out of something I can use again and again. We all should."

Shaka lifted up her glass to show him. She had taken it from the bar weeks ago and kept it in the kitchen. She'd even taken the label maker and made a name tag for it, sticking the "SHAKA" tag right below the Bud Light decal. She used it only because she felt that her drinks tasted better in a glass than in plastic. She didn't disclose her motivation though.

"Uh oh. Looks like we've got a new top humanitarian in the kitchen," Jim said and smiled to himself.

"Way to go, Shaka!" Jason said. "Way to make good choices. That's what I'm gonna start doing tomorrow. Thanks, girl. You know what's up."

"I try," she said and turned back to the row of tickets in front of her and Jim.

"I'm real proud of you too, Shaka," Jim said sarcastically. "I'm real proud to see you drinking out of a glass."

Shaka giggled as she set her glass back down.

"You can laugh," Jason said, "that's cool. You're still doing something good."

Before the lunch rush ended, Jason had told them all about the migration patterns of sea turtles, which digressed to his dream of surfing, then to him wondering if he could surf Lake Superior. He invited Jim to come along when he tried. Jim told him he'd thought about doing that himself, but when he was twenty years younger. Still, if Jason would do it, he'd do it too, he promised.

"Shaka," Jason said, "you coming?"

Her mind went to her diving into the lake, then stretching and shifting into a wolf. She wasn't one for the beach if she wasn't going to change, but she also knew there was a very slim chance this surfing expedition would even happen.

"Yeah, count me in, why not?"

When her shift ended at seven, she felt lighter. The routine work and Jason's monologues had helped to get her mind off the people in the woods. It occurred to her that she could cancel her date with Adrian and walk around looking for Winston, but that seemed like such a long shot that it made her feel ridiculous to even consider it. He would come to her. She just had to wait.

Back at her apartment, she put on a black skirt and a dark red lacy shirt. She curled her hair and put enough mousse in it that when it dried, it was crunchy to the touch. She worried that it was now incredibly flammable and prayed she wouldn't bump into someone's cigarette. She put on heavy black eyeliner and red lipstick, and added silver hoop earrings she'd bought when she was in high school, then took a step back and looked at herself in the mirror. She looked like she belonged in another decade. She felt foolish. The dread that had been building since the night before had washed out any of the excitement she'd felt to see Adrian. "Too late to back out now," she said to herself as she turned from the mirror. She went to the back of her tiny closet and found her little black boots. They laced up the front and had square heels. They ended in a frill of black lace just above her ankles. They were a bit showy, but they had deceptively good traction, for whatever the night might bring. Then she grabbed her black clutch purse and left her apartment.

CHAPTER FIFTEEN

SHE DIDN'T GET TO THE HALLOW UNTIL A QUARTER AFTER eight. The bus stop was further away than she remembered. When she walked in, she found the place nearly empty. There was a couple at the bar who looked like they were arguing, and a few young men playing pinball. She strained to see into the dark corners of the room, but didn't see anyone. She wondered if he had already left, or maybe not come at all. She looked at her phone. Nothing. She felt both disappointment and relief at the thought of him standing her up. But she knew he had wanted this date bad enough to track down Rena and get her number. It wouldn't make sense for him to not show up.

She made her way to the bar and ordered a whiskey sour. As she took her first sip, she saw him, dressed in black with messy hair that threw a shadow over his eyes, and a diamond stud earring. He was walking toward her from the back corner. She must have missed him when she scanned the room. He approached her with a sneer on his lips, but as he got closer, it turned into a smile.

"Hey, punk," he said as he leaned in to hug her. He smelled like fresh soap and sandalwood.

"Hey, killer," she returned. "Love what you've done here." She motioned up and down at his outfit.

"I thought you'd like it. You seem like an eighties girl."

"Well, I do own Journey's greatest hits."

"Oh, look at that: style and taste," he teased and took a long drink of his beer.

Shaka watched him as he drank carefully and set his glass down. His hands were muscular—not what she would expect from an artist turned lawyer. Her eyes flicked up to his hair, a dark nest of tangles. She wondered what it would look like in the morning, then felt a little thrill in her chest as she wondered if she would see him in the morning. He turned and smiled at her, as if he could read her thoughts. She blushed and took another sip of her drink.

"So, you worked today?" he asked. "You work in a kitchen, right?"

"Yes and yes."

"I have to admit, I'm a little envious of that. Some days I wish I'd chosen a career that didn't require me to talk to people, especially clients. Do you like what you do?"

"Um, yeah, but I don't know if I'd call it a career," she said as she considered it for second. "I like being able to just focus on making something, then never see it again. Plus, I'm not great with the customers. It's hard to smile and say 'yes, ma'am' all day."

"I know. It's a skill you develop. I used to be horrible at pleasantries, but after a couple years of practice I got pretty dang good at it."

Shaka smiled at him. She liked the unhurried way he spoke. It had been a little while since she'd had a conversation with anyone other than Rena or Salem, and both of them tended to control the conversation. It was nice to feel heard, to feel like she had time to respond. Adrian and Salem seemed so different that she had a hard time imagining them as friends.

"So, you must be a good cook, then," he said. "What are the chances that I could get you to cook me dinner sometime?"

"Hmm... Not great. I mean, I live in a studio apartment and only own two pans."

"What about my place, then? Not to boast, but I have more than two pans, and a kitchen table. I could even buy the groceries, if you tell me what to get."

"Whoa. Sounds like a palace! I'd have to buy the groceries though, just in case you buy the cheap stuff."

"You know me so well already," he said. He took a long drink from his beer and placed it neatly before him. He tried to shake his hair out of his eyes, but it barely moved—only enough to reveal the clip-on diamond earring. Shaka laughed.

"Were you wearing that earring last time I saw you?"

"What, you like that? Maybe you can borrow it sometime. You just have to ask my grandma first."

"Sweet! Thank you! And thank you to Grandma Lois too."

"Mabel."

"Oh, sorry, Mabel. So, tell me about this Mabel. What's her deal, other than having impeccable taste?"

"Grandma Mabel lives in a retirement community in St. Paul with her new husband, Herman. She likes to knit, and to talk about her grandkids."

"And you devil, you haven't given her any grandkids, have you?"

"One," he said, watching her face closely.

"Oh. You have a child?"

"Yes. I had to give Mabel her dues." He gave a nervous laugh. Shaka watched him, smiling.

"So, what are the details? Boy or girl? How old? Where does he or she live?"

"A boy, Collin. He's four and he lives with his mom in California. She's remarried. I'm not really part of the picture anymore."

For the first time that night, Shaka didn't have his full attention. He looked off into the corners of the room while he swallowed the rest of his beer.

"I'm sorry. I don't have kids, but I get that that would be hard. When was the last time you saw him?"

"Last summer. I usually have him for a couple months in the summer, sometimes over Christmas too. He forgets about me though. He forgets I'm his dad."

"Well, he's young. He'll get it as he gets older. My parents split up when I was young. I can count on one hand the times I've seen my mom since she left, but she's still my mom. I'd still love to know her."

Adrian smiled at her and held her eyes for a minute. "You're a good person, Shaka. Not knowing you is her loss."

"Thank you," Shaka said sincerely. It had been ten years since she'd seen her mother last. She didn't even know if she was still alive. She didn't think about her all that often anymore, yet the sympathetic look Adrian gave her made her feel vulnerable. She was relieved when the bartender interrupted their conversation by bringing another round of drinks.

"So, you got the clothes right, and the hair, and Grandma's diamond earring, but something about your face isn't right. You just need more apathy, more disdain," she said.

His expression darkened on command, and the sneer returned to his lips. "How's this? ... Not that I care."

"Better. Much better."

"So, do you know where your mother is now?" he asked.

"No," she said coolly. "And that's okay. She's not an important person in my life." She picked up her glass and sipped, hoping he would let the topic go.

"How about your dad? Are you close with him?" he asked.

"Not really. Not at all actually. He lives in Chicago now. We were never really a great team. I spent a lot of time with my grandpa growing up, way more than I did with either of my parents. He lived in a cabin outside of Two Harbors. He used to pick me up from school on his motorcycle. I loved that."

"So, you were the bad-ass bitch of the middle school, huh? Do you still talk to old Clem?"

"His name is Arnold, and no, not in a while. He was always kind of reclusive. I think he moved further north. He was always talking about that."

Adrian squeezed her shoulder gently, then let his hand drop and settle against the small of her back.

"How about your parents?" she said. "Are you close with them?"

"I am with my mom. She's always in my corner. My dad is another story. I don't think he's ever forgiven me for going to art school."

"Wow. Gotta love that old-school judgement. Imagine if you'd been gay!"

"Oh, I don't think he'd care about that. My cousin Shelly is gay, and he loves her. She went to school to be a nurse though. That's a choice that makes sense to him. She never wasted time or money trying to live out a fairy tale."

"Well, just because you followed your dreams doesn't make you a bum. I mean, as a lawyer who owns more than two pans and a dining room table, it sounds like you've done pretty well."

"Yeah, I do okay. I don't know. I guess maybe he just doesn't like me."

"Well, cheers to parents we never asked for," Shaka said as she lifted her glass. He clinked his pint glass against hers.

For a moment they sat quietly and took in the atmosphere, the music, and the ambient conversation. Somewhere in the bar, someone was playing a piano. It clashed with the music that came through the sound system. There were a few more people filtering in now, most of them dressed in everyday clothes, jeans and sweatshirts, half of them throwing Adrian and Shaka curious glances.

"Do they have food here?" Adrian asked, unaffected by the veiled attention they were getting from the newcomers.

"Yes, but it's not very good," Shaka whispered.

"Should we leave our post and go somewhere where it is?" he whispered back.

She flicked her eyes from side to side suspiciously, then nodded. "Ten-four."

Adrian flagged down the bartender and paid the tab, then they made their way out to the street. Outside it was twilight.

The first brave stars shone as a soft pink still hugged the horizon. Adrian took her hand in his, and they walked east down the street. She knew his costume wasn't fooling anyone, though it was getting a lot of looks. He was tan, and smiling, two things that exposed him as fake right away. Shaka, on the other hand, could have fooled anyone. Her skin was fairer, her hair darker, but mostly it was the darkness in her eyes. Her smile came often, as did her laugh, but there was something there that betrayed it, a sadness that clouded her, a secret.

"Do you like Indian food?" he asked.

"Of course," she answered, smiling at him.

He opened the door to a small Indian restaurant. Shaka was wrapped up in the warm feeling of his arm around her. With each breath, she drank in the scent of his cologne and his skin. Everything had become so engaging that she had completely forgotten about the night before.

But as soon as she walked into the restaurant, all of that changed. The man in the baseball cap and the woman from the night before were sitting in a booth near the kitchen. When Shaka saw them, she froze, then quickly remembered herself and kept moving.

"You okay?" Adrian asked.

"Fine," she answered as she stepped up to the hostess stand.

They were seated in a booth opposite the man and woman from the woods. Shaka chanced a glance in their direction.

They were engrossed in conversation she couldn't hear. She told herself to relax, act natural, and not draw attention. She took one deep breath and looked up at Adrian. He was watching her closely, a hint of a smile on his lips.

"You seem tense. You know somebody here? You want to go somewhere else?"

"No, no. I think I just need to eat. I didn't have lunch," she lied.

As the waitress approached, Adrian ordered two waters and a basket of naan.

"So, tell me something awkwardly personal about yourself," she said daringly. It was the first thing she could think of to pull her mind back to her date and away from the two hunters at the other table. "How many girlfriends have you had?"

He gave a half laugh, half snort. "Cutting right to the chase."

"Or something else ... but something thrilling, even sobering."

"Oh, is that how that works? Personal secrets to keep the booze from affecting you?"

She felt like her clumsy attempt to distract herself might have turned the date in a bad direction. For a moment, it worked. She thought about how she didn't want to ruin it with Adrian. She liked him. She didn't want to chase him off by being crass or rude. But then, she also knew that their time together had a glass ceiling, so maybe cutting her losses early was the best way to go.

"Sorry if that was a bit much. A couple of whiskeys can go a long way on an empty stomach."

He smiled at her, but his smile didn't reach his eyes; the twinkle seemed to have disappeared. *Good job*, she thought with an internal sigh.

"I've had three serious girlfriends, and a handful of not-so-serious girlfriends. Your turn."

She smiled as the conversation picked up again. "I've had one boyfriend and a handful of non-boyfriends."

He watched her for a second, not smiling. For the first time, he was hard to read.

"If we're being candid, I have two questions for you. Number one, how long did it last? And number two, why only one?"

She smiled a fake smile for the first time that night. She had dug her own grave. "About six months," she said, and he made the same half snort, half laugh he had made before. She watched him without smiling until his eyes met hers again. "He didn't trust me, so I broke it off," she continued. "And there just hasn't been anyone else. I don't know why."

"Well, trust is paramount," he said.

The waitress returned with the naan and the waters. Shaka grabbed a piece of it and devoured it. She actually was hungry, and a little buzzed. The soft, buttery bread was delicious.

"Why did you break up with your girlfriends?"

"The first one, Candace, broke up with me, because I was broke all the time and smoking too much pot. College days."

Shaka worried that by saying her name, he had brought her to life and placed her between them. She wondered if he had meant to do that. But she had asked him specifically about these women, so who was she to get offended when he answered truthfully?

"The second one," he continued, "was Jessie. She screwed a friend of mine. You may know him: his name's Salem. That girl I really loved. I would have forgiven her, but then she dumped me and moved to Europe."

He took a drink from his water glass, then flagged down the waitress and ordered a beer. She was gone before Shaka could order a drink for herself. "The third and most recent ex-lover of mine was Molly, quiet as a mouse. She's my son's mother, and I ultimately dumped her because she just didn't excite me. I tried to make it work for almost three years after he was born, but we just didn't have anything in common. The relationship was starving. And the strange thing is..." The waitress arrived with his beer, and he took a long drink from it, then ordered two red curries. "...The strange thing is that when I met her, I was sure I would marry her. She was so kind, she was a kindergarten teacher, and the kind of woman that would stand by me and be my moral compass. But I guess kindness and morality and a family just aren't enough for me."

When he finished, Shaka didn't say anything. He wasn't looking at her, anyway. He was looking off into the distance, staring at nothing.

Shaka glanced across the room at the other table. They were both looking over at her and Adrian. They saw her. And in a glance she could see that they knew who she was.

She tried to play it off like it was nothing. Adrian, who had returned his attention to her, glanced their way too. His eyes seemed to linger on them calmly for a few seconds before he looked back at her.

"Freaks," he mumbled, and she gave a little smile. It felt for a moment like some of the tension had lifted. Then he said, "Rena says you're unknowable," and leveled his eyes at her. But she was too worried about the man and woman sitting across the dining room to answer him. She glanced at them again. They were getting up, and the man was throwing cash down on the table. As they walked to the door, her eyes flicked up to them twice. They didn't look at her once.

Adrian watched them walk out too.

"You know them?"

She bit her tongue. She wanted to say, "No, I'm unknowable," but she knew that would be pointless, even childish. She hoped their evening could be salvaged now that the two people she'd seen in the woods were gone.

"No, they just look like assholes."

"I'm sure they are."

"Rena knows me," she finally answered. "And I know her. I don't know why she would say that. Other than my grandfather — "

"Arnold," he inserted.

"Yes, Arnold. Other than him, Rena knows me better than anyone else. I don't know why she would say I'm unknowable; she knows nearly everything about me. She knows that I hate tomatoes, and that I want to live in a yurt in the woods, and that my favorite Disney movie is *Bambi*, plus a million other meaningless details."

"Yeah, she's probably lying. She gets a little aggressive whenever you come up. She said she thought you were keeping something from her, that you didn't trust her."

"A person doesn't need to disclose every detail to be trustworthy."

The waitress returned with their curries.

"You probably hate that I ordered you red curry if you don't like tomatoes," he said.

"It won't kill me ... but I do know how to order for myself, for future reference." She smiled at him. He gave her a weak smile in return and started eating. They ate in near silence.

After they finished, they spoke only on light topics: his plans to go jogging, and her coworkers wanting to surf Lake Superior. When the check came, Shaka felt that she should pay her part. It had been a strange dinner for them both, and there probably wouldn't be another one, so she felt bad letting him pay for her. But when she took her wallet out, he motioned for her to put it away.

"My treat," he said. "Besides, next time, you'll be cooking."

She smiled, unsure if he actually planned on there being a next time.

As they got up to leave, she felt anxiety start to creep up from the pit of her stomach again. What if the couple from the woods was waiting for her outside? She looked down the street for a white van, but didn't see one. As they left the restaurant she walked close to Adrian—so close that he had to put his arm around her or their arms would bump and rub.

"I'm sorry if I was a jerk tonight," he said to her. "I haven't dated much recently. I'm rusty."

She smiled. "Likewise. I hope we can have a do-over."

"Oh, there's many do-overs to come."

She walked snuggled beside him all the way to the bus stop.

"Let me be a gentleman and see you home," he said. "Don't worry, I'll leave you an honorable woman."

"Well, that might be harder than you think," she answered, grinning.

"Oh, a woman of the world, huh?" he teased her.

She rolled her eyes as they got on the bus together. She scanned her bus card twice.

"My treat," she said, smiling.

They sat down beside each other, his arm wrapped around her, his chin on top of her head as she leaned into his chest. She wanted to bring him up to her apartment and touch his bare chest, his stomach. She wanted to kiss him while trailing his jawbone with her fingertips. She rested her ear against his chest and heard his heart pounding. He was nervous. She smiled.

When her stop came, they stood up and got off together without saying a word. He held her close as they walked to her building.

As they came near, she noticed a man sitting on the stoop. *Shit!* she thought. *It must be one of them!* Her mind spun with ideas of how she could get out of this trap. *Just walk the other way, she thought, just turn around and go the other way. Say you lost your keys.* But as she got a little closer, she saw that the man on the stoop didn't look like the men from the woods. This man had darker skin and a smaller frame.

As he came more into view, she suddenly realized it was Winston. He was staring ahead and smoking a cigarette. Even when she was right in front of him, he didn't look at her. She played along and ignored him too. When she and Adrian reached her front door, she turned around to face him.

"I'd love to have you up, but my apartment is a horrible mess," she said to him.

"I said I'd leave you honorable, and I meant it, my lady." He lowered his voice, leaned in, and added, "But are you gonna be okay with that guy on the steps there?"

"He's harmless," she said dismissively.

Adrian leaned back with his arms around her waist and looked up at the side of the building.

"Somebody hates trees," he said, unknowingly looking at her windows.

She looked up and shrugged, hoping he wouldn't press the topic.

He didn't. Instead, he leaned forward and kissed her, his mouth both soft and firm. She leaned into the kiss, her hands trailing up his chest until they found his neck. He squeezed her back and tilted in toward her. She felt a jolt of fear and excitement. Then, with a last gentle kiss on the corner of her mouth, he stepped back. She couldn't contain her smile, and she giggled as he backed down the steps.

"Good night, punk," he said.

"Good night," she echoed.

She watched him until he reached the end of the block,

then unlocked the door and went inside. She left the door ajar for Winston to follow her in.

CHAPTER SIXTEEN

SHAKA WALKED UP THE STAIRS WITHOUT LOOKING BEHIND HER. She knew Winston was back there, but she didn't want to leave the thrill of her time with Adrian until she had to. She wanted the buzzing in her body, the warm feeling in her chest to continue as long as possible. She unlocked her door, replaying the kiss in her head, but as Winston's quiet footfalls got nearer, she retreated from her dream step-by-step. Her door clicked open, and she stepped inside, holding the door for him as he followed her in. She let the joy of the night slip away. She knew this conversation with Winston was leagues more important than a kiss from a new man.

She took a deep breath and turned around to face him. He was locking the door behind him. He had a vacant, nervous look on his face.

"I didn't mean to interrupt your evening," he said.

"No," she said instantly. "Thank God you're here. I need to talk to you. I saw them. You were right. They're out there, and they're looking for you."

"Okay," he said calmly. "Tell me what you saw."

"Well, I was in the woods last night, and I saw them—three people, two men and a woman. They had these weird wands that they were using to scan the woods. I think they were looking for you. I mean, they were looking for owls, and when they saw one, they shot it with a tranquilizer dart, then one of the men ran a wand over its body. When they figured out it was just an ordinary owl, one of them broke its neck. I heard him say he had used enough sedative on the owl to take down a man. Why would a person use that much sedative on an owl unless they were trying to capture you?"

Winston turned his back to her and faced the window. He stood behind the picture of the trees and pinched the bridge of his nose. She watched him closely, waiting for his reaction. She hoped he wouldn't break down or panic. She wanted him to keep calm. Something horrible was beginning, and she needed someone calm to explain it to her.

After a minute, to Shaka's relief, he turned back around, his eyes heavy but clear. "And then what?" he asked.

"Well, I was hiding in the woods, and it was like their wands picked up on me. They waved them back and forth and spread out to flush me out. I thought about changing and attacking them. I mean, if they were looking for an owl, they would have been pretty surprised to find a wolf. It almost came to that. I shifted and was waiting for the woman to reach me, but her hair got stuck on a branch, and that gave me just enough time to get away. It was hours before I came back. They were gone by then, but I felt like they were watching me. When I came out of the woods, there was no one around, but there was a white van on the side of the road. I know they were in there. I don't know if they saw me or not, but I think they found my clothes in the woods." She took a deep breath. It was more difficult to recount all of this than she'd thought. "Then tonight, when we were at dinner, I saw two of them eating in the restaurant. I couldn't get close enough to hear what they were saying. They made me nervous enough the way it was. They mostly kept to themselves, but they did look at me a couple times. I don't know how much they know about me, and I don't know what to do now. All I know for sure is that I can't shift with them lurking around, and neither should you. Do they know what you look like—I mean, as a man?"

Winston shook his head. "I don't think so, but then, I didn't know they were so close to finding me either. I don't know what they know. But Shaka, we have some cards to play too. I found their headquarters. It's west of Minneapolis, in an industrial zone. They have their own building, under the guise of a drug research company. The lab is on the main floor. That's where they're keeping Rachel."

"How did you find that out?" Shaka asked.

"I drove down there after we spoke, and I spent two days following unmarked white vans around the city. Eventually, I found a garage that had several of them that wasn't a catering company or an office supply store. I was trying to figure out what kind of business it was when I saw one of the men who was there the night Rachel was taken: an old man with white hair and round glasses. I knew him immediately. I waited until it was dark, then shifted and snuck in through an air exchange vent. I looked into almost every room in that building. Then, I saw Rachel in a jail cell with nothing but a toilet, a sink, and a tiny cot. She didn't look good — not that I expected she would. She was so thin. She looks old and frail now, and she's my little sister! I wanted to tell her I was there, that I'm going to get her out, but I couldn't take the chance. If they'd caught me too, neither of us would be getting out."

He stopped talking for a moment and looked down at his hands. His palms were sweating. He squeezed them together, took a deep breath, and continued. "I watched them bring a young man in. He was probably about your age. He was screaming and swearing and trying to wrestle free as two men forced him into an empty cell. His eyes were red and foggy, like he had been drugged. Once he was in the cell, the two men held him against the wall as a woman came in and gave him a shot in the arm. He lost his fight pretty quickly after that. He fell to the floor and sort of crumpled up. He moaned for a bit, then his body twisted and shrank, and he became a rattlesnake. Whatever they gave him made him shift, and he couldn't stop it. As a snake, he moved sluggishly, and a man in a lab coat caught him with a wire noose on a pole. Then he drained venom from his fangs into a glass jar and tossed the snake back onto the pile of clothing. The snake slithered inside it and stayed there for hours. It was morning before he shifted back."

Shaka felt a chill run down her spine. That could have been her, if she hadn't escaped them in the woods. She felt ill. She sat down on the couch, and Winston sat down beside her.

"I should have believed you before," she said.

"You didn't know. And it wouldn't have made any difference. Now we know where they are. That's something."

"What are we going to do?" she asked, half to him, half to herself.

"I don't know yet," he said, "but something. You should sleep now. We can figure it out tomorrow. Just don't do anything out of the ordinary. They may be watching us. It could be just a little detail that gives you away." Reaching into his pocket and pulling out a little notebook, he tore out a page and handed it to her. It said, *2385 Nightingale Ave., Bloomington.*

"If anything happens to me, this is where they are. Just be careful, and be clever. The key to survival is not only strength, but also fear."

She took the paper from him hesitantly. "Please don't let them catch you," she said.

"I will do everything I can not to." He looked down at his hands and squeezed them again, then back up to her. "But if I do, could you see that Michal gets to his grandparents in Wisconsin? He won't want to go, but he knows how to get there."

"Of course," she said, though she was uncomfortable with the idea of being responsible for a child, even if it was just for a drive across the river. She had a feeling that in the days and weeks to come, she would be doing many things that she wasn't quite ready to do. Shaka gave him a sad smile. "You don't know anyone else like us, do you? I feel like we'd have a better shot if there were more than just the two of us."

"I wish I did," he answered, "but no one that can be trusted."

"Is there anyone? Even if they don't have our abilities?"

He gave her a guarded look. "Not really. Like you, I have few relationships." Again, he squeezed his hands together. "In my culture, the owl is an omen of death. Most of those who know of my gift regard me with fear. Not many of them would stand up to help someone they believe is the angel of death. And speaking of bad omens, that man you were with—be careful with him. He looks familiar. I can't place him, but he gives me a bad feeling. We don't know who we can trust, so we must assume we can trust no one."

Shaka felt a flicker of irritation as soon as he mentioned Adrian. "Well, you two do live in the same city, so there's a good chance you have actually seen him before."

He nodded. "I know. Just be careful. And you'd better take those pictures out of your window. People will wonder about you." He gave her a little smile.

"I will. They've served their purpose."

"Tomorrow, meet me at 10:00 a.m. on the beach," he said as he rose. "We can troubleshoot."

"I'll be there."

He walked to the door. "Good night, Shaka."

"Good night."

As he pulled the door shut behind him, she went to her window and took down the pictures. She saw him on the steps below, jogging out to the street. His pace slowed to a brisk walk as he turned down the sidewalk, throwing a suspicious look over his shoulder as he went. It was clear that overnight, the world had become a hostile and dangerous place for both of them.

CHAPTER SEVENTEEN

SHAKA DIDN'T SLEEP WELL THAT NIGHT. IN HER FIRST DREAM she was running down the street as headlights bore down behind her. She woke up in a breathless sweat but was able to fall back to sleep. In her second dream, she was chasing Adrian through the woods as a wolf with a blood-stained muzzle. He was fast, but she steadily gained on him and eventually took him down. When she did, she awoke with a violent gasp and was flooded with relief, knowing Adrian was safe on the other side of the city. She tossed in bed, wondering if spending time with him would put him in danger. Of course she would never really attack him, but what if the man and the woman in the restaurant started wondering about him as well? She knew that the sooner she let him go, the better it would be for both of them. Her heart sank at the realization, but her mind calmed, and eventually she fell back to sleep.

The next time she awoke, it was light out, and the birds were singing. She got out of bed and dressed quickly. She made herself a cup of tea and poured it into her travel mug, then hurried out of her apartment towards the bus stop.

She got to the beach at nine— an hour too soon. She killed time by strolling down the boardwalk and on through the nautical-themed neighborhood that separated downtown from the beach. When she finally reached the beach, it was empty, just as it had been last time. Only driftwood and seagulls populated the shoreline.

She found the old stone house in the same condition, but there was a new pile of beer cans in the center of what had once been the living room. She kicked one across the floor and watched as it came to rest against the opposite wall. Turning around, she looked through the missing wall at the lake. It was a windy day, and the water was punctuated with thousands of small whitecaps, yet to her, the lake looked inviting. She felt the urge to dive in and swim along the torrential bottom, then come up as a wolf and paddle back to this very beach, where she would run along the shore, chasing gulls. She knew the urge was pointless, even silly, but it was so strong that she felt tears burning her eyes.

She shook her head to get rid of the thought, then stepped out of the house and into the open air, where she let the breeze dry her eyes and run its wispy fingers through her hair. The air smelled like cold water and seaweed. She opened her mouth and tried to taste it. Then an unwanted thought intruded into her mind, and fear pricked in her belly. What if they took her from this? What if she ended up in one of those cells and could no longer feel the sun or smell the air? The prickle of fear quickly turned into a knot, and she shook her head, trying to banish it. She couldn't afford to indulge every anxiety that occurred to her. There were too many; she'd never be able to feel normal.

Behind her she heard footsteps, and she turned around, expecting to see Winston. But it was a man she'd never seen before. He was walking up to the house slowly, like a tourist. He was dressed like one too, wearing khaki pants and a dark blue sweatshirt. His shoes were polished brown leather. She wondered what he had been thinking, wearing those shoes to the beach. Shaka felt goose bumps rise on the back of her neck.

After a couple more steps toward the house, he noticed her and gave a little jump.

"Oh, hi!" he said cheerfully. "I didn't see you there!"

"That's okay. I was just on my way out," she said as she turned toward the wooded trail that led inland from the beach. She gave him a shy smile as she walked past.

"No need to leave on my account, miss. I'm harmless," he said.

Shaka tried to hide the shiver that ran down her spine. "I'm sure you're great, but I have to meet someone," she said and kept walking toward the trail. Once she passed through the first trees, she heard rustling in the treetops and looked up to see two owls. She watched them take flight above her, and they disappeared westward.

She chanced a glance over her shoulder and saw the dark-haired man watching her from the doorway of the empty house. When he saw her look back at him, he stepped forward as if he was going to follow, but stopped once he was outside the building, an expression of mild curiosity on his face. She kept walking at a steady pace; she didn't want to alarm him by running. When she was far enough down the trail that he could no longer see her, she broke into a run, her flight fueled by fear. She leapt over rocks and branches on the path without thinking. As her heart raced, she wondered if she was overreacting. She didn't even know who he was. He could have just been a friendly tourist... But that assumption wasn't enough for her.

She kept running until she reached a park. At the far end of the parking lot, she saw an unmarked white van and froze. Was it them? Was that man one of them? She visibly shuddered at the thought. How had they known she would be here? Had Winston inadvertently led them here? She felt like they were coming at her from all sides.

A voice in her head demanded that she keep walking, act natural. She took a deep breath and started walking again. A group of kids were playing kickball on the baseball diamond to the west. She was relieved to see them. She doubted they would take her where there were so many witnesses. She hoped that Winston and Michal had made it out of the neighborhood. She didn't dare look up at the trees again and alert the hunters that there was something up there. She just kept walking. *One foot in front of the other, like a normal person,* she told herself.

When she reached the boardwalk, there were enough people around that she could disappear among them. "Thank you, tourists," she muttered.

She sat down on a bench, not knowing what to do next. She felt helpless. Again, her eyes burned as she blinked back tears.

Just then, her phone buzzed in her pocket. She pulled it out quickly and looked at the screen. It was a text from Adrian.

Good morning, beautiful. Coffee?

She quickly stuffed it back in her pocket. Thinking about him right now would distract her, and she was already vulnerable ... though it was hard for her to push him out of her head, especially when she felt totally alone. She wished he was with her now; it would give her a veil of safety. She stood up and started walking again. It quickly occurred to her that a veil of safety was not true safety; on the contrary, it was dangerous and would bring her guard down.

She walked to the end of the boardwalk and took the stairs up to the street, then she walked north. She didn't know where she was going, but she knew she couldn't just stay still. She had no idea if her home was safe or not, or how she could find Winston again, or how to identify any of the people who were after her. They could be anyone. She scanned the pedestrians ahead of her, and looked over her shoulder at those behind her. She felt she should get off the street.

Shaka walked past a coffee shop and felt eyes on her. Giving a quick glance to the window, she saw a familiar face. She spun on her heels and went into the coffee shop. Winston and Michal sat on stools by the window. Winston's eyes were wild with panic; they gave him the look of an animal, or a man about to lose control. He motioned to the back of the room, and she followed them to a table in the corner. It was dark and crowded, and no one was paying attention to them.

She ordered a chai tea and a bagel from the waitress and sat down, trying to look natural. Winston and Michal sat opposite her with solemn expressions on their faces.

"Did you see the guy at the beach? Was he one of them?" she asked.

"I don't know," Winston said. "I haven't seen him before,

but there are many of them, and I've only seen a few. I'd be hesitant to trust anyone at this point."

Shaka felt her hands tremble as he spoke. It was one thing to think it, but another to hear someone else say it. "Do you think they know where I live?"

"I don't know, but it's always safest to assume the worst. Is there anywhere else you can stay?"

"No," she answered quickly.

"I think they followed me out there," he said. "I don't know if they know about you yet. We probably shouldn't be together in public. We'll have to keep this short. I'm going back to Minneapolis tonight. We need to know as much about these people as they know about us: where they live, who their families are, what cars they drive. I need more information about the lab too. I need to know door codes, where the supply rooms are, the security schedule, what the guards are like. If we can't stop them, we should at least figure out how to free the prisoners."

Shaka was surprised by Winston's determination. It impressed her, but it also made her uneasy. "What if we went to the press?" she asked. "Do you think if everyone knew what was going on there, they would shut that place down?"

"That's a gamble," said Winston. "We couldn't do that without letting everyone know that people like us exist. Imagine the reaction! The public may end up donating money to those guys to keep our kind under control, or to clone us, or something worse."

Michal listened to the conversation with wide eyes as he sucked down a chocolate milkshake. Shaka wondered if he understood what was happening. She worried for him. If Winston was captured, Michal surely would be too, and how frightening would it be to be a child in their custody?

Her phone buzzed against her leg again. It was another message from Adrian.

Maybe you're sleeping past coffee today. Text me when you can. ☺

Shaka stuffed her phone in her pocket.

Winston was looking at her gravely. "Remember," he said, "we can't trust anyone."

"I know," she replied, "we need our guards up. But Adrian and I met through someone I've known for many years. He's not one of them."

Winston didn't say anything.

"So, you're going down there tonight?" she asked.

"Yes. After dark. And I was going to ask you a favor." He paused and looked searchingly at her. "Can Michal stay with you while I'm gone? It will only be a couple days at most. I'm afraid to take him to his grandparents' house. I don't know if they're being watched too."

"Yes, he can stay with me," she said. "But it may not be safe there either."

"True, but his chances are better with you. We know for sure that they're watching me; we don't know if they know about you."

"Aren't you afraid they'll come for your parents?"

"No. They don't share our gift. It came from my grandmother."

Shaka had never thought of it as a "gift" before, but he was right: it was a gift. That was why they were being hunted for it.

"Well, can't say I'm good with kids, but I guess I can learn," she said, looking at Michal.

He looked down at his hands with a scowl on his face.

Winston smiled at her and looked to Michal. "I need you to listen to her, Michal. It will only be for a couple days."

"Yes, sir," he said quietly. Shaka couldn't tell if he was being polite or sarcastic.

"I'll bring him over tonight at dusk. I'll bring you a burner phone tonight too. I don't know if they're tracking our phones, but we'd better not risk it. And let us leave first. We shouldn't be seen together."

Shaka nodded, and before she could say anything else, Winston and Michal rose and headed for the back door.

The rest of that day, Shaka sat nervously in her apartment. Every so often, she looked out the window for a white van on the street. She didn't see one, but that didn't calm her nerves.

As she paced her floor, her phone buzzed again. She saw Adrian's name on the screen and looked away. She wanted to answer—she even felt a little flutter in her chest at knowing he was still thinking about her—but she was afraid to let herself get distracted by him. She walked over to her dresser and stuffed her phone in the sock drawer. She would call him back later, when she no longer feared she was being watched.

She turned her attention to cleaning up her apartment and making space for Michal. It was hard to imagine an extra body in her small apartment, but she made up a bed on the couch and cleaned off her coffee table. If he was like every other boy she'd known, he was going to want to be close to the TV. She checked her cupboards for food and found them almost empty. This got her out of her apartment and sent her to the corner store to buy junk food: hot dogs, mac and cheese, hamburgers, Doritos, and Pepsi. She was going to have to assume he ate like she had when she was his age. After all, Winston hadn't asked her to teach him healthy eating habits; he had just asked her to keep him safe for the next couple days.

When dusk came, she turned the TV down and nervously waited to hear the ring of the doorbell. It wasn't long before she heard it and buzzed them in. In less than a minute, they were at her door. Michal had a duffel bag slung over one shoulder and an Xbox tucked under his other arm.

"I hope you know how to hook that up, because I don't," she said.

Michal gave her a quick nod and looked around the apartment.

"Okay," Winston said. "Come here, boy." He squeezed Michal in a bear hug, Xbox and all. "You be good. This is important. I love you."

Michal nodded. "Yes, sir," he said weakly, and this time his voice held no sarcasm.

Winston turned to Shaka and pulled a Tracfone from his pocket. "My number is under the missed calls. Don't be afraid to use this."

As Shaka took the phone from him, they heard a knock at the door. They both shifted uneasily. She cautiously went to the door and looked through the peephole, then gave a short sigh of relief and opened the door. Adrian walked in. He was smiling and opened his mouth to say something to her when he saw that they weren't alone. The smile fell from his face as he saw Winston standing in her apartment. A look of confusion flashed across his face.

"I'm sorry," he said, taking a step back, "I should've called. I mean, I did call— twice—and that's why I decided to come here and check on you. But I don't want to intrude."

"No," said Winston, "I was just leaving." He gave Shaka a hard look of warning, then turned to Michal and gave him a softer look before walking out the door.

Adrian looked at Michal, then back at Shaka. "I'm sorry, Shaka," he said as he stepped toward the door. "I shouldn't be here."

"Wait a minute," she said, going after him. She stepped out into the hallway and pulled the door shut behind her. "He's my neighbor, and he has to go out of town for a couple days. I agreed to watch his kid. That's all that's going on here. And I'm sorry I didn't text you back. I just had a crazy day, you know?"

He nodded. "I know. I mean, I can see that."

"I've been thinking about you though."

The smile came back to his face as she said it.

"My life is just flipped upside down right now," she continued.

"You gonna tell me how you became the Fresh Prince of Bel-Air?" he joked, but his smile faded when she didn't laugh. In fact, her eyes were heavy with tears. "I'm sorry," he said as he stepped forward and embraced her. "What can I do? Do you want me to stay?"

"Yes," she said instantly and wrapped her arms around him. She held him close to her until she was able to say what she knew she must say next. "But I need you to go. I can't tell you why. I'm sorry."

To her surprise and disappointment, he didn't argue with her. "Okay," was all he said, but he didn't let her go right away.

She pressed her hot cheek against his chest, afraid if she said anything, her voice would crack. She pulled out of his embrace and wiped her eyes.

"You don't have to explain anything to me right now. I trust you," he said. "Just know that I'm here if you need anything."

"Thank you," she whispered and looked up at him. He gave her hands a squeeze and dropped them, then slowly turned his back to her and walked back the way he'd come. She stood in front of her door until she heard the building's front door close, and the hallway return to silence.

CHAPTER EIGHTEEN

SHAKA STEPPED BACK INSIDE AND SHUT THE DOOR SOFTLY behind her. She leaned against it and looked straight ahead, seeing nothing. From the couch, Michal glanced at her shyly. Her expression was hard. She was trying to push something away, to make something disappear. She reminded herself that she was probably being hunted at that moment. She also reminded herself that there was a boy who was being hunted too—a boy who she was responsible for. Dating was a luxury she just couldn't afford. She steeled herself and stepped away from the door.

"Love stinks," she said. "Don't mess around with it."

Michal didn't say anything, but watched her as she walked to the bathroom and gently shut the door behind her. A few minutes later she came out, composed, and found Michal still sitting quietly on the couch.

"Did you hook up your Xbox?" she asked.

He shook his head.

"Why don't you? I'm gonna get ready for bed. I just want this day to be over with."

Shaka went back to the bathroom and showered. When she was done, she found that Michal had hooked up his Xbox and was playing a zombie war game.

"Are you hungry?" she asked.

He glanced at her and nodded.

She went to the stove and heated some instant mac and cheese for him. She couldn't bring herself to eat it though. Since she'd started cooking for a living, she found it increasingly difficult to eat bad food, no matter how convenient. She made herself an Italian salad and toasted a couple slices of French bread. She sat down on the couch beside Michal as they ate.

"How is it?" she asked.

"Good," he said. His bowl was already empty. "Why are you eating a salad?" he asked with a look of disgust.

"Because it's delicious. Don't worry, I won't make you eat one. I have plenty of junk food for you to get by on 'til your dad gets back."

"*If* he gets back," he mumbled.

Shaka thought carefully before she responded. "Your dad

seems like a smart and resourceful guy. I bet he'll be back with a plan to get your aunt out before the week is over. He knows we're depending on him."

Michal clicked away at the controller as one zombie after another fell into a screeching, bloody pile on the screen. She watched for a few minutes, remembering her teenage years: she and Rena sitting awkwardly between boys at parties as they competed against one another at some game that looked almost painfully simple. Their idea of flirting was handing Shaka the controller and trying to teach her to play. Shaka and Rena could tolerate about half an hour of that—maybe forty minutes if the boys were really cute—but that was it. Now her days of pretending to be interested in video games were behind her.

"Do you need anything?" she asked.

"No, ma'am," he answered.

She smiled at the formality. "Okay. Well, if you would be so kind as to turn the sound off, I'm going to go to bed."

Michal jumped forward and turned the sound down. "What time do I have to go to bed?" he asked.

"I don't know. Midnight?" she asked more than told him.

Michal didn't say anything, but turned around and smiled at the TV. Shaka climbed into bed and pulled the covers over her head. She could hear the clicking of his controller and thought about retracting her allowance of games until midnight, but before she could, she fell asleep.

When she woke up, it was quiet and dark in her apartment. She could hear Michal breathing heavily on the couch. Her phone was vibrating. She picked it up and looked at the screen. Rena was calling her. She rubbed her eyes to make sure she had read it right. There was no mistake: there was the familiar picture of Rena on her phone, smiling and holding up a martini. It was a picture Shaka had taken when they took a riverboat ride on the St. Croix the year before.

Shaka grabbed her phone and walked into the bathroom. She touched the accept button and tentatively said, “Hello?”

“Hi,” came Rena’s voice, sounding smaller than normal.

Shaka opened her mouth and closed it. She didn’t know what to say.

“Listen,” Rena began, “I’m sorry for being so horrible. I don’t know why I said those things, but I did, and I’m sorry.”

Shaka found herself smiling. Rena always repeated herself when she was nervous. It was good to hear her voice. “I probably deserved it. I can be a lumberjack,” Shaka replied.

“Yes, but I’ve always loved that about you ... and I miss you,” Rena replied.

“I miss you too.”

“If I promise not to be a complete bitch, will you meet me for coffee tomorrow?” Rena asked.

"Of course. Can you meet me at the grille at three?"

"Yes. I'll be there."

Shaka hung up the phone and gave a happy sigh for the first time in days. She crept back to her bed, crawled in, and was asleep within minutes.

CHAPTER NINETEEN

SHAKA SLIPPED OUT OF THE APARTMENT EARLY THE NEXT morning. She left Michal a note directing him toward the food. When she was twelve, she had already been babysitting the neighborhood kids for two years, so she assumed if she could care for others at his age, he should be able to care for himself.

By 8:00 a.m. she was behind the line and beside her least favorite coworker, Ken. He must have been filling in for Jim. Ordinarily, she would have been nervous all morning, but he didn't frighten her as much as usual now. His big, imposing presence didn't feel as threatening when there was a real threat somewhere out in the streets. She kept herself on her end of the line and tried her best to anticipate his unspoken needs as he glared at the tickets that came through. They made it through the morning this way, and up until 3:00, when Jason came in to replace her. He smiled at her and waved as he walked past the grill to get his apron.

"Hey, boss. Hey, Chakra," he said as he joined them behind the line. At his words, the corners of Ken's lips curled. It was the first thing resembling a smile Shaka had seen from him all day.

"Hey, Jason. Soups are all made, and there's more in the cooler," Shaka said as she took off her apron. "I'm meeting a friend at the bar, so I'm gonna go."

"Oh, so Shaka's getting day drunk!" he teased her.

Shaka gave two quick shrugs as she came out from behind the grill.

"Have fun, girl!" he yelled as she left the kitchen.

The cool air of the dining room washed over her, and the classic rock from the kitchen was instantly transformed into smooth jazz. There weren't many customers in the dining room; the middle of the day was always slow. Shaka sat down at the bar. She thought about ordering a beer, but decided to wait for Rena. It seemed like the polite thing to do.

In less than five minutes, Rena walked in. She was wearing orange leggings and a black blazer, a combination that Shaka could never have pulled off, but she had known Rena long enough to know that she could make any outfit look good. Aesthetics were her gift.

When Rena noticed her, she smiled. Shaka smiled back naturally. She had missed her friend.

After Rena sat down beside her, Shaka leaned over and hugged her. "Hi. It's good to see you."

"Good to see you too, even if you smell like a fryer."

Shaka pulled back with a giggle and signaled to the bartender. She ordered a Budweiser, and Rena ordered a martini.

"How have you been?" Rena asked. "What have I missed?"

"I've been okay," she lied. "How about you?"

"Oh, you know, same story. I have an art show next month, a series of trees I've been working on," Rena answered.

"That's cool. What types of trees?"

"All different: oak, aspen, white pine, cedar. They're all standing alone and painted at a different time of day, so when they're all lined up, you can see the sun rise and set through the series. What do you think? Corny?"

"No way, it sounds great. Where is the show?"

"At the Institute. You should come to the opening. I get tired of listening to Salem kiss everybody's butt at those things. It'd be more fun if you came."

"I'd love to come," she said, but in the back of her mind, she couldn't quiet the thought that she didn't know what her life would be like in a month.

"To be honest," Shaka began tentatively, "I haven't really been okay. Things have been sort of messed up."

Rena dipped her finger in her martini and put it in her mouth. "Do you want to elaborate?" she asked.

"I don't know. I don't know who to trust. I saw some creeps in the woods looking for someone to assault a few nights ago, and since then, I've just been nervous. I feel like they're looking for me." Shaka tried to be as honest as she could without revealing too much.

"Why do you think they're looking for you? What would they want with you?" Rena asked.

"I don't know. Maybe I'm just being paranoid," Shaka said, suddenly feeling like she had indeed revealed too much.

"Is it because of Adrian?" she asked.

"No," Shaka replied. "I like Adrian. He's sweet, and he's fun. But I don't know how to make room for him. You know my motto: 'trust no one.'"

"I'm familiar," Rena replied. "But you've got to learn sometime. You don't have to run to the chapel, but you could just give him a chance. I mean, you don't want to be alone and stuck babysitting for your neighbors forever, do you?"

"How do you know about that?" Shaka asked, suddenly suspicious.

"How do you think? Adrian came over last night. He spilled his guts to Salem, who of course told me everything."

"What's 'everything'?" Shaka asked, curious to hear about the evening from Adrian's perspective.

"Oh, you know, just that you ignored him all day, then he went to your apartment and found another man there, and that you're now spontaneously caring for this guy's child, which sounds remarkably un-Shaka to me. Then how you hugged him desperately and cried and told him you couldn't be with him."

Shaka looked at her half-empty beer glass. He had left nothing out.

"So," Rena pried, "what's going on with you?"

Shaka took a long drink of her beer, wishing she'd had at least one drink in her before she had to start coming up with answers for these questions.

"I can't tell you, and I can't tell him. If I were clever, I would come up with a lie that explains everything, but...well, you know me." She turned to Rena and gave her a weak smile.

Rena's eyes searched her.

"If I could share it with you, I would. In fact, I'd like to share it with you, but I can't. I know this is an impossible favor to ask, but could we just leave it at that?"

Rena gave a quiet scoff and turned to her martini. She sipped it as Shaka watched her, then carefully set it back down. She turned and looked at Shaka, then reached out and patted her arm, letting her hand come to rest there. She shut her eyes, and the sounds of the bar seemed to fade away. The air moved around them as if a breeze were blowing through the place.

Shaka looked at Rena, whose eyes were still closed. She knew what she was doing. It was the same thing she'd done when they were in high school, despite her promise to never to do it again: she was looking inside Shaka's mind. And Shaka wanted to let her. She longed to tell someone her secret, but it was too risky. She pulled her arm away.

"What is up with you and that wolf?" Rena asked. "And you shouldn't go into the woods at night, you know. That's female safety 101."

"Rena," Shaka said sternly, "don't."

Rena scowled and took another sip of her martini. "Fine," she said. "We can do it your way."

"Thank you."

"You've never been real forthcoming, Shaka. It's irritating, but I've grown accustomed to it."

"Do you think Adrian could grow accustomed to it?" she asked.

Rena shrugged. "Doesn't hurt to ask. I mean, if Salem had said to me 'I like you, but I have some disturbing secrets involving a wolf that I can't share with you,' I would have assumed he was a serial killer and smothered him in his sleep."

"Yeah, you talk big, but you couldn't smother a sick cat if it came down to it," Shaka teased her.

Rena gave her a theatrical look of rage and went on. “But that boy has it bad for you, Shaka. He just might put up with this double life nonsense, so long as he gets to be part of one of them.”

Shaka felt a flutter in her chest at hearing this. She pulled out her phone and checked it. No messages. She slid it back into her pocket. As she did, Rena pulled her phone out as well.

“Great,” she muttered. “I have to go. Salem locked himself out again.” She stood up, swallowed the last of her martini, and set a ten on the bar. “I’m sorry for being so awful before. I accept you as you are, secrets and all.”

“Thank you. And Rena...please don’t tell anyone what you saw,” she said with a pleading look.

“Your secret is safe with me. I’ll call you tomorrow,” she answered as she walked to the door.

As soon as the door closed behind her, Shaka ordered one more beer. Just like that, Rena was back in her life. At least one thing in her life felt normal again.

Halfway through the beer, her phone buzzed. It was Rena texting her: Call Adrian.

Shaka smiled as she sipped her beer. When she finished, she went outside. It was a gray afternoon, and the air smelled like rain. She took a deep sniff and noted several scents the air carried: the lake, car exhaust, fried food, and cigarettes.

With that scent, she looked around until she spotted a middle-aged woman smoking while she waited to cross the street. Shaka bummed a cigarette from her and walked to the bus stop. She was early, her bus wouldn't be coming for another twenty minutes.

She smoked the cigarette slowly. She always liked to enjoy her cigarettes, listen to them crackle, taste the smoke that passed through her mouth. Rena always told her it was a disgusting habit, but she didn't find it disgusting. She liked the feel, the scent, the entire act. It was like a ceremony for her, one she reserved for special occasions, and by doing so, she kept it from becoming a habit.

When she stubbed out her cigarette, she took out her phone. She felt herself tense up as she started typing Adrian a message.

Hey. Sorry about last night. Think we could talk? She hit send and tucked her phone back in her pocket, then she sat listening to the gulls and felt the first drops of rain as the bus pulled up. By the time the bus reached her stop, it was pouring.

When she got to her building, she rushed up the steps and fumbled with her keys at the door. She dropped them, and while bending over to pick them up, she saw an unmarked white van pass by. She looked at the driver. It was a man she'd never seen before. He was wearing a blue shirt and a matching baseball cap. He paid her no attention. Still, her hands shook as she finally slid her key into the lock. Once inside, she pushed the door shut and ran to her apartment. She locked the door behind her and ran to the window. The white van was gone.

"Did you see any white vans drive by today?" she asked Michal. He was on the couch, wearing the same clothes he'd worn yesterday, killing zombies.

"No," he replied without looking at her.

She looked at him with irritation.

"Have you eaten anything today?" she asked.

"Mac and cheese," he said and motioned to the empty bowl that sat beside him on the couch.

"Okay. Gross. Well, I'm going to shower, and when I'm done, you'd better shower too,"

"Yes, ma'am," he replied.

The warm water felt nice on her skin after the cold wash of the rain. She stood in the shower for almost thirty minutes, and when she stepped out, she found herself in a cloud of steam. She wiped the fog from the mirror and looked at herself. She looked fragile. A thin red scar ran over her right breast. Years ago, she had cut herself on a rock while running through the woods with her grandfather. As a man, he had moved slowly, but as a wolf, he was as fast as the wind, and she had to work hard to keep up with him. One day as she was running beside him, her lanky new legs got tangled, her back paws stepping on her front, and sent her skidding to the ground, chest first. She felt a sting as she slid, and when she stood up, blood ran down her thick gray coat. Her grandfather led her down to the water, where they waded for a bit, and the cool water stopped the blood from flowing. That evening, they returned home at a trot so her wound wouldn't tear open. When she shifted back, she had a delicate new scab on her chest. Its mark had been there ever since.

She carefully ran a fingertip over it, trying not to remember her grandfather. She tried not to imagine the feeling of running through the night on her four leathery paws, her nails tipping in and out of the earth as she covered ground, putting miles between herself and whoever was watching her, chasing her.

She grabbed a towel and dried off quickly, then dressed in sweatpants and an old T-shirt and left the bathroom, hoping to reclaim the TV while Michal showered. When he went into the bathroom, she plopped down on the couch and soon realized she didn't know how to watch TV with his Xbox hooked up to it. She reached for her phone instead. Adrian had replied while she was in the shower.

Of course. When? Where?

She quickly typed back, Now? Call me? She lay back on

the couch with the phone in her hand and waited. A minute passed, then two, and then her phone vibrated. He wasn't calling; it was another text.

Can't. Working. And I would rather see you. Can I stop by later?

She replied: Yes, but the kid's still here.

Deal breaker. (joking) Be over at 8, he answered.

He was coming back! She felt relief wash over her and then her nerves started quietly buzzing. What was she going to tell him? She couldn't tell him the truth, he'd try to have her committed. No, the truth was not an option—but she didn't want to lie to him either. A big lie so early in the relationship would seal the fate of their time together. Even she knew that. The best she could do would be to give him the same proposal she'd given Rena and hope he took it too.

CHAPTER TWENTY

SHAKA TOLD MICHAL THEY WOULD BE HAVING COMPANY later. For a minute, he looked excited. But when she told him it would be Adrian, the man who had been over the night before, his features fell into a look of indifference. He sat down on the couch, but didn't immediately return to his video game. He watched Shaka as she filled a pot with water.

"Why are you having him over?" he asked.

Shaka glanced at him. "We didn't leave things on a good note last night, so I just want to talk to him."

"Does he know you're a wolf?" he asked.

Shaka straightened up when he said it. It was so rare that another person acknowledged her secret ability. She wasn't used to hearing it mentioned in casual conversation.

"No," she answered. "I don't tell people about that. Does anyone know that you're an owl?"

"Just Dad, and Mom, when she was around, and my aunt Rachel, and my grandparents, and my dad's ex-girlfriend, Mabel. I told my friend Ray at school, but he didn't believe me." Michal stopped talking and looked up at the ceiling as if he were trying hard to remember. "And my dad's other ex-girlfriend, Sonya, and probably her son. He was almost as old as my dad." Michal looked at her as if he expected a reaction.

She looked at him and said nothing.

He went on, "My uncle who's in jail right now knows, and my cousin Cody. Oh, and my dad's friends Jay and Irvin, and my aunt Rachel's friends and her boyfriends."

"Is that all?" she asked, taken aback.

"And you," he added. "How many people know you're a wolf?"

"My grandfather—he's a wolf too—my parents, and you and your dad."

"That's it? Don't your friends know?"

"No. They don't need to know. My grandfather always warned me not to let people know my secret. I guess your dad didn't feel the same way."

"He said it was a gift and we should share it. But we haven't told anyone but you since my aunt was taken away. Now we have to hide it."

Shaka turned back to the stovetop and poured a box

of penne pasta into the boiling water. She couldn't help but wonder if it had been their lack of discretion that had gotten Rachel captured in the first place. She knew her grandfather would tell her to get away from these people, that if the captors didn't suspect her yet, the more time she spent with Winston, the sooner they would. But she felt it was too late to back out, and the truth was she didn't want to. As long as there were people out there who wanted to hurt people like her, she would never be safe. It didn't matter that she wasn't their target yet; one day she would be.

That night, she made Michal turn off the TV and eat dinner at her tiny kitchen table with her, only because she needed a break from the soundtrack of zombie groans and gunfire.

"Don't you have to go to school?" she asked him halfway through dinner. It hadn't occurred to her until then.

"Dad pulled me out last week. He said it's too dangerous."

"You don't have any lessons to do or anything?" she asked.

"No," he said, giving her a look that implied that much was obvious. "Dad pulled me out of school," he repeated.

"Okay," Shaka said and dropped it.

She was impressed to see Michal get up and clear the table after he was done eating. He tried to fill the sink with dishwater, but the stopper had never quite fit, and the water drained away almost as fast as the sink filled. He instead washed the dishes under the steady stream from the faucet. He did this slowly and carefully, then stacked the dishes in the dish drainer. When he finished, he went back to the couch and resumed killing zombies.

Eight o'clock came and went, with no buzz from the front door. Shaka tried to remain patient, but when it was nearly nine, she walked down to the front stoop and looked down the sidewalk. She didn't know what difference it made, but she felt like she had to do something. She felt like there must be a reason why he wasn't there. She couldn't imagine he would just stand her up now.

It was a little after nine, and she sat on her stoop, listening to the night and still foolishly hoping to hear his footfalls when he actually rounded the corner and stood in front of her. He was wearing dress pants and a white shirt. His hair was combed back, and he was almost freshly shaven. He was a professional. She suddenly felt self-conscious in her sweatpants and black Fender T-shirt. She was barefoot and had painted her toenails pink only hours before, the only part of her appearance that had received care equal to what Adrian gave his entire look. She kept her neatly painted nails visible.

"Hey, Shaka," he said quietly as he approached her. "Sorry I'm late."

"I wondered what happened to you," she said.

He gave her a quick smile and sat down beside her. He interlaced his fingers and let them hang between his knees as he watched a moth flutter beneath a streetlight. Shaka followed his gaze. He was occupying space she couldn't enter, he was pulling away from her, and she could feel it.

"Moths fly into the light because their navigation is directed by the moon," she said. "They think our lights are moonlight."

"Huh," he said. "We sure have a way of ruining everything."

"If that light went out, the moth would probably find the moonlight and be on its way."

Adrian nodded, then picked up a loose piece of brick from the wall of the stoop and stood. He hurled it at the light and the bulb popped and shattered. Darkness reclaimed a small piece of the city.

Shaka felt the hair on the back of her neck stand up. She hadn't seen him behave aggressively before. She felt both uneasy and curious. Unconsciously, she pulled her legs in and tucked her newly painted nails out of view.

"My good deed for the day," he said as he sat back down. Then a moment later he added, "That was probably stupid."

"Maybe," Shaka said. She didn't know how to respond.

"Think at least the moth appreciated it?" he asked her.

"As much as a moth can," she said and smiled at him.

He looked at her but didn't smile back. "Shaka," he started slowly, "what's going on with you?" He paused for a moment, but when she opened her mouth to reply, he continued, "We had such a great date the other night, then yesterday you wouldn't even text me back. Then you had that guy in your apartment, and now you're watching his son indefinitely?" He gave her a searching look for a moment. "You were a wreck last night. I didn't feel like you wanted me to leave, even though you told me to. It's like you're pushing me away with one hand and pulling me in with the other. I don't know what you want, or what I should do."

Shaka sat for a moment, letting his words sink in. When she drew a breath to speak, he went on.

"These games, or whatever they are... I wouldn't put up with them, except I like you, and if you're in trouble, maybe I can help. It can't be that bad, I just need you to open up to me."

This time he sealed his lips and waited for her to respond.

"We'd better go inside," she said as she stood up and reached out for his hand. He half scoffed, half laughed, but reached up and took it. She led him into the building and up to her apartment, where inside, Michal still sat in front of the TV, pausing only momentarily to look at Adrian as they walked in. Adrian waved to him, and Michal nodded in return, unwilling to remove his hands from the controller.

"Can he go back to his apartment or something?" Adrian whispered to her.

"Michal," she said, "could you go down to the lobby for a few minutes?"

"What am I supposed to do there?" he asked.

She pulled the first book she saw off her bookshelf and handed it to him. "Read," she suggested.

He glanced down at the book in his hands: *The Novice's Guide to Cream Sauces*. He looked back up at her with an *"Are you serious?"* look.

"Please," she begged. "Ten minutes."

With his shoulders hanging, he turned and walked out of the apartment, pulling the door shut behind him.

"Beer?" she said, turning to Adrian.

"Please."

She grabbed two bottles from the fridge and handed him one. After she took a drink, she turned to him. "Adrian, I like you too. A lot. But there are things about me that I'm not ready to share with you. I'm not trying to play mind games or irritate you. I just can't tell you everything. I know how that sounds, and I don't expect you to just accept it. But if you could try to see it my way, we really don't know each other that well yet, and I'm not ready to spill my darkest secrets. So, what I'm gonna ask of you—and I know it's a long shot—but could you ever just accept me, even though you don't know the whole story yet? I can assure you I'm not a bad person. It's just that I'm not ready for full disclosure yet."

When she finished, she sat very still and watched him with wide, searching eyes. He looked at her without giving any indication of his thoughts. She noticed the distinct line of his jaw, the softness of his mouth, and the deep blue of his eyes. She wanted to kiss him, to reach over and rest a hand on his knee and lean into his space. But she stayed where she was.

He picked up his beer and swirled it around in the bottle, then set it back down and gave a sigh of resignation. "You win," he said.

She gave him a minute to elaborate, and when he didn't, she asked, "What does that mean?"

"I'll do it. But not forever," he said as he looked at her sternly. "Someday you have to let me in."

"Yes," Shaka said, smiling, and she leaned over into his space. He wrapped his arms around her and squeezed her tight. He still smelled like soap and sandalwood cologne. She felt warm next to him, warm and happy. She didn't know yet what she would do when that someday arrived, but she supposed she would figure it out by then. She was just happy to have him beside her now.

He kissed her sweetly and slowly, until they heard a knock at the door. Michal opened it and poked his head in.

"Done yet?" he asked.

"I suppose we can be," Adrian said.

Michal walked in and nervously eyed Adrian.

Adrian gave Shaka's shoulder a squeeze and released her. "What are you playing?" he asked Michal. "Resident Evil?"

"Yes, sir," he replied.

Adrian turned to Shaka. "So, that's where you're learning your manners," he said to her, then turned back around and picked up the controller. "Mind if I give it a go, bud?"

"Go ahead," Michal said shyly and watched the screen as Adrian explored the virtual mansion, collecting weapons and herbs. Soon Michal's health status was back up to one hundred percent, and he had an arsenal of new weapons. Adrian outsmarted one zombie after another, then beheaded an undead dog while Michal watched as if in a trance. Shaka sat down beside Adrian as a giant spider appeared in front of his avatar.

"Damn!" Adrian said, "where did he come from?!" He slashed at it over and over until it died but depleted his health in the process. "Sorry, kid," he said. "I'll get you filled back up." Again, he roamed around looking for more herbs to restore his health. In the course of his search, he found a new map. Michal gasped audibly.

"You want to check out the map?"

"Yes!" Michal said excitedly as he grabbed for the controller.

"I didn't know you were so skilled at this game," Shaka said.

"Of course. I was a boy once, you know."

"Well, maybe we could watch a movie or something. I mean, I'd like to pretend I have any interest at all in this," she said, motioning to the screen, "but I just can't."

"I just found this map though," Michal pleaded.

"It really doesn't unlock much for you," Adrian told him. "You'll be done with it in ten minutes, I bet."

"Ten more minutes, then?" Michal asked Shaka.

"Okay."

"If we're going to watch a movie, I propose we watch *Resident Evil*, the movie," Adrian said as he smiled at Shaka.

She rolled her eyes.

"Yeah!" Michal agreed.

"Ugh. Fine," she said. "I'll make popcorn. But you guys have to figure out how to order the movie."

"We won that round," Adrian said to Michal.

Michal nodded in smug agreement.

The movie wasn't as bad as Shaka had been expecting, though she wasn't entirely paying attention to it. She leaned closer and closer to Adrian as the movie went on until she was nestled against his chest, her ear close enough to his skin that she could hear his heartbeat. He wrapped his arm around her shoulders and pressed her close to him. For the first time in several days, she was able to forget about the uncertainty and the threats that waited outside. She felt a veil of safety cover her—or maybe she just didn't feel alone anymore.

When the movie ended, it was after midnight. Shaka asked Adrian if he wanted to stay over.

"Definitely," he replied.

Michal was asleep on the couch minutes after Shaka turned out the lights. She could hear his heavy breathing. She climbed into her bed and watched with quiet interest as Adrian undressed down to his T-shirt and boxer shorts. She wished they had the apartment to themselves, but she felt secure knowing there would be time for that later. He wasn't going anywhere, not yet, anyway. Maybe one day he could even be trusted with her secret. She let the thought come and go from her mind without indulging it. She knew it was more than half fantasy, but she didn't want to think about the alternative. Instead, she let herself be warmed by him and fell asleep to the rhythmic sound of his breathing.

At half past two, she woke up to the shrill ring of the burner phone. She stumbled out of bed, grabbed it off her kitchen counter, went into the bathroom, and turned the fan on.

"Hello?" she said quietly.

"It's me," Winston said. "How is everything?"

"Fine. Michal's sleeping. We're fine."

"Yeah, sorry to call so late. Are you alone right now?"

"I'm alone in the bathroom, but Adrian is here, and Michal, of course."

"Damnit," he muttered suddenly. "Shaka, Adrian isn't who you think he is. You've got to get away from him. I told you not to get close to anybody. We can't trust anyone."

"Whoa! I think you're overreacting, especially since, according to Michal, you've told every person you've ever dated about your little... idiosyncrasy."

"Shaka, this is different. I remembered where I know him from. He was there the night Rachel was taken. He was younger then, but it was him, I'm sure of it. He was sitting in the van, watching everything. I didn't put it together until today, when I overheard the old doctor talking about his son Adrian who's working in Duluth. Shaka, he's setting a trap for you. You and Michal have to get out of there—now!"

CHAPTER TWENTY-ONE

Shaka dropped the phone and froze. There were so many thoughts racing through her mind that she couldn't grab hold of a single one. The most she could do was bend over and pick up her phone.

"Are you sure?" Shaka whispered. "That was a few years ago, right? And it would have been dark. I met him through a friend I know I can trust. You must be mistaken, Winston."

"I'm not! I know what I saw. That night is seared into my mind, and it seems a bit too coincidental that this man running the laboratory has a son in Duluth by the same name, doesn't it?"

"Yes." She felt her hands start to tremble again. "But none of that proves it. You might be wrong."

"I might be, but do you want to risk it?" he asked.

"What am I supposed to do? He's here in my apartment right now!"

"You need to wake up Michal and get out of there. Adrian might not know what you are, or even what Michal is, but at the very least, he knows what I am, and that Michal is my son. I'm sorry, Shaka. I'm sure you have feelings for him, but make no mistake, he is there to trap you."

"This doesn't make sense! I met him before he even knew that I knew you. How could he know about me?"

"Maybe it doesn't make sense now, but trust me, it will. Right now, you just need to get away from him."

"Okay," Shaka agreed, "I'll call you when we're out of here."

She switched off the bathroom fan, hoping it had covered up her voice. She quietly opened the door and listened. Michal was still breathing heavily, and Adrian was softly snoring. She tiptoed over to Michal and gave him a gentle shake.

"Huh?" he said loudly as he woke up.

"Shhh!" Shaka shushed in his ear. "We have to leave, just you and me. Be very quiet. We don't want to wake up Adrian. I'll explain once we're outside."

Michal rubbed his eyes and sat up. Clearly, he was used to taking orders with no explanation from his father, and Shaka was grateful for that. She grabbed her shoes, her purse, and a sweater. She stuffed the Tracfone in her pocket and backed up carefully toward the door. Michal started putting on his shoes. Shaka leaned toward him and shook her head. She held up the hand she carried her shoes in. He picked up his own shoes and followed her to the door in his socks.

The door squeaked when she opened it. Adrian stirred in bed. She saw him reach over to her side of the bed, and finding it empty, he lifted his head and looked around. Shaka's heart jumped and hammered in her chest; she felt the blood rushing in her ears, it was almost deafening. She took a deep breath, calling on the calm confidence of her inner wolf. In a moment, her heart slowed a little, and her hands steadied. Adrian was just a man; he had no special powers.

"Shaka?" he asked. "You going somewhere?"

"Yes," she answered, surprising herself at how natural her voice sounded. "Michal's dad called. He's coming to pick him up."

"It's the middle of the night," Adrian observed.

"I know, I think he's just passing through town on his way to his parents' house. I shouldn't be too long."

"I'll come with you," he said, climbing out of bed. "You guys shouldn't be outside alone at this hour. I'm surprised he would ask you to do that. No offense, bud," he said to Michal.

Michal just watched the conversation without speaking.

"No, don't," Shaka said pleadingly. "I don't think he would

be happy with me if he knew I had a man stay over while his son was here."

"Screw him. He shouldn't be asking you or Michal to go out in the middle of the night. Why can't he come up and get him himself, anyways?"

"I don't know, but I just want to do this the way he asked me. Please make this easy on me and go back to bed. I'll be back in ten minutes, fifteen at the most."

Adrian ran his hands through his hair and sat back down on her bed. "Okay," he said. "Maybe I should head out too."

Inside, Shaka felt a surge of hope. Maybe he would just leave on his own. But she knew if she didn't try to smooth things over, he would be even more suspicious of her than he already was.

"Michal, wait for me in the hall?" she said, and Michal walked out into the hall without question, pulling the door shut behind him.

She walked over to Adrian and dropped her purse and shoes on the floor. She sat down beside him and linked her knee over his, slightly turning him toward her. "You should stay. I've been wishing we were alone all night. So, just let me bring Michal to his dad, then we can finally be alone." She squeezed his knee in hers and ran her fingertips slowly up his back. She couldn't help but recognize that part of her really did want to be alone with him. It made convincing him to stay that much easier.

He turned toward her. "Do you always get your way?" he asked, smiling.

She gave him a little nod and smiled back. He leaned forward and kissed her. It was a deep kiss that stirred her in her belly. The part of her that wanted to be alone with him was growing quickly. She pressed the front of her body against him as his hands ran up her back, under her T-shirt. Then she gently pulled back from him.

"Just hold that thought," she said as she bent down to pick up her things and walked slowly toward the door. She looked over her shoulder at him. He grinned at her, and his eyes sparkled.

How could he be lying? she thought. *It just doesn't seem possible*...But she kept moving and slipped out the door.

Michal was waiting downstairs; his shoes were on. She put hers on quickly. Michal didn't ask questions but waited for instructions.

"Let's go," she said, and he pushed through the door. She was right behind him. She pulled her sweater on and tightened her purse strap across her chest. When they reached the sidewalk, she pointed right, and she and Michal both quickened their pace to a jog.

Standing at her window, Adrian watched them round the corner.

CHAPTER TWENTY-TWO

THE FIRST TIME SHAKA CHANGED, SHE HAD BEEN TEN years old,and she was scared. She had grown up listening to her grandfather tell stories about the wolves in the family. She had always known there was a chance that she too would be able to turn into a wolf one day. With the stories also came warnings of how dangerous people could be when they were afraid, and how they feared what they didn't understand.

The mysterious ability that ran in Shaka's bloodline had missed her father, and perhaps because of this, he had always regarded her grandfather with fear and subdued disgust. She never understood why; her grandfather was a kind and wise man. But once they knew she too had the gene, her father distanced himself from her as well. She often wondered if things would have been different for her and her father had she not inherited the gene. But she didn't know any of that yet on the first day she changed shape.

She had followed her grandfather down a deer trail into the woods. They had been walking for more than an hour, and Shaka's bug spray was wearing off. Her grandfather kept on steadily, walking stick in hand and a deep-seated smile on his face. He was always smiling when he was in the woods, a sentiment Shaka shared, even as a child.

"Grandpa, a woodpecker!" she yelled, pointing up into the trees.

He looked up to the sound of the *tap, tap, tap* and saw the red head hammering on the tree among the leaves. "So it is," he said approvingly.

It was the better part of an hour before they reached their destination, a small rocky lake, from which the nearest home was almost two miles away. There were no roads or trails, the place was nearly impenetrable for modern-day explorers. Shaka knew it was necessary to stay hidden. She'd heard the story of what happened to her great uncle James when he and her grandfather were boys.

They both had the gene and would run through the woods together often, sometimes staying out all night. Unlike Arnold, James was wild and sometimes reckless. One night, he decided to visit their neighbor's house and kill all his chickens.

Their neighbor was a grumpy old man whom they both despised, and at the time it had seemed like a good prank.

The two of them went to the old man's house after dark. Arnold watched from the tree line through his cautious wolf eyes; he didn't have his brother's daring. In minutes, James had dug into the chicken coop and grabbed one chicken after another in his big jaws, ripping them apart. As soon as the job was done, James slid out from under the coop and happily loped toward Arnold—but as he did, a shot rang out. James stumbled and rolled as he reached the tree line. He'd been hit in the back leg. He pulled himself up with his front legs but struggled to stand on his hind ones.

The old man was climbing down from his porch.

Arnold whined for his brother to get up, but blood was pulsing out of James's back leg. When he did manage to stand, he took a step and fell. Arnold jumped forward to help him up, but James growled and snapped at him.

Not knowing what else to do, Arnold shifted back, ran out of the woods, and picked up James. The old man stopped in his tracks and stood stunned for a moment, but in a matter of seconds, he had raised his gun again and was firing blindly at the nude boy who carried the wounded wolf into the woods. Arnold heard the shots cut through the leaves around him, but none hit him.

He carried his brother two whole miles back to the house, running the entire way. He kicked open the front door and laid James on the kitchen table, where his parents were playing cards. As soon as they saw him, they jumped up and hastily tried to apply pressure to the wound, but his cold glassy eyes told them it was too late: James was already dead. He had lost too much blood. No matter what they tried, his soft wolf body stayed limp and lifeless.

When Arnold's mother and father had accepted that James was gone, they turned their efforts to gently cleaning the blood from his fur and wrapping him in blankets. That night, their father dug a deep hole under an old oak tree, and the three of them laid James to rest. There would be no funeral, as there was no body. James had gone off to live with his cousins in Kansas; that was the story they would tell. But his mother's broken heart told another story, and their old neighbor told yet another, of his farm being attacked by werewolves on the night James Reed went missing.

The townspeople laughed, and Arnold's father laughed with them, though his eyes remained somber. People spoke of the old man losing his mind—but they also distanced themselves from Arnold and his family. As time went on, Arnold learned that the cost of his gift was having to keep it concealed. After James's death, he changed only when he'd traveled deep enough into the woods that there were no signs of humans. This practice had become a strict habit for Shaka's grandfather, and so it was all she ever knew. That was why she knew better than to complain about the bugs or the distance as she followed him into the woods that day.

They didn't know if she had the gene; they would find out when she went into the water. Her grandfather coached her on how to stretch out her limbs and will herself to change, to see herself becoming a wolf. If she had the gene, that would be all that it took. Her body would *want* to change.

"Will it hurt?" she asked.

"No, honey, it won't hurt. It will feel a bit like stretching, and it will be over before you know it. Are you ready?"

Shaka nodded nervously.

"All right. I'm going to turn my back now, so you strip down and get in the lake, and we'll see if a wolf or girl comes back up," he said to her, his eyes twinkling. Then he turned around and faced the trees, whistling softly.

She went to the water's edge and quickly undressed. She waded into the water and steadily walked out until it was up to her shoulders, then she dove under and thought about wolves: wolves running, wolves hunting, wolves howling, wolves playing. Picturing herself standing on the bank of the little lake in the lanky body of an adolescent wolf, she spun around in the water. She thought of herself swimming across the lake with four wolf paws paddling beneath her. Her mouth opened, and she unexpectedly let out something like a bark underwater. She impulsively reached a hand to her mouth—but now her arm was shifting and wouldn't bend that way. She kicked her legs beneath her, but they were shrinking and couldn't propel her to the surface. Her torso stretched out, and she felt her face growing long and narrow. She was now kicking with four legs as she desperately rose to the surface, where she broke the water with two pointed ears. As her head emerged, she let out a sharp yip. He grandfather turned around, and his smile turned to laughter when he saw her.

"Look at that gorgeous wolf!" he said. Shaka was paddling toward him; it was hard to get used to paddling with four small feet. She let her paws relax and spread out, then found she was moving faster, smoother. She reached the shore and shook the water off her coat.

"Look at you," her grandfather said admiringly. "You're just beautiful!"

Shaka could hear him, but she couldn't understand him. She stood looking at him expectantly as he approached her. She didn't know what he was doing, but she knew she trusted him. He ran his hand over her wet coat; her eyes followed his arm as it ran down her back. Then she saw her long, fluffy tail and spun around to nip at it. Her grandfather laughed and pulled his hand back. "You found a new toy," he said. "All right, Shaka."

Recognition sparked in her eyes when he said her name, and her ears perked up.

"A little privacy?" He shooed her away with his hand.

She turned on her new feet and trotted into the woods. She sniffed the air; it held more scents than she could name. She didn't know which one to follow, so she danced in place, leaning this way for one, that way for another. On the soft ground, her paws felt light and agile. She felt limber when she trotted. Then a gray ball of fur darted past her, giving her a quick, gentle nip as it passed. It was her grandfather.

She gave chase but couldn't catch him. In human form, he didn't do things quickly, but as a wolf, he was large and fast.

She did her best to dodge the hanging branches and leap over the fallen trees, but she was clumsy on her new legs and tripped more than twice. He was getting further and further ahead of her. When she could no longer see him, she found that she could smell him and followed his scent.

When she found him, he was standing in a stream, lapping up cool water. She joined him and awkwardly copied his behavior. Every several seconds, he would stop and listen, so she did the same. They heard only rushing water, birds, and squirrels. They were alone.

That day had changed her, body and spirit. It awoke a wildness inside of her. From that day on, more than anything, it was running in the woods with her grandfather that she looked forward to. While other girls talked about boys, tried out for sports teams, and went to school dances, Shaka thought only of running through the woods and smelling the night air with her wet wolf nose. After she learned about her ability, she began to distance herself from her peers. She had a secret, and she needed to protect it.

Shaka knew even before she became a teenager that life would be different for her, all the way to the end. She could be a wolf, and she could be a girl, but she would never fully be either one. Yet she wouldn't have traded her gift for anything, even if it meant being an outsider. Slumber parties and boyfriends were no comparison to being able to run through the woods at night with speed and agility that even the best athletes at school didn't have, or to clearly see every leaf and rock in the darkness with her sharp wolf eyes, or to send her own haunting howl up into the night air. She loved her ability, even if it meant she would lead a lonely life.

CHAPTER TWENTY-THREE

THREE DAYS SHE WAITED IN A SUPER 8 HOTEL WITH MICHAL. They ordered pizza and watched movies. In the lobby, she found a deck of playing cards, and they played every game Michal knew, but it wasn't enough to keep her anxiety at bay. She kept the window open for the fresh air and the sounds of the city, which made her feel less alone. The thought crossed her mind that she was already their prisoner, but she squashed it out quickly. She knew any of their captives would have gladly traded places with her. She shuddered when she thought about those people locked in their sterile cells, being inhumanely tested on and who knew what else.

Her fear spilled over into anger, and she prayed there would be a reckoning. One way or another, she knew that her life would not return to the way it had been. She was going to see this all the way through. As long as she was free, the people running this laboratory were a threat. She would have to do everything she could to stop them; she just didn't know what that was yet. She knew she wasn't doing any good hiding in a hotel room, but she was afraid to leave. If Adrian was one of them, they knew exactly who she was, and they would be looking for her.

She was still in shock about Adrian's betrayal. She tried not to think about it, but it wasn't easy. He had texted her five times by the third day. The first two showed casual concern: Where are you?, and a half hour later: Are you coming back? What happened?

But soon they cycled on to anger: What happened last night? Where the hell did you go? Then to desperation: I don't know what I did that upset you, but call me so we can talk. And finally, honesty: Please just let me explain. It's not what you think.

He was crazy if he thought Shaka was going to take the bait. Every time he texted her, she surged with anger and sadness. Eventually, she just had to turn her phone off. She wanted to call Rena and ask her about him. She wanted to know when he and Salem had reconnected, and how well they really knew each other, but she couldn't guarantee that Rena was on her side either, as much as it hurt her to admit it. She didn't know who could be trusted anymore.

She used the room phone to call her work, telling them she

had a family emergency and had to leave town for a while. She wasn't sure when she'd be back. Jim had taken her call. He didn't ask for details, and as relieved as she was by this, she got the feeling it was only because he didn't really believe her. When he asked if she was in some kind of trouble, her suspicions were confirmed. "No," she said and repeated her story about a family emergency.

"Do what you need to do, Shaka. Don't be too big to ask for help though."

"Yes. Thank you," she'd said, feeling simultaneously guilty and grateful. It was the only honest part of their conversation. She felt even worse about it because Jim was a trustworthy man. She suspected that even if he knew the whole truth about her, he'd still treat her kindly and offer his help.

She steeled her heart. She was alone. She had to remember that.

On the third day, she left the hotel and went to a pharmacy across the highway. She bought things she'd never bought before: blonde hair dye, fake eyelashes, and bright lipstick. After the pharmacy, she took a taxi to the mall and bought two dresses and a pair of heels. She looked over her shoulder every other minute. No one was watching her. If she was ever going to leave the hotel, it couldn't be as the woman they were looking for. She bought a baseball cap and a hooded sweatshirt for Michal. She could become another woman easily enough, but Michal would be a twelve-year-old boy no matter what he wore. If he could just keep his head down, look anonymous, maybe he could keep out of their sight. She bought a pair of shears too; they would both need haircuts.

Her savings account was quickly dwindling. She couldn't afford to stay in the hotel much longer, living on the run was expensive. She hoped Winston would come back soon, though she didn't know what she was going to do when he did. Her best idea was to hitch a ride to the Boundary Waters Canoe Area, change to the wolf, and disappear. She knew they'd never find her, but she also knew she wasn't going to run away while people like her were being captured.

It took two hours for her to become a blonde with a pixie cut and too much makeup. She practiced smiling so her teeth showed and being ready to laugh at any remark. The girl she saw in the mirror was an extrovert and a flirt, two things Shaka was not. In her new short green dress and black heels, she could have even fooled herself. She did not look like a woman who went into the woods. Michal, on the other hand, still looked very much like himself. Despite his protests, she had cut his hair and dyed it blond as well. He covered it shamefully with the baseball cap.

That evening, she paced the floors, trying to come up with

a plan while Michal watched cartoons. Every so often, she would stop and ask him a question.

"Didn't your aunt live in Minneapolis?" she asked. He shook his head. She started pacing again. A few minutes later she asked, "Are you close with your grandparents?"

He shrugged.

"Think they would help us?"

He shrugged again. He wasn't paying much attention to her. He was clearly still angry with her for dying his hair blond.

Shaka kept pacing. She knew he was upset with her, but she couldn't address that now. She had to come up with a plan. "Do you have any family close by?" she asked. Again, he shrugged. She sighed, but didn't push him. It seemed more and more like it would be up to Winston to find them a safe place to hide.

It was just after dark when there was a quiet knock on their door. It startled both of them. Michal was up first. He crept to the door and slowly rose up to the peephole. As soon as he looked through it, he swung the door open and threw his arms around Winston. Winston squeezed him back.

"I missed you, son," he said. "I missed you so much!"

"I missed you too," Michal said, sniffling.

As they pulled apart, Winston pulled Michal's hat off, and a look of disappointment fell across Winston's face.

"What's this about?" he asked Michal.

"Ask her," he said, pointing to Shaka.

Winston turned to her for an explanation, then exclaimed, "You two look like a couple of clowns!"

"Well, hello to you too," she said. "And you're welcome for keeping your son safe."

"Except for that bit about sleeping with the enemy..."

"You know I had no idea about that," she scolded him, "and not to mention, I didn't have to help you. I mean, it is you that they're looking for, not me."

He and Michal both looked at her silently.

"I mean, it's in my best interest to be as far away from you two as possible."

"True," Winston said. "But you aren't going to leave us."

"What makes you so sure?"

"Because this is about you too now. They have one of your people," he said.

The room was suddenly quiet and still. "Who is it?" she asked, the words coming out in a choked whisper—but even before she asked, she knew that there was only one person who it could be.

"An old white man who turns into a wolf," he answered.

Shaka carefully walked to the bed and sat down. Her head was spinning. How long had it been since she'd last seen him? Almost two years. He would be seventy-five years old now, and spending his golden years locked up in a cage. Her stomach turned, and her eyes welled with tears.

"Was he hurt?" she asked. She looked up at Winston pleadingly.

He walked over to her and sat down next to her on the bed, giving her forearm a gentle squeeze. "No, he's not hurt, but he doesn't look healthy. No one in there does. He had some books in his cell—John Muir, I believe."

Shaka let out a short laugh. That was her grandfather, all right. He used to read to her from *My First Summer in the Sierra* when she was young. He'd wanted to make sure she loved nature, whether she was able to shift or not. Shaka took a breath and imagined a lotus flower closing, the petals folding in on each other in an organized pattern. It was a trick he'd taught her when she was young. When the flower had returned to a neat bud, she had regained control of her emotions. She turned to Winston, ready to hear what else he had discovered.

"Do you think we can get them out?" she asked.

"I do," he said, "but it will be difficult. We should start planning now." He grabbed a notepad from the dresser with the Super 8 logo on it. He drew a maze of hallways and rooms, with one big room in the center, over which he wrote, *Lab*. "There's a back door here that isn't patrolled often. It will be easy enough for me to get into the air ducts, but you'll have to travel another way. Every night, a security guard comes out of the door at least four times. How do you feel about mauling a man?" he asked.

Shaka scoffed. "I feel like your plan is pretty sloppy."

"Just listen," he went on, "if you took him out, you could take his ID badge and get into any room in the building. If you put on his uniform, no one would suspect you."

Shaka shook her head.

"One way or another, we will need an ID badge," he said.

"Another way. First off, there's a good chance he'd kill me if I attacked him. Security guards usually have some kind of weapon, right? Second, I'm not big on murdering random people."

"There's nothing random here," he responded vehemently. "You haven't seen what it's like in there, and we need to stop them before they create a drug that will give our ability to anyone who can pay for it. I think that is what they're trying to do."

Shaka shuddered. She felt a chill run up her spine at the thought of everyone being able to shape-shift. She pictured hordes of violent and fearless animals crowding the woods. She hoped that wasn't possible.

"That's horrible," Shaka said. "I'll do whatever I can, but we need a better plan than mauling our way in. Do they sleep at night?"

"Most of them do, but there's always someone there. And there are cameras, of course. I don't know if there's someone watching them, but we'd have to assume there is."

"Yes. How long do we have to come up with a plan?" she asked.

"I don't know, but they're going to keep looking for us until they find us again. I have to bring Michal to stay with my cousin, Terry. He lives on the reservation. I don't think they've been looking out there."

"What?" Michal spoke up. "But I want to go with you!"

"I know, son, but I won't be able to watch out for you."

"I can watch out for myself."

Winston smiled kindly at his son. "I know you can. But I won't be able to do the things I need to do if I'm worried about you. We all have to make sacrifices, and my boy, I'm afraid yours is that you will have to be kept hidden."

Michal crossed his arms and scowled at the floor.

"Well, I for one cannot afford to keep living in a hotel, especially when I'm not working," Shaka added.

"We can stay with Terry until we figure out a plan. It's probably even safe to shift there."

Shaka felt a weight lift from her chest. She suddenly realized that if she could just change and run, she could clear her head and then come up with a plan.

"Okay," she said, her voice noticeably calmer. "I need to get some things from my apartment first."

"You'd better be careful. Your boyfriend is probably still watching your place."

Her expression hardened at the mention of Adrian. She felt so stupid for having been tricked by him. "I'll go tonight," she said.

"I can give you a ride to the neighborhood, but I don't want to be seen either."

"I know. A couple blocks away would be fine. I can walk if you can wait."

Winston nodded, and Shaka began packing up her things. The three of them were in Winston's Buick ten minutes later, anonymously cruising through the city.

He dropped her in front of a bar three blocks from her building and drove away. She walked quickly and confidently down the sidewalk, trying to appear as a person who had nothing to hide. She exaggerated the movement of her hips as she walked and swung her shoulders a little. She was a different woman. A man whistled at her from across the street, and her first impulse was to glare coolly at him, but she stopped herself. Instead, she threw him a quick flirtatious smile and kept walking.

"Come back, beautiful!" he yelled after her. One of his friends teased him, and they both laughed. She kept walking;

she was almost to her apartment. She chanced a glance up at her window. It was dark. He'd be crazy to be hiding up there, she told herself, but she didn't know anything about him or what he wanted with her. Maybe he *was* crazy. She kept going. To stall was to break character, and she was determined not to be herself.

She unlocked the front door and let herself in. The hallway was quiet except for the sound of a TV coming from her downstairs neighbor's apartment. She steadily walked upstairs, her heartbeat quickening as she gripped the railing. Her door was closed. She tried the handle; locked. *Why would he lock himself out?* she wondered. She unlocked the door slowly and flicked the light on. It was empty. She went to the bathroom and opened the door... Empty. She quickly grabbed clothes, her phone charger, and her toiletries and stuffed them into a messenger bag. Having collected everything she needed in less than two minutes, she turned toward the door. It was then that she saw the note on her fridge.

Shaka,

I'm sorry I wasn't honest with you. I know about Winston, and about your grandfather. I'm here to help you. I'm sure you don't believe me, but it's the truth.

I know Winston is in trouble, and you will be too if they find you helping him. I don't know how you two know each other, but PLEASE, be careful. If you could just give me a chance I could explain everything.

Call me. —A

Shaka ran her fingertips over the surface of the paper a few times, then set it down on the counter. She stood staring at it for moment, thinking about him, feeling both hopeful and stupid when she considered the possibility that his letter was honest. She picked it back up and slipped it into her bag. She would think about it later.

She made it back to the same bar where Winston had dropped her without arousing any suspicion. She stood next to the doorway and waited, with one leg turned out. A car of college-aged boys drove by, whistling and catcalling at her. She turned her leg back in, thinking maybe she was overdoing it. She reached into her purse and pulled out a cigarette. She didn't smoke it in her usual slow, mindful way; she smoked it quickly, taking long drags and tapping the ash almost compulsively. It was getting easier and easier to be someone else. She felt safe behind the act.

Halfway through her cigarette, Winston rounded the corner. He slowed in front of the bar, and she jumped in the back seat. Winston drove steadily toward the interstate that would take them west out of the city.

Shaka gave a sigh of relief as the glow of the city lights fell behind them. They rode without speaking, each one's thoughts turned inward. They all felt hidden and safe under the darkness of night and within the steady stream of traffic—but it was a presumptuous safety, because less than a mile behind them, under the same darkness, Adrian too headed west.

CHAPTER TWENTY-FOUR

THEY DROVE THROUGH THE TOWN OF CLOQUET HALF AN HOUR later, and soon the lights from that town also dimmed behind them. They passed a couple of small housing developments, then turned down a gravel road, then another, and another. Forty minutes from Cloquet, Winston pulled the Buick down a long driveway that led to a log cabin. There was a porch light on, and a middle-aged man sat in a rocking chair, smoking a cigarette. His long, graying dark hair was pulled loosely into a ponytail. His expression revealed nothing as he watched Winston come to a slow stop and kill the engine. Then a woman with wide hips and a long black braid came out onto the porch, being careful not to slam the door. She stood behind the man, placing one hand on the back of his chair, and watched. Winston killed the lights and stepped out of the car.

"Get out," he said to Michal before he shut his door. Michal obeyed. Shaka followed them out.

"Winnie," the man on the porch said as he rose from his chair. "Get up here." A smile spread across his face. "You been living off of field mice? You're thin as a pole," he said as he pulled Winston into an embrace.

It's good to see you, Terry," Winston said to the man. "Thanks for taking us in."

"Of course. Any time, cousin. Mikey, I see how your dad got so thin," he said as he turned to Michal and poked him in his soft belly. "Come over here and hug your uncle."

Michal did as he was told. "Hi, Uncle Terry," he said, and when he stepped out of the embrace, he turned to the woman who had been watching them with a wide smile. "Hi, Aunt Whisper."

"Hello, love," she said as she reached out to him. "What have you done to your hair?" she added.

"He had a mishap with a bottle of bleach," Winston chimed in before Michal could answer. Shaka knew he was trying to protect her. Little good it would do, she thought, since her hair was the same color.

"No matter, my boy," Whisper said. "I'll shave it off in the morning, and you can start over."

Shaka silently walked toward the porch, feeling like she

was intruding on this little reunion. Everyone turned and looked at her simultaneously, and the warmth on Terry's and Whisper's faces seemed to fall away. Winston gave her a tiny smile of encouragement.

"This must be the mishap," Terry said, the laughter gone from his voice.

"This is Shaka," Winston said. "She's the girl I mentioned. She's traveling with us."

"Hi," Shaka offered.

"Oh," Terry said as he looked at her. "She's not what I expected." He could have meant anything— that she was younger or older or smaller or quieter than he'd expected— but Shaka knew he meant that he hadn't expected her to be white. She stood awkwardly in front of the porch. She felt she should wait to be asked up. When no one said anything for a moment, she started to worry that they might not let her stay. Her mind raced to find a solution, and a solution came quickly: she would change and go into the woods. At the thought of it, she felt lighter and carefree, and the tiniest smile touched the corner of her lips.

"Any friend of Winnie's is a friend of ours," Terry finally said to her, the smile returning to his face.

She realized he had just wanted to see her squirm. She was glad she hadn't. She glanced at Winston, who was looking up at the treetops. She thought he must have been thinking about changing too. Surely, he felt the need, like she did. Sure, he had changed to sneak into the lab only a couple days ago, but that wasn't the same as soaring through the treetops at night.

She turned to Terry. "Thank you," she said as she stepped onto the porch.

"Come on in, you three. Whisper made some sugar cookies for you."

The house was small and neat inside, and as promised, it smelled like fresh-baked cookies. Hanging over the fireplace was a print of a wolf. Shaka walked up to it immediately. She examined the brush strokes that made up the wolf's thick fur, and the way its eyes seemed to hold the observer in place. She wondered if they knew about her. If they didn't already, she would just as soon they didn't find out. She worried that Winston, having trusted so many people with his secret, might start trusting people with hers.

She turned away from the picture. She doubted it mattered much either way now, these people weren't going to turn her over. They could hardly do that without exposing Winston.

"Hey, *waabishka ma'iingan,* you want a cookie?" Terry called to her from the small kitchen she had just passed through. She was glad she didn't know what he had called her. She realized that she was hungry; she hadn't eaten since lunch, and it was late in the night.

"Please," she said as she walked into the kitchen.

Whisper held out a plate of cookies to her. Shaka picked one up and took a step back. "Go on, take two," Whisper said. Shaka leaned forward and picked up another one.

"Thank you," she said, giving Whisper a smile, but Whisper wasn't looking at her anymore. Terry held out a glass of milk to her. "Thank you," she repeated to him.

They ate quietly for a few minutes. She let her eyes wander around the kitchen. A small woodstove sat in the corner, and a sink with only one basin sat in the center of a small counter. It was no bigger than the kitchen at Shaka's apartment. The fridge and the oven took up most of the space. The fridge was covered in finger paintings made by a small child. One of them said *Ashley* in purple letters. She wondered if there were others who lived here. After a few days of being stuck in a hotel room with Michal, she longed for privacy, though she knew she wouldn't be getting any—not yet.

When they had all finished eating, Whisper led them to a small room with two twin beds. "Two of you can sleep here," she said, "and the other will have to sleep on the couch."

"I can take the couch," Winston offered.

"No," Shaka interjected, "I'll take it. You and Michal should sleep together."

Winston gave her a knowing smile. Though she tried to frame it as an act of generosity, they both knew that what she was really after was her own space.

"That's kind of you," he said through his smile.

"We get up early, so be warned," Whisper said to her.

"Okay," Shaka answered.

"And it's past our bedtime," Terry added. "So, on that note, I'm headed to bed." He climbed a spiral staircase that stood in the corner of the living room, leading to a loft. Shaka saw two bedroom doors coming off of an open center space that had a bed in it. The little house seemed to use every inch of space for something. She was grateful there was room for her. She was exhausted, physically and emotionally.

She sat down on the couch and dropped her bag on the floor. Reaching inside, she touched the letter from Adrian. She hadn't told Winston about it yet, but she knew it wouldn't matter if she did. Winston was sure beyond all doubt that Adrian was the enemy. She wished she shared his conviction.

CHAPTER TWENTY-FIVE

SHAKA LAY DOWN AND TOLD HERSELF SHE WAS JUST GOING to take a nap, then when the house was quiet, she was going to go into the woods and shift. But she woke up to the sound of footsteps thundering down the spiral staircase and the smell of frying beacon. She cracked her eyes open and counted four kids in the kitchen, none of them Michal.

"Joseph, give me your plate," Whisper said, and the tallest boy handed over his plate. Two younger ones, a boy and a girl, were arguing over some kind of toy. "You two stop that, or I'm going to throw it away," Whisper demanded.

Then the door swung open and Terry stepped in. He went to the smallest child, a girl with two long braids who looked about five or six years old, and kissed the top of her head. Shaka rolled over and faced the back of the couch, burying her head under her blanket. She couldn't help but feel like she was intruding. The blanket muffled their conversations, but not by much.

"Where's Michal?" one of them asked.

"He's sleeping. He was up late last night."

"When can we see him?" a small voice whined.

"When you get home from school." The kitchen was filled with the sounds of clinking silverware and hurried eating.

"Robin, plate," Whisper said, and then it was quiet again for a minute.

"Who's that?" she heard a child quietly ask.

"Uncle Winston's friend," Terry answered in a hushed voice. "Now eat up, it's almost time to go."

A moment later, she heard chairs pushing back from the table and Whisper instructing the kids to put on their shoes and jackets. Then there was the padding of footsteps out the door and a chorus of "Love you," and the door pulled shut. Just like that, it was quiet. A minute or two later, Shaka heard Whisper running water and piling dishes next to the sink. In the quiet, Shaka found that her eyes were heavy, and her body was too. She drifted back to sleep.

When she woke up an hour later, the house was silent and smelled like coffee and cigarettes. This time when she opened her eyes, she found that she was alone. She kicked her legs to the floor and rubbed her face. She felt like she'd been sleeping for a week. She rubbed her neck, which was stiff from the armrest of the couch, then she stood to stretch and noticed the front door was open. She could see the toes of Winston's boots. She poured herself a cup of coffee and walked out to the porch.

Winston sat in the rocking chair where Terry had sat the night before. A cup of coffee steamed in his right hand, and a cigarette smoldered in his left.

"Good morning," he said, looking up at her.

"Morning," she replied. "May I?" she asked, reaching for his cigarettes.

He nodded and looked back out to the driveway. Woods surrounded them. In the trees above them, two crows were calling back and forth to each other.

"Sleep okay?" he asked.

"Yeah."

"You weren't wakened by the troops this morning?"

"Yeah," she repeated.

Winston chuckled. "Not a lot of peace and quiet around here."

Shaka nodded. "It's nice though." She turned her back to the soft breeze and lit her cigarette. "We're safe here?"

Winston looked over to her. "Safe as anywhere."

"Okay." Shaka took another drag off her cigarette, exhaled a stream of smoke, and followed it with a sip of coffee.

"I can promise that no one here will turn us over," he added.

"Okay," she repeated. "I guess that's the best we can hope for. So, now that we're safe-ish, what is our plan?"

"To lay low here until we know exactly how to break into the lab. I can probably find a few people around here who will help us."

"Are there other shape-shifters here?" she asked.

"None that will help us," he said as he crushed out his cigarette on the side of the Folgers can beside his chair.

Shaka found his comment startling. The only shifters she'd ever met, other than her grandfather, were Winston and Michal, and that ability alone had united them in a common cause. She found it hard to imagine that Winston knew other shifters, and that they wouldn't help them. She wanted to pry, but something in his tone told her he didn't want to discuss it.

"Are there any trails close by?" she asked.

"Yes, I can show you," he answered. He took one last swig of his coffee and stepped off the porch. Shaka followed.

He took her down the gravel road about a quarter mile. They didn't pass another driveway before they came to what looked like a deer trail. Winston turned down it, and a minute later, they were surrounded by woods. Shaka felt herself relax immediately. The damp air, the scent of leaves and dirt, and the sound of small animals running through the underbrush all helped her to forget what she was doing out in these woods in the first place. She gave a happy sigh and followed Winston down the trail.

They walked for twenty minutes before they reached a small lake, more of a swamp, really. One end of it was thick with cattails; the other end was a deep blue. Winston walked along the side of the lake until he reached a bench made from fallen trees. He sat and smiled out at the water.

"I know it's not home, but it will work in a pinch."

"It's perfect," she said. The breeze made the cattails rattle. Shaka shut her eyes and listened to their whisper. "Do you like to change in the water too?" she asked.

"No. That doesn't work so well with feathers. I just shift beneath a tree and try to get up into it as quickly as I can."

"Makes sense. Does everyone out here know about you?"

"Most have probably heard the rumors. My father was proud that his children were able to shape-shift. Sometimes he even gloated about Rachel and me, as if he had passed the ability down himself. It was from my mother though. She didn't have the ability, but her mother did. Grandma Gladys. She died when I was five. Her own mother outlived her. Her name was Sarah, and she was a white woman who had married into the tribe. Neither she nor her husband had the gift. We all assumed he had been the one carrying the gene. We believed it was a gift that was for the Anishinaabe people, but now we know it wasn't just given to us."

He looked over at Shaka gently. "There are others," he

started again, "a family that lives out on the west edge of the reservation, the Fishers. They don't speak to us. When they learned about our gifts, they told us we must have made a deal with the devil. At first, I thought they were just afraid of us, but it turned out they had shifters in their family too; they just didn't celebrate it like we did. They found the gift shameful and thought we should too. A week after Rachel was taken, my father saw Bea Fisher smiling smugly at him in the grocery store. She seemed to be saying, 'I told you so.' It bothered him so much that he became convinced she'd had a hand in Rachel's capture. His paranoia grew until he didn't trust anyone, not even old friends. That's when he and my mother decided to move to Wisconsin. I moved into the city shortly after they left."

Winston pulled another cigarette from his shirt pocket, then struck a match in his cupped hands. "So, to answer your question, Shaka," he said while holding the cigarette in the corner of his mouth, "yes, everyone here knows about me, and I don't think it's a good thing."

"I suppose not," she said. "But I've never told a single person, and it gets lonely."

"You have to trust someone once in a while," he said.

"Yeah, well, apparently I'm not a great judge of character."

"I'm sure Adrian has been well-versed in the art of deception. Don't beat yourself up over it. Lord knows I've trusted the wrong people before."

"Hmm," Shaka reflected as she turned her face to the breeze. She smelled wood smoke on the wind. It must have been from Terry and Whisper's house. "Thank you for showing me this place."

"Of course. If it's privacy you want, this is the place. There's no one for miles. I'm going to get out of your hair too. Michal's probably up by now." And without another word, Winston rose and started back down the trail.

At last, Shaka was alone. She sat quietly and listened to the sounds of the forest, letting her thoughts drift away. Then she stood, stripped off her clothes, and walked into the water. The coolness of it made goose bumps rise on her skin. She dove under, and the forest was instantly silenced. Beneath the rippling surface of the lake, she changed. The stretching and morphing of her body was a sensation she had missed, and she was still enjoying it when her thoughts changed to the keen visual thinking of a wolf. She rose to the surface and paddled with four wide paws to the opposite shore.

As soon as she stepped out of the lake, she smelled it. It was a familiar scent, but one she knew didn't belong here: soap and sandalwood cologne. Her instincts told her to run, to hide. She made it to the shore and took two leaps into the woods, then spun around and faced the direction the scent came from.

She heard a branch break, and then she saw him, a tall man with light brown hair: Adrian. He was standing at the opposite edge of the lake. She remembered that she knew him, and that he was a traitor. He stood there looking helpless and clumsy across the lake. He was not armed. He leaned left and right, peering into the woods. Clearly, he was looking for her; he must have been following her. A growl escaped through Shaka's bared teeth. She knew if she ran into the woods, he would never catch her, but as she watched him, her fear ebbed away. He looked lost, nervous, as if he was just realizing he was in too deep. He had come there to hunt her, to threaten her, but he was in her world now.

She trotted silently around the lake, staying hidden in the woods. When she reached the edge of the trees, she stopped and watched him. He turned and looked behind him, then turned back to the lake. He scanned the woods, then took a few steps to his right, his back to Shaka.

She made another low growl in her throat, just loud enough for him to hear. He stopped in his tracks and carefully looked over his shoulder. As he did, she stepped out of the woods. He slowly turned to face her. She could smell his fear; the air was thick with it. His eyes darted from her to the trail and back. She hoped he tried to run; she wanted to chase him, though he wouldn't get far.

She took another step toward him, head low, lip curling in a snarl. He took a step backwards and stumbled, but quickly straightened up. She took two more steps toward him, long and steady, her hackles raised and her muscles tense, ready to leap on him. Her instincts urged her to attack.

"Easy now," he managed, as if she were a house pet. His voice shook. She took two more steady steps toward him, and he took another quick step backwards, this time tripping over a log and falling onto his back. He was at his most vulnerable. She snarled loudly, showing him the long white knives of her teeth. He pushed himself backwards. "Please don't," he said in a gasp, his breathing erratic. Then he struggled to his feet and turned to run.

With another chilling snarl, she leapt on him, knocking him to the ground. She mercilessly sunk her teeth into the flesh of his arm and shook her head wildly; she felt muscle tearing and blood oozing into her mouth. A scream escaped him, full of terror and pain. Her instincts urged her to move to his neck and sink her teeth into something more vital, but underneath, something felt wrong. Her human thoughts scrambled to make sense of what was happening. She didn't want to kill Adrian. He was struggling, in pain, and afraid. Something new to her wolf mind surfaced from the depths of her human thoughts: sympathy for the enemy.

She faltered and for a second loosened her grip, allowing him to pull his arm out of her mouth. He pushed himself back from her a few feet and sat cradling his arm and gasping for breath.

"Please, please..." he begged her as he struggled to his feet.

She watched him while her two identities became conflicted for the first time. The wolf in her urged her forward. He was an enemy weakened and ready to be finished. But the human in her fought to stop, to leave him alone, to disappear. She stood in place, unable to move in either direction. Slowly her lips curled back, and again the low growl returned.

Adrian had backed himself into the woods. There was nowhere for him to go without turning his back to her.

She took another step toward him. The urge to attack him was growing stronger by the second. It all bvut drowned out her fear that this time she wouldn't be able to stop herself from killing him. There was only one thing she could do. She lay down on the ground in front of him and shifted back. Then she stood before him, naked, as he looked at her in stunned silence.

"It's you," he finally choked out. "This is bad. This is so bad..."

She took a step toward him, and he instantly took a step back. "No!" he cried. "Stay back!"

She stopped and nodded, almost apologetically. She could tell that his blood was still on her face. She turned around and walked into the lake and dove under to wash herself off, then found her clothes and dressed. Slowly, she approached Adrian again. He watched her suspiciously as he hugged his torn arm against his body.

"I'm sorry for that," she said. "I lost control. It's not easy to think rationally when I'm a wolf. I just know that you're a threat now."

"I need to sit down," he said.

"There's a bench." She pointed to the bench where she and Winston had sat only minutes before.

He walked over to it unsteadily and sat down hard. Shaka cautiously approached and sat down on the other end.

He didn't look up at her, he looked down at his feet. "I'm not a threat," he finally said.

"Oh, really? Even though you clearly followed me here?! And we both know that you knew about me and Winston all along." She paused to control her anger before she continued, "And that you were only spending time with me to figure out how to trap us. I mean, what are we going to do now? If I let you leave this place, I'm as good as caught, and Winston too."

"Why not just kill me, then?" he asked.

"I can't do that. Though I suppose I'll have plenty of time to regret it when I'm locked up in a cage beside my grandfather."

"I'm not a threat," he said again. "I didn't know you were one of them. I only knew about Winston, and I came to help him."

"You can drop the act," she said firmly. "He remembers seeing you the day his sister was kidnapped."

"I know..." He trailed off.

Shaka looked at his hand and noticed blood steadily dripping from his index finger. "We'd better stop that bleeding. I think I really messed you up," she said.

"Yeah, I think so too."

"Let me look at it."

He slowly sat upright, exposing his arm. She rolled up the sleeve of his shirt, revealing two deep tears that went into the muscle. She was sure if she manipulated the wound, she would be able to see bone. Luckily, her grandfather had taught her how to dress a wound in the woods. She got up and looked for moss near the boggy end of the lake, them came back and placed it over the wounds. She used her teeth to rip a hole in the sleeve of her shirt, then tore it into strips which she wrapped tightly around the moss. She tore off the other sleeve too and tied it into a sling.

"Okay. We've got to walk," she told him.

He stood, and he looked more stable than she expected. They walked down the deer trail slowly and steadily. When they were near enough to see the gravel of the road, she asked, "Where is your car?"

"About a mile up," he answered, motioning with his hand. "Behind a big oak tree. You can't see it from the road."

"Give me your keys." She held out her hand.

He slowly rummaged through his pockets and finally pulled out the key to his Subaru.

"Just stay here. I'll be right back," she ordered.

He nodded and sat down on the ground.

When Shaka returned fifteen minutes later, she found him asleep in the same spot.

"Wake up. Let's go," she said, and his eyes cracked open slowly. "Come on. We need to get out of here before anyone sees you."

He nodded and awkwardly stood, then made his way to the car.

The nearest town was Cloquet. She found a drugstore there and loaded up a shopping basket while Adrian slept in the car. She worried that he had lost too much blood and would need a transfusion, but taking him to a hospital wasn't an option. All he had to do was call his father, and it would all be over. She grabbed a bottle of iron pills instead. It was the best she could do. She filled the basket with dressing supplies: antibiotic ointment, iodine, gauze, elastic bandages, sterile water, Tylenol, and Advil.

"Let's not waste time," she said as she got back in the car.

He opened his eyes and looked at her, as if waiting for her to say more, but she just shut her door, started the car, and drove.

She stopped beside an empty baseball field. "Let's do this outside. I'm guessing you don't want your car to smell like blood and iodine."

He didn't reply, but watched as she took the bags from the back seat and walked across the field. A moment later, he joined her in the empty dugout.

The moss had stopped the bleeding, but it was an ugly wound. His skin was already changing color. She rinsed it twice, first with water, then with iodine. She put antibiotic ointment in the wound bed, doused some gauze in sterile water and stuffed it into the wound, then covered it with dry gauze and wrapped it up in an elastic bandage.

"If we do this every day, it might not get infected," she said.

"Great," he said flatly.

"Look, I said I was sorry. And let's not forget that you were trying to kidnap me and do God knows what to me."

"I told you, I'm not working with my father. I'm out here to help you."

"Right. Well, let's just go back. We'll need to figure out what to do with you," she said as she stood and marched toward the car.

By the time they reached the place where Adrian had hidden his car, it was getting dark. She pulled the car back in behind the brush. He was asleep again. She didn't like the idea of leaving him there alone for the night, but he certainly couldn't come back to the house with her; that was out of the question. She knew Winston would not be as kind to him as she was, and though she thought of him as a traitor, she couldn't deny she still didn't want to see him hurt. There was a pillow and blanket in his back seat, along with water jugs and a bag of food. Clearly, he'd been planning on staking them out for more than just a day. She grabbed the blanket and draped it over him.

He cracked his eyes open. "Thank you, Shaka. You won't regret this."

"I already do," she said skeptically. "If you don't take us prisoner, Winston will kill me."

"No. I'm on your side. I can help you two. I can."

"You keep saying that, but I'm still taking your keys, and your phone," she said as she stuffed the keys in her pocket. He obediently pulled his phone from his pocket and handed it to her.

"Battery's dead anyway," he mumbled.

She stuffed his phone in her pocket with the keys and watched him for a moment. He closed his eyes and was asleep again almost instantly. She quietly shut the door, snuck back onto the road and walked to Terry and Whisper's house. As she neared the driveway, she could hear the sound of children laughing and yelling. They quieted as she walked down the driveway.

"Hi, guys," she said as she passed them.

"Hi," Michal replied while the others just watched her curiously.

She saw Terry and Winston sitting on the porch. They had pulled a kitchen chair out for Winston. They were smoking cigarettes and drinking Old Milwaukee beer.

"Hey, stranger. Looks like you had a good day," Winston said as he looked at her shirt. She followed his gaze and found that in addition to the torn sleeves there was blood smeared across the front.

"Oh. Oops."

"Waabiska ma'iingan returns from the hunt," Terry quipped. She glanced up at him, then quickly back down to her shirt. She had no idea what he was calling her, but his smile told her it wasn't anything too unkind.

"You missed a good dinner, *ma'iingan*," he added. "Fried perch."

"That sounds good. I lost track of time."

"I bet you did," he said with a knowing smile. "Whisper!" he yelled towards the door. "Heat up some dinner for *ma'iingan*. She's back, and she's hungry."

"Okay!" Whisper called from inside.

"Thank you," Shaka said, half to the open door and half to Terry. "Did I miss anything else today?" she asked, turning to Winston.

"No. Just me drawing out a map of the lab, and Terry counting his guns."

"How's an owl gonna carry a gun?" She laughed as she tried to imagine it.

"Winnie ain't going in there alone," Terry said. "I'll carry the guns."

"Oh. Are you coming too?"

"Of course. You're not the only one with a family member in there, *ma'iingan*. Rachel is my cousin."

Shaka was surprised to learn that Winston had told Terry about her grandfather. Today, two people had learned secrets about her. It felt unnatural. She was at the mercy of their discretion now. All she could do was shake it off and hope they could keep her secrets quiet.

"I'm glad our numbers are growing, then," she finally said, and excused herself to go inside and eat leftover perch and mashed potatoes.

CHAPTER TWENTY-SIX

ALL NIGHT HER SLEEP WAS RESTLESS. ADRIAN HAUNTED HER dreams. In one dream, she went to his car and found him gone, then helicopters flew in and circled overhead as she heard tires grinding toward her on the gravel. She looked up to see three white vans. Adrian sat in the driver's seat and smiled at her. She awoke in a sweat, relieved to find it was only a dream, then fell back asleep, only to find him drowning in the lake. She wanted to save him, but her legs were heavy and stiff, each step an excruciating test of her will. After a while, she realized too much time had passed, and she just gave up and sat beside the quiet lake as his body sank.

She woke with relief again to find herself in the quiet living room of the small house in the heart of the reservation. She looked at her phone. It was 3:00 a.m. She thought about just staying awake until daybreak, then going to find him, but it wasn't long before she drifted off again. This time, Adrian wasn't there. She stood in the woods, listening. She was human, as she usually was in her dreams. Birds sang in the treetops, and sunlight filtered through the leaves in rays that came to rest on the forest floor. She reached her right foot forward into a sunbeam and watched her skin turn yellow in the light. She felt the warmth, a smile came to her face, and she shut her eyes.

"Shaka," said a familiar voice.

Her eyes shot open, and standing twenty feet from her was her grandfather. She didn't move toward him, nor did he approach her. In many ways, they mirrored one another: their blue eyes, their quiet dispositions, the way their toes pointed to one another. She waited for him to speak, but he just stood there with a kind look on his face. Just then, a hawk screeched from high above and she looked up as its wingspan cast a moving shadow over the forest floor.

"Red tail," her grandfather finally said.

"Yes, female," she replied, and he beamed at her with a proud smile. The wind picked up and shook the leaves. Both of them turned their faces to it to see what scents it carried. Shaka smelled water, pine, and an animal—no, a man, his natural scent almost disguised with perfumed soap. She looked back to her grandfather, but he was gone. The wind was blowing harder, plastering her hair against her face. Soon all she could smell was the soap and sweat of a man. She tried to run, but again her legs were heavy. She tried to scream, but the wind drowned it out. The rays of light were squeezed from the sky, and darkness covered the forest. A hard, mean rain pelted her.

She looked behind her and saw the shadow of a man standing not ten feet away—no features, just darkness, and that scent. It sickened her. She tried again to run, but her legs wouldn't move. She chanced another look over her shoulder, and the shadow was moving closer, its dark hands opened up. She crouched down, ready to change right there and fight, when she was wakened by the drumming of footsteps coming down the spiral staircase. She opened her eyes and found a brown and white dog, a pit bull mix, sleeping on her feet.

"Good morning, buddy," she mumbled as she reached out to pet him.

"Daisy is a girl," a young boy corrected her.

"Oh, okay. Sorry, Daisy."

The boy stood in front of her and stared.

"What's your name?" she asked.

"Braden."

"I'm Shaka." She pulled her feet out from under the dog and sat up straight on the couch.

"My dad says if we're bad, you'll eat us," he added boldly, and with a fearful, serious face.

Shaka laughed, which, made Daisy bark. Shaka looked at Braden, who had a small smile forming at the corners of his mouth. She motioned for him to come closer, and he took a small step toward her.

"You're too small to eat," she whispered.

"Braden! Breakfast!" his mother yelled, and he ran into the kitchen.

Again, Shaka's body ached from the couch. She stood and stretched, then moved to the bathroom to get dressed. When she came out, the house was quiet except for the sound of the coffee pot percolating. She grabbed a mug from the cupboard; it had a red heart on it that said, *Someone in Texas Loves You!* She filled the cup with coffee, then started down the driveway.

It seemed a short walk to Adrian's car. When she saw the big oak tree, she looked around to make sure no one was watching, then ducked into the tall grass of the ditch. Somewhere in the treetops, two crows were calling back and forth. She was alone. She tapped on the driver's side window with her nail. She could see Adrian sleeping in the passenger's seat. He didn't look like he had moved much since she'd left. He was so still. She felt her heartbeat speed up. She tapped again on the window, this time louder and more frantically.

He took a sharp inhale, and his eyes cracked open. He looked in her direction, then, seeing it was her, he rubbed his eyes, shifted in his seat, and unlocked the driver's side door.

"How are you feeling?" she asked as she handed him her half-full cup of coffee.

He wrapped his hand around the warm mug and took a deep inhale of its contents. "Coffee," he said quietly and took a drink.

"So? How are you?" she asked again.

"Um..." He swallowed. "You mean, since you tried to kill me?"

"No. I mean since you tried to entrap me and bring me to a testing facility."

His eyes widened. "How do you know about the lab?"

"So, it is true, then?" She looked ahead thoughtfully.

"Yes, but I'm on your side, believe it or not. I told you I want to help."

"Then unlock your phone for me," she demanded as she handed him back his fully charged phone. To her surprise, he put in his passcode without arguing and handed it back to her. She scrolled through his texts. She was the last person he had texted, and that had been three days ago. She looked at his call history and his email too. He hadn't communicated with anyone in the last two days.

"Do you have another phone?" she asked suspiciously.

"No, Shaka, this is my only phone," he insisted.

She tossed it back toward him, then thought better of it and grabbed it and put it in her pocket with his keys.

"Now who's keeping who prisoner?" he asked.

"You're the one who came out here to spy on us. You must have considered the risks. It's not like this is your home turf."

"How many times do you want me to say that I'm here to help you? I just need you to let me explain. And Shaka, this isn't exactly your home turf either." He pulled the two bottles of pain relievers from the glove box and tried to open one of them. He fumbled with the cap, unable to grasp the top with his injured hand. Shaka took the bottles from him without saying a thing, opened them, and handed them back. He pulled two pills from each and swallowed them down with the last of the coffee.

"If you're going to explain yourself, you'll have to do it to all of us. This isn't just about me," Shaka said.

"I know, but somehow I doubt anyone else will listen."

"You're right," she said flatly, "they won't be happy to see you out here, and I can't just walk you up to the front door either. They'd probably shoot you on sight." She stopped talking and thought for a minute. "Maybe Winston will come down here and meet you. If he's the one to bring you in, they'll be better to you, although I don't know how Winston will react to seeing you. He seems like a collected guy, but he's not exactly a fan of yours."

"Yeah, I know, he hates me. I'd hate me too," he said.

"I mean, you did help kidnap his sister." Suddenly the sight of him angered her, and she felt foolish for even considering that he was being honest with her. "Do you even know what they do to people there?" she asked as she glared at him.

"I have an idea," he said. "But I didn't help them capture her, I was just there. I couldn't have stopped them if I'd tried. I wasn't there because I wanted to be. I was being groomed for the family business."

"And now?" she asked.

"Now I'm here, in the middle of nowhere, with my arm torn up, trying to keep anyone else from getting abducted. It would just be a lot easier if you would believe me."

"It's just such an unlikely story. We'll see what Winston thinks of it." Shaka got out of the car and slammed the door. She started down the road without looking back.

When she reached the house, Winston sat alone on the porch, coffee in one hand, cigarette in the other. He looked calm and content. She knew she was about to change that. When she stepped up on the porch, he smiled at her and said, "Good morning."

"Hey. Can I bum a cigarette from you?" she responded hastily.

He reached into his shirt pocket and pulled one out, handing it to her with a book of matches. She took it from him and lit it, taking a long drag that she exhaled in a blue cloud. "I have to tell you something," she said. "I'm afraid you may not like it."

Winston stopped rocking in his chair and looked at her patiently.

"Adrian followed us here." She glanced at him and saw his look of patience pull into a hateful scowl. "I found him in the woods yesterday, and I attacked him," she continued. "I ripped up his arm pretty good, but I shifted back before I could kill him. Then he was weak and shaky and bleeding everywhere, so I took him to Cloquet and bandaged him up and brought him back here. He's in a car about a mile down the road right now. He claims he wants to help us get Rachel and my grandfather out."

Winston ran his hands through his hair. "He's probably already called back to the headquarters and told them right where we are."

"No, he didn't, because I have his keys and his phone," she said as she patted her pocket.

"Okay," Winston said sounding a little relieved, "that's good." He ran his fingers through his hair one more time and went into the house. Seconds later, he came out with a rifle. "I don't fault you for not killing him. I know you two were close. If you just tell me where he is, I'll take care of it."

Instantly, panic flooded Shaka's thoughts. She had expected Winston to be mad, but she hadn't expected him to immediately want to kill Adrian.

"No," she said, trying to sound calm, though she felt her voice shake. "You can't just kill him. That's not why I told you."

"Whose side are you on, Shaka?" he asked her, with a darkness in his eyes she hadn't seen before.

"Maybe he *can* help us. He says that's what he came here to do. I know it sounds crazy, but I checked his phone. He hasn't called anyone since he got here. He hasn't told anyone about us."

Winston looked at her for a moment, then pushed past her and started down the driveway. "I thought you were smarter than this," he said.

"Okay, so say he's lying. He's still worth more to us alive than dead. Maybe we can use him as collateral for them to release Rachel and my grandfather. Maybe we can get him to tell us some secrets about the lab," she pleaded.

Winston didn't even look at her as she spoke. He turned right out of the driveway, the way she had come in, and looked at the gravel for her footprints. He found a few on the soft sand near the edge of the road and followed them.

"Winston, please, can't we just hear what he has to say? We have nothing to lose by listening to him!"

"We have nothing to gain by listening to a liar," Winston growled as he walked on, looking at the gravel, the muzzle of the rifle pointing up over his shoulder.

"You don't have to forgive him. You can hate him, beat him up, I don't care, but please don't kill him! If you kill him and he was really trying to help us, I couldn't live with the guilt."

"You couldn't live with the guilt." He whirled around and faced her. "But he does fine with it! How many people do you think he's helped capture? How many people has he reduced to lab rats?!" he yelled, then paused and started again more quietly. "Rachel had her whole life ahead of her. Now, if we even get her out, she's going to spend the rest of her life trying to figure out what happened to her. Maybe *you* can't live with the guilt, but I will sleep just fine tonight."

"But just think about it, Winston," she continued, undeterred by his rage, "if you kill him, you'll be doing it for revenge. That might feel good, but we can't use that to get Rachel out." She spoke clearly, trying to keep her voice steady.

He turned his back to her and kept walking in the direction of her tracks. They were getting closer; she could see the oak tree ahead of them.

"If you want him to pay, make him work for us. Please, Winston! You're not a killer."

"You don't know that," he growled.

She trailed after him, but as the oak tree neared, she slowed down. She didn't know what else to do. Winston wasn't hearing her. He was running on anger, and anger doesn't listen to reason. Maybe he was right; maybe Adrian was still lying to them. Maybe he would always be the enemy. Still, she couldn't watch him die, and she couldn't stop his death, so she stopped walking. She watched Winston as he reached the oak tree and followed her tracks down into the ditch. She squeezed her eyes shut and covered her ears. Tears spilled out from her clenched eyelids and ran down her face. She knew the shot was coming; she knew she would feel it vibrate through her body.

She felt she should have known better than to trust Winston; she knew how badly he hated Adrian. Now she had sealed his fate. She squeezed her ribs with her arms and pressed her hands so tightly over her ears that her head hurt. She told herself that after it was done, she would bury him. That was the least she could do.

She waited. What was taking so long? Why was Winston dragging it out? She vowed that after Adrian was in the ground, she was going to leave. She would find a way to get her grandfather out without the help of a murderer. What use was Winston if he couldn't control his emotions? He would only put them in danger. Still, she waited, but there was no shot. Could she have missed it somehow?

She cracked open an eye, and to her surprise, Winston was walking Adrian down the road. She dropped her hands from her ears and jogged toward them. Adrian was bleeding from his nose, and his left eye was starting to swell. He walked with his hands in the air, Winston pointing the rifle at his back.

"You didn't kill him!" Shaka said, relieved.

"Not yet," he answered grimly. "And I mean that!" he yelled at the back of Adrian's head. "This doesn't mean you're safe."

"I got that," Adrian said as he looked at Shaka.

"Good. Maybe he can help us, Winston."

"His only use is as collateral," Winston said, then turned to Adrian. "There are two reasons you're not dead, and neither of them are because I believe you want to help us."

When they turned down the driveway, Winston pushed Adrian toward the woodshed. "Open the door," he said to Shaka, and she obeyed. "Get in," he said, this time to Adrian, and he ducked into the dark shed. "Now lock it up," he said to Shaka, and again, she obeyed. When she turned around, Winston was staring at her.

"Thank you for not killing him."

"If we can't use him to get our family members out of that place, you'd best prepare yourself for his fate."

Shaka nodded, then asked, "Is it so hard to imagine that someone who's been inside that place would be disgusted by it and want to shut it down? If he helps us, we could just slip in and make all the captives disappear overnight. We wouldn't need to wage a war."

"Yes, Shaka, I understand; it would all end in rainbows if he were telling the truth. But if he's not? Here's what we know about him," he said as he stuck one finger up in the air. "He was once on their side, regardless of whether he is now or not." He stuck a second finger up in the air. "He feigned an attraction to you and lied to you to learn more about your abilities and to get closer to me." He pointed a third finger in the air. "He followed you for days, then tried to confront you alone in the woods. And," he pointed his fourth finger in the air, "when he found himself at the mercy of a wolf, he told you he wanted to help."

"I know it looks bad—"

"That's one way to put it."

"And you might be right. But we don't know that for sure yet."

"*You* don't know that for sure. I do."

"Okay, fine. You don't have to listen, but I'm going to see what he will tell me."

As she spoke, Terry's truck turned down the driveway. They both looked at it and took a step away from one another. The old truck rolled to a stop with a squeak from the brakes, and Terry killed the engine. Then Terry, Whisper, and Michal all jumped out.

"Dad!" Michal yelled as he ran toward Winston, his arms giving short, abrupt swings as he ran. "Do you want to go to the quarry today?"

"I've got work to do, Mikey," Winston said.

Michal's eyes fell on the rifle in his dad's hands.

"Can we shoot guns then?" he asked.

"I just told you I've got work to do."

"Oh," Michal said dejectedly.

Terry walked up to them. "Come on, cous, a quick target practice never hurts."

"Michal, go inside," Winston said, ignoring Terry's comment.

Michal turned around with his head hanging and walked slowly back to the house. When he was out of earshot, Winston turned to Terry.

"Shaka has something to show you. She took in a stray that I'd just as soon put out of its misery." He pointed to the woodshed and glanced at her. Once more, she stepped up to the latch and unhooked it. The doors swung open, and Adrian sat cross-legged on the dirt floor in the center of the room.

"Jesus Christ!" Terry exclaimed. "You kidnapped a white man? What the hell are you thinking, Winnie?!"

"It's okay, though," Winston answered. "He wants to *help* us," he added sarcastically.

Shaka stood quietly watching him, then her gaze switched over to Terry, who looked at Adrian with panic all over his face.

"I don't know what you're trying to do here, cousin, but he's gotta go. Now."

"If it were up to me, he'd already be gone."

"Winston, you *bagwanawizi*! You kill a white man out here and in a week this place will be crawling with feds! You'd better apologize real sweet to him and get him the hell out of here."

"He's one of them. He was there when they took Rachel!" Winston said.

"And you brought him *here*? Winston, you even use that head of yours?!"

"He followed us here," Winston corrected him.

"He says he wants to help us get the captives out," Shaka added. "I want to hear what he has to say."

"Not here, *ma'iingan*. What do you think it will look like when the kids find him chained up in the woodshed? First thing Braden will do is tell all his little friends at school, and we'll have the tribal police out here tomorrow. He's got to go." Then turning to Winston, he said, "This is your mess. Clean it up." And he walked to the house.

Winston watched him go, the fury gone from his face.

Shaka stepped into the woodshed and looked down at Adrian. "I guess we're going back to the car."

He struggled to his feet, gritting his teeth as he stood. "Okay," he said, "sounds good to me."

"Don't think you're safe just because he's afraid of you," Winston said, pointing the barrel of the gun toward the house.

"Yeah, I'm not safe. I know that much."

Winston turned to Shaka. "Give me his keys and his phone," he said, holding his hand out. She handed them to him, and he held out the rifle to her. "You might not think you need this, but you might be surprised."

She took it from him and headed back down the road with Adrian.

"I didn't know he was going to want to kill you," Shaka said quietly when they were well down the road. "I wouldn't have told him if I'd known that."

"He's not wrong," Adrian replied.

Shaka gave a frustrated huff. "Yes, he's wrong! You've done bad things, and maybe you're trying to make up for them now, maybe you're not—but either way, killing you is an impulsive solution."

"I didn't know you were such a bleeding heart," he said sarcastically.

"I learned from my grandfather to respond with reason, not emotion."

"Sounds like a wise man."

"Well, you should know; your father has been holding him hostage."

Adrian didn't respond to this. They walked the rest of the way to his car without speaking. When they reached it, he got in the passenger seat and covered up with a blanket. She laid the rifle in the back seat, then sat down in the driver's seat. She took her phone out of her pocket, opened her camera, and set it up on the dash. She positioned it so Adrian filled the screen. His dirty, swollen face made it look like more of a ransom video than a recorded explanation of how he planned to help them.

"Okay. Start at the beginning," she said.

On the screen, he looked at her, then down to his hands. "My father started out as a doctor. When I was born, he was a family doctor, if you can believe it. He wasn't very popular though. He never did well with people. He didn't like explaining things, and he hated being questioned. He had trouble keeping a steady nurse around, and as his patient load dwindled, he decided to go back to school for pharmaceutical science. He worked at the University of Minnesota until I was a teenager. By then, he and some colleagues had found enough investors to open their own testing facility. I was probably about sixteen by this point. I didn't really know what went on there; he never brought me with him. It wasn't that he was trying to keep anything hidden, it was just that he never liked me hanging around. My sister, on the other hand, was right beside him the whole time, pretending to care about his work. He ate it up, and by the time she was a sophomore in high school, she was his little lab gopher. She sucks with people too, but she's great with science. That's how this all turned into what it is. He started it with two colleagues, then bought one of them out within the first year. I suppose the old man had a different vision than him. Then it was just Dad and Dr. Milton. When they learned about your kind, they went on an expedition and came back with their first test subject—"

"Victim," Shaka corrected.

"Right. Well, to them they aren't victims, they are test subjects. It was a young woman from Arizona. I don't know what her name was; I don't know if they even knew. All they knew about her for sure was that she could turn into a scorpion. That poor woman was poked and prodded and zapped and given who knows how many types of drugs for two years. She finally killed herself one night. Hung herself with her bedsheet in her cell. They burned her body. Her family will never know what happened to her. By the time of her death, they had others, so it didn't stop their research. My dad went right back to work as usual, but Milton struggled with it. He must have finally felt a little moral conflict at what they were doing. He took a month off, and when he returned, he proposed they release the subjects and take their work in another direction. But he must have known when he asked that that was impossible. My father wouldn't have stopped their work if they had been court-ordered. Tension rose in the lab, and finally one day, Milton stopped coming in.

"It wasn't long after that that your grandfather was brought in. Everyone in the lab was afraid of him. Most of the others turned into smaller animals that they could easily control if attacked, but they knew if they weren't careful with your grandfather, he could kill them. Part of me wished he would. But now I see he taught you to be a pacifist, so I was betting on the wrong horse. In fact, he never hurt them, never even growled at them. He would just do as they asked. They grew to like him for his obedience. He got special privileges, better meals, books, longer time periods in the gym. If my father has a pet, it's him. I've never understood why your grandfather was so willing to submit like that. I mean, they had kidnapped him and put him in a cell smaller than this car, and he just smiled and said 'please' and 'thank you.'"

"It's easier to attack a friend than an enemy."

"But Shaka, he's not going to attack. He's been there for almost two years."

His words stung. She looked out the driver's side window. Her eyes burned for a moment, but she blinked back her tears. How could her strong, resourceful grandfather have been held captive for so long?

"I'm sorry, Shaka," he said, but she didn't hear his apology.

"I just need a minute," she said and stepped out of the car.

Outside there were only the sounds of nature. She looked up at the rattling aspen leaves and closed her eyes.

CHAPTER TWENTY-SEVEN

SHAKA'S GRANDFATHER HAD BEEN MORE OF A PARENT TO HER than anyone. She'd always felt her gift made her seem threatening and unknowable to her actual parents; the only one who truly understood her was her grandfather. He was the one who'd taught her about the differences between the wild world and the domesticated one. Everything she knew about human nature grew from a foundation he had built. She had been the only child of an only child, so there was no one to compete with for his attention, and there was nothing that seemed more important to him than her.

Her mind drifted back to the day he had come to school to pick her up after she'd gotten in a fight with a girl from her reading class at recess. Shaka had seen her throwing rocks at a squirrel's nest. The girl yelled out to anyone within earshot that there were babies in the nest, and she wanted to see them.

Their recess supervisor stood idly by and watched as a crowd of curious children gathered.

"I could get it down faster than that!" a boy said, and he too picked up a rock and hurled it at the nest. Then the girl's next rock hit the nest, and a chorus of squeaks erupted from it. A fat gray squirrel squawked wildly at the crowd as it ran up and down the tree and jumped from branch to branch.

"Watch me hit the mama!" another boy yelled.

"Leave them alone!" a girl yelled. She was younger than Shaka and had red hair fashioned into two pigtails on top of her head.

"Shut up, Marcy," someone yelled as another rock hurtled toward the nest. The supervisor just stood with one leg kinked at the knee. It was clear that he too wanted to see what was in the nest.

Shaka stood up from her swing. Even at the age of eight, she hated to see pointless violence toward something that couldn't defend itself. She knew she needed to intervene; she just didn't know how to do it gracefully.

She quietly bent over and picked up a rock of her own. No one was watching her when she pulled her arm back and launched it toward the girl who had started it all. It sailed through the air and hit her squarely on the side of her face. She fell to the ground, her sobs reaching all corners of the playground. Finally, the supervisor moved. He ran to the girl and looked at the side of her face. Blood ran from a cut on her cheekbone. The crowd of children lost interest in the squirrel's nest and turned to form a circle around her.

"Serves you right!" the red headed girl yelled.

"Marcy!" the man yelled. "Go to the office!"

"Why should I?" she demanded, but he wasn't paying attention to her anymore.

"Who threw that rock?" he yelled at the children. His question was answered with silence. "Who threw it?" he demanded again. "If no one answers you will all be sitting out recess for the rest of the week."

Shaka liked that idea. With the exception of the little red headed girl, she hated them all that day. She sealed her lips.

"Shaka did it," a small voice spoke up. "I seen her."

Shaka looked at her accuser, a young boy she'd never seen before. How he knew who she was, she had no idea—but then, the younger kids always seemed to know the names of the older ones.

"Shaka," the man asked, "is this true?"

She said nothing.

"Why?" he demanded.

"'Cause she should throw rocks at someone who can throw them back," she answered through clenched teeth.

"Go to the office. Now," he said sternly.

Shaka didn't protest; she turned her back to them and left.

She sat in a hard chair outside the principal's office for almost an hour before she was called in.

Mrs. Larson, the principal, sat behind her desk with her hands crossed in front of her as Shaka came in. There was a coffee mug in front of her that steamed. The smell of coffee reminded Shaka of her father.

"So, Shaka, what happened on the playground?" she asked.

Shaka shrugged. She didn't feel like talking.

"Mr. Jacobs said you hit Becky with a rock. Why?"

"She was throwing rocks at squirrels."

"So, you thought it would be okay to throw a rock at *her*?" she asked as her eyebrows knit together in concern.

Shaka shrunk under her gaze. She knew this was a question that you weren't supposed to answer. Then the door creaked open, and her grandfather walked in. Shaka sat up in her chair and beamed at him. He would be on her side; he always was.

"Mr. Reed," Mrs. Larson said, "please come in and have a seat."

"Thank you," he said and sat down next to Shaka without looking at her. She settled back into her chair a little, wondering why he didn't say hello to her.

"There was an incident on the playground today."

"Yes, they explained it to me on the phone. I can assure you, we do not teach Shaka to resolve her problems with violence. We're going to have a good discussion about this tonight." He gave Shaka a disapproving look, and she shrunk a little in her seat again.

"To be honest, Mr. Reed, I was surprised to hear about this too. Shaka has never been violent or disruptive before. Is there anything at home that could be troubling her right now?"

"No, ma'am. No changes at home. But Shaka never has been one to tolerate pointless cruelty. I suspect that if the other children had been stopped from throwing rocks, Shaka wouldn't have felt she had to step in and stop it herself, crude as her intervention was."

Mrs. Larson straightened a pile of papers on her desk as she considered her response.

"Mr. Reed," she finally said, "I do see your point, but the welfare of our children is paramount here. I believe you when you say you will instill in Shaka the importance of kindness toward other students, no matter the circumstances. In the future, she can tell a teacher, or she can ask the child to stop. There are other options than violence."

Shaka squirmed in her seat. She wanted to speak up and say that those options had been tried, but she knew she was supposed to keep quiet. She let her grandfather do the talking.

"Of course," he replied. "I will make sure she doesn't do this again."

"Thank you. Our school has a policy of two days' suspension for any physical fighting between students. Since this is Shaka's first fight, and we hope her last..." She turned and looked at Shaka. "I'm willing to reduce it to one day. But I would also like her to write a letter of apology to the girl she struck. *Capiche?"* she said to Shaka.

"Capiche," Shaka answered quietly.

On the drive home, her grandfather hummed an old folk song to himself. His window was down, and the breeze blew through his graying hair. Shaka was scared to speak. She was waiting for him to reprimand her, but his lecture never came. She was surprised when he turned not toward her house, but onto the road that led to his cabin. She chanced a question: "What are we doing?"

"Shaka, darling," he answered lightly, "you're going to stay with me tonight."

"Can we have a fire?" she asked excitedly. Staying at her grandfather's cabin was always fun. They would go out in his little boat on the river or walk through the woods. Every night ended with a bonfire, even in the winter. Beside the fire, he would tell her stories. Some were funny, some were scary, but she loved them all.

"Hmm. Not tonight. You've got a letter to write tonight."

"I can write it tomorrow."

"Tomorrow you'll be stacking firewood with me. Winter is on its way, and I need to get ready for it."

Shaka looked out the window. She hated stacking firewood. It made her arms sore, and if she didn't stack the pile straight, her grandfather would make her take it all down and restack it.

"If your arms are strong enough to throw rocks, they're surely strong enough to stack wood."

"She threw rocks too," she defended herself.

"I know. But there's nothing I can do about that. I know you were trying to stop her from hurting those squirrels, and I'm proud of you for that. But you should have used your words to stop her, not your hands, and certainly not your hands before you've said anything at all."

"Yes, sir," she answered him.

That night, she wrote a letter to the girl, apologizing for hurting her. She said she wouldn't throw any more rocks if she would please just let the squirrels be. Her grandfather read it patiently, then handed it back to her.

"No," he said. "This letter is an apology for hurting her, not a plea for her to leave the squirrels alone. If you want to ask her to leave the squirrels alone, you need to write two letters."

She took the sheet of paper and started over. Forty minutes later, she handed him two letters. He read one, then the other, and handed them back to her.

"Well done, honey." He winked at her. "That's how you use words to make a point!"

When Shaka returned to school, she had blisters on her hands from stacking wood. The other kids whispered as she walked past them and gave her a wide berth in the hallway. She passed the little redheaded girl, who beamed up at her. Shaka smiled back. At least one person had agreed with her. She handed her letters in to Mrs. Larson, who thanked her and asked her if there would be any more trouble. She answered with a short "No, ma'am" and was dismissed from her office.

At recess, the squirrel's nest was the first place she went. She worried that the kids had knocked it down yesterday, but as she got closer, she found it was still there. She could see the tail of the big mamma squirrel sticking up within it. A sign had been nailed to the tree. She read it slowly: Anyone throwing rocks at the squirrels gets automatic detention!

Shaka smiled. She may have stopped one girl from throwing rocks at the squirrels in the moment by throwing a rock herself, but through discussion, her grandfather had made sure none of the other kids would throw rocks either.

Now, many years later, as Shaka stood beside the gravel

road, she made a silent apology to her grandfather, who had tirelessly taught her to be a pacifist. This time, she could not use language to resolve conflict. This time, she was going straight for the rocks.

CHAPTER TWENTY-EIGHT

"CAN WE FAST-FORWARD TO YOUR ROLE IN ALL OF THIS?" Shaka said as she got back into Adrian's car.

He gave her a cautious smile and nodded. "I'm sorry that this is how we met," he said.

"That doesn't matter. Let's just focus."

"It does matter though. I'm not an asshole. I'm not my father."

"Then I want you to prove it. I want you to tell me how we can get my grandfather out of there."

"I don't know all the ins and outs of the lab, but I know that to get the cells open, you'll need a fingerprint from someone who works there."

"Will yours work?"

"Yes, he gave me authorization a year ago. I never liked what he was doing. When I first found out, I told him he should let all his captives go. He told me I had no idea how important the work he's doing is. The next time we talked, I told him if he didn't let them go, I was going to tell the police. He laughed and said there's nothing illegal about what he's doing. He said he's holding a clinical trial, which is quite common in pharmaceutical science. I told him he was crazy. Those people hadn't agreed to anything. Then he showed me releases they had all signed, agreeing to submit to testing. He must have forced them to sign at gunpoint or something. But he had his crooked lawyer work everything out, so it did look like what he's doing is perfectly legal.

"A year passed, but I couldn't stop thinking about it. When I returned for Thanksgiving, I heard my sister telling my mom about how important their work is and how close they were to finding a serum that would give ordinary people the ability to turn into animals. At first, I felt nothing but anger—but then I got the idea to try to shut them down from the inside. All I had to do was pretend to be interested in what they were doing.

"The next week, my dad called me and asked if I'd 'changed my position' on his work. I told him yes, and he said he was going to need a new lawyer in a couple years and asked if I would be interested in that. At first, I said no. I only had a bachelor's degree at the time, and in art, no less. Law school would take years. But the more I thought about it, I would need years if I was going to infiltrate that place and regain my father's trust. So, he sent me to law school. A year ago, I passed the bar exam and have been doing his bidding ever since. Now I know it doesn't matter if what he's doing is illegal and immoral; he has the protection and funding of some very powerful people. He's untouchable. The best I can do right now is try to keep new people from being captured." He shifted in his seat, took a drink of water from a bottle in the cup holder, and continued.

"My father's been trying to find Arnold's family since they captured him. When I heard they had a lead on a woman who'd been seen with someone affiliated with the Kowalski firm, I came up here to see for myself. One call to Salem was all it took to be welcomed back into his circle. I saw you at his girlfriend's art opening. You were easy to spot; you have the same eyes as Arnold. You move like him too. And you know the story from there."

"But what about Winston? I thought you were after him?"

"They've been trying to capture Winston for years. He always gives them the slip. I came up here for you. If I can keep Winston out of their reach too, all the better. But if I'm being honest, I don't feel like doing that guy any favors right now. I just wanted to find you before they did."

"Do they know about me yet?" she asked.

"Not quite. Those people you saw in the woods—"

"I didn't tell you about that!" she interrupted.

"Yeah, but I heard about it though. They didn't see you change, but they saw you come out of the woods. You weren't just being paranoid. They were watching you. They only kept their distance because they know I'm getting close to you."

"Or I'd already be in a cage," she said quietly.

"Maybe. They don't know for sure that you're a shape-shifter. I'm the only one who knows." Adrian reached over and squeezed her hand. "And I'm not gonna let them get you."

Shaka threw his hand off. "If they want me, they'll take me. Who were those people in the woods?"

"The woman was my sister, Amanda, and the younger man was her boyfriend. I went to high school with him. He's always been an idiot. The other man was my dad's assistant, Mitchell."

"What do they know about us?"

"I've been telling them lies they can't disprove. I told them you're quiet and serious and it's hard to get you to open up. I guess on second thought, I've been pretty honest with them, but it buys me time to figure out what I'm doing. I told them I met Winston, and he's quiet and serious too. I told them it would take some time before either of you spilled your secrets to me. They're getting impatient though. They're hoping I can lead them to more people of Winston's bloodline. I don't think they know about Michal yet."

"At least there's that. What about Salem? Is he in on it too?"

"No, he's clueless. He's just a guy I met while I was getting my undergrad, remember? I told you that."

"How am I supposed to know what's true?"

"That part was true. I never really liked him all that much though. He's obnoxious, and after he slept with my girlfriend junior year, that sealed it for me. Luckily, he's horrible at picking up on those subtle signals. When I called him, he welcomed me in like an old friend and offered to set me up with a beautiful young woman, just as I had been hoping he would."

"God, I'm an idiot," Shaka muttered.

Adrian reached over and squeezed her hand again. "Don't say that. You're not just some stranger I was trying to keep away from my father. I mean, it may have started out that way, but when I saw you at the restaurant that night, I knew you would be more than that to me. You're so beautiful, and self-possessed. When you stormed out, I just excused myself and followed. I really didn't care if you led me to Winston or turned into a wolf, I just wanted to know you better. And when I did get to know you better, I halfway hoped Winston would just disappear, and you would have no idea that shape-shifters existed, and we could just date like normal people."

"How quickly you can be dissuaded," she said with the tiniest smile.

"Yeah, because I like you, Shaka—even when you turn into a wild animal and try to rip my arm off, and even when your friend threatens to kill me with a fifty-year-old hunting rifle. And that's another thing: if they think they're going to just bust in there, guns blazing, and overthrow the place, they're in for a surprise."

"Winston was able to sneak in undetected twice."

"He was lucky. His luck is going to run out eventually. Do you know how he's planning to break in?"

"No. All I know is they plan to get a bunch of their buddies together and pool all their guns."

Adrian scoffed. "It's not the Wild West. It might be easy enough for a bird to slip in under their radar, but ten men with guns? A wolf? Please. You won't make it out of the corridor. They have two sets of security doors, and nothing gets through them. Whether they like it or not, they're going to need a man on the inside."

"Well, we don't have a whole lot of time to convince Winston."

"I know that. I just hope he'll listen to reason. It's his skin, after all." He looked at Shaka, and his gaze softened. "And yours." He took a deep breath and started again. "I know what you're going to say, but I have to say it: if you and I just disappeared, no one would know. They wouldn't look for us. We could go live in Mexico and sit on a beach for the rest of our lives. Whenever you wanted to turn into a wolf, we could drive to the middle of the desert, and you could run through the canyons at night. We could drink margaritas and eat tacos every day..."

"Really? I was thinking more like Alaska. If we're going to disappear, might as well be somewhere with enough space to never be seen again."

"I don't know if I'm manly enough for Alaska," he joked.

"Well, then it's your fault that we have to stay here and see this through."

He watched her, saying nothing.

She didn't allow herself to indulge in the fantasy of a future where the testing facility was gone and she and Adrian could disappear. Fantasy had no purpose. It would only take her further from the present, a place that required all her attention. She stopped recording the video on her phone and sent it to Winston. He had been too enraged to listen to Adrian in person, but maybe through the filter of the screen, he could hear what Adrian had to say.

Adrian opened his door and stepped out. He walked into the sunlight and shut his eyes. His swollen face made him almost unrecognizable from the handsome, clean-cut stranger she had danced with weeks before. She considered for a moment that everything he was saying was true, and he had been doing all of this to keep his father from taking her and Winston captive. If that were the case—and she was starting to believe it was—she and Winston had both been horrible to him.

She stepped out of her side of the car and walked up to him. He didn't open his eyes.

"If you're really trying to help us, I hope you can forgive me," she said.

A little smile came to the corners of his mouth. "It's my fault for not having a plan. I should have been honest with you from the start."

She didn't answer, but stepped closer to him, lifted his arm, and ducked underneath it. He squeezed her against him. When she was this close to him, she smelled sweat and dirt mixed with the day-old scent of his cologne. His heartbeat raced like a snare drum, though his face was calm. He glanced down at her, then looked away. She reached up and touched his cheek, and he looked back down at her. She leaned forward and kissed him. His mouth opened slowly at first, then he turned his body toward her and kissed her confidently. The sunlight warmed them, and she ran her hands softly over his chest, until she touched a sore spot, and he winced.

"Sorry," she whispered.

"I'm a mess right now. Maybe this will have to wait for Alaska," he said.

"Maybe."

He stepped back from her and opened the car door. Reaching into the back seat, he pulled out a towel and a small backpack.

"Want to walk to the creek?" he asked her. "I should probably wash some of this dirt off myself."

She nodded. She didn't know of a creek, but the land was thick with woods and swamp, so she doubted they could be far from water.

Slowly they wound down a deer trail, and soon she heard gentle running water. In the trees, birds called to each other without worry. She knew to listen to them. They would announce when something was wrong, just as they announced her and Adrian's arrival at the creek.

He took off his shirt awkwardly, revealing blooms of new bruises on his back. Winston hadn't gone easy on him.

"I'll give you a minute. You probably don't need an audience," she said and walked down the creek bank. She found a pine tree laid across the creek from bank to bank. She hopped on it and walked in a straight line to the other side. She could no longer see Adrian, though she could smell sweat and soap on the wind. She wanted to shift, to run down the creek, to follow it into the woods. She realized she could; there was little danger to her out here, and she had nowhere to be. But she doubted Adrian wanted to see her as a wolf again so soon. Instead, she turned her back to the creek and inhaled deeply through her nose. She took in all the scents of the forest: the running water, the rocks, the wet, juicy leaves, the soil, the dead foliage, even the scent of a nearby rabbit hidden in its burrow.

"Shaka," she heard Adrian call from down the creek, and she turned back to the river. She walked again over the pine tree and planted her feet on the bank.

"Shaka!" she heard him call again, this time with more urgency. She ran up the creek bank until she saw him standing where she'd left him with a clean shirt on and the dirt washed from his face. He held out a hand to her. "Come on, we need to go."

She took it and asked what the hurry was. He didn't answer right away, so she asked again.

"There's someone else out here. They're watching us."

"Probably Winston," she said.

"It's not Winston. This person was hiding."

"Where were they?" she asked.

Again, he didn't answer. They reached his car, and he pushed her into the passenger seat, then jogged around and got in the driver's seat. He felt both of his pockets, then turned to Shaka. "Winston has the keys."

"What did you see?" she asked again.

"I heard a rustle in the woods and saw something white. I couldn't see it very well, but it looked like a person."

"Hmm," Shaka said.

"Just don't change into a wolf, no matter what. It could be someone from the lab. They don't know for sure that you can shift yet."

Shaka felt violent relief wash over her that she hadn't shape-shifted on the creek bank. If she had, she could have been running for her life at this moment.

"There!" she yelled, pointing to the woods. Adrian followed the direction of her finger and saw a girl standing at the edge of the woods, watching them. She was young, maybe eight or nine years old. She wore a white dress and sandals. Her long black hair fell freely down her back, and she watched them through dark eyes with no fear or kindness in her expression, only a cool curiosity. Shaka opened her door.

"No!" Adrian yelled. "Shut your door!"

Shaka shut her door and turned to him. "She's a little girl. What are you scared of?"

"Is she a Fisher?" he asked.

"I don't know who or what she is, other than a little girl in the woods."

"Just stay put," he said, looking back at the girl. They sat in the car, watching her, and she stood watching them back. Her dress danced in the breeze, and the tips of her hair fluttered next to her skin. She watched them without speaking or moving for almost two minutes.

"Okay, this is getting creepy," Shaka finally said.

Then the girl turned her head and looked over her shoulder into the woods, as if someone had called her, and she disappeared back into the forest.

"What was that about?" Shaka asked, disturbed.

"I don't know. I think she was a Fisher," he answered.

"Winston told me about the Fishers. They're another family of shifters that live out here, right?"

"Yeah. But you need to stay away from them. They work with my father, and they'll turn you over to him in a second if they find out about you."

"Winston's dad was right," she said.

Adrian looked at her for an explanation, but she didn't offer one. Instead, she looked at her phone and found a new message from Winston: Okay. I'll talk to him, but if you're wrong about him, we're all doomed.

Shaka quickly stuffed her phone in her pocket. She felt the weight of Winston's words, but the truth was they didn't have much of a chance either way. They were both right: Shaka couldn't prove that Adrian wasn't setting a trap for them, but without Adrian's help, they had no chance of getting into the lab, let alone getting anyone else out. They would have to gamble.

"Guess who's coming around now that you're sharing privileged information?" she said.

"I figured he would, if he could just keep from killing me long enough to listen."

"Should we go make peace?" she asked.

He sighed and opened his car door.

Shaka got out too. As she stood next to the car, she sensed that something was different. The breeze still rustled the leaves, but something had changed... The birds had stopped chirping. She felt eyes on her as she stepped away from the car.

"Grab your things. We're not coming back here," she said, aware that her tone had changed. "Let's not waste time." She started quickly toward the house. Adrian followed closely behind. She didn't know what it was about the girl in the woods, but something was off about her. The air held a scent Shaka had never smelled before, and when she thought of the way the girl had watched them, cool and fearless, it made the hair on the back of her neck stand up. She felt the girl was still watching them now. She scanned the woods for white.

It was the movement that caught her eye first. Shaka let out a gasp, and Adrian, not knowing what had scared her, pushed her behind him and looked into the woods until he saw it too. The girl was watching them again, but her teeth were bared like a growling dog, though no sound escaped her. Her brown eyes glowed.

Shaka started to throw off her clothes so she could shift.

"No," Adrian said and put his hand on her shoulder. "Don't. Let's just keep walking."

Shaka looked at the girl, who stood completely still except for the quivering of her snarl.

"What is *wrong* with her?" she mumbled.

"Just put your shirt on, and let's go," he said.

She did as he said and started walking again, keeping her eyes on the girl. As they moved forward, the girl broke from her stance and moved forward as well. She was walking parallel to them in a swinging, leaping gait. She didn't step so much as crash forward. As they neared the driveway, Shaka wondered if the girl would follow them up to the house. She figured Terry would know who she was and who to call to come and get her, but she hoped the girl would just disappear into the woods again. It chilled Shaka to look at her.

As they turned down the driveway, the girl stopped and stood across the road from them in the ditch, her lips curled, her dark eyes lit.

CHAPTER TWENTY-NINE

WINSTON WAS WAITING FOR THEM ON THE PORCH, THE RIFLE propped up against the wall behind him. When they reached him, Shaka looked over her shoulder. The girl was gone.

"Did you see her?" Shaka asked Winston.

"See who?"

"That creepy little girl! She followed us from his car."

"I didn't see any little girl. Maybe bad spirits are following you," he said, his gaze shifting to Adrian. "You can come in and tell us what you know about the lab. If it's helpful, we may let you live."

"Who's 'us'?" Shaka asked.

Winston motioned with his head to the front door and picked up his rifle.

Shaka walked into the house first with Adrian close behind. The kitchen was filled with faces she had never seen before. There were seven men in the tiny room, including

Winston and Terry. They stood shoulder to shoulder around the table.

"Is this him?" a deep voice asked, and an older man stepped forward, putting a hand on Adrian's shoulder. His touch looked soft, but his eyes were full of hate. Shaka watched Adrian squirm as the man's grip tightened around his shoulder like a claw.

"Dad," Winston said as he stepped forward. "Let him go. We'll listen to him first."

The old man gave one final squeeze before releasing him and stepping back among the other men.

"Sit," Winston ordered, and Adrian obediently sat down at the table.

A man who looked like Terry, but younger, stepped forward and set a notebook and pencil in front of him. "Will you draw the lab?" he asked.

Adrian picked up the pencil and began sketching. He included as many details as he could. The room was silent as he drew.

"Where's Rachel?" Winston asked. Adrian wrote her name in one of the little boxes that lined a wall of the lab. As he did, Winston's father appeared at the table again.

"Where's my grandfather?" Shaka asked, and he wrote *Arnold* in a box beside Rachel's.

"How many are there?" an unfamiliar voice asked. It was a

blond man in a camouflage shirt. His blue eyes glared down at Adrian as he leaned forward.

"I don't know," Adrian answered without looking up at him. "Less than five."

"So, how are you going to get us in there?" he asked.

"I can't get you all in there. That's not possible," Adrian answered.

The group broke into angry chatter, throwing out questions and accusations. Adrian remained still, his eyes averted.

"Quiet down," Winston said, and the chatter quieted to mumbling, then stopped. "So, how do you suggest we get them out?"

"I have access. I can get one of you in without looking suspicious. Once we're inside, I can arrange for all the staff to leave the lab, and whoever comes with me can free the captives."

"How do we know you're not trying to trick us?" Winston's father asked suspiciously from across the table.

"You don't," he answered. "You just have to trust me."

"How will you get one of us inside without being noticed?" Winston asked.

Adrian glanced up at him, then around the room nervously. "I would bring you in as a captive."

Immediately the room grew loud with protest.

"You think one of us is going to just peacefully walk in there with you?" the man in camouflage asked sarcastically.

"It couldn't be just anyone. It would have to be someone who can shift," Adrian answered.

"You're lying!" the man yelled as he leaned over the table and slammed his hand down. "You're only pretending to help Rachel when what you really want is to bring in another one of us. I got a better idea: how about *you* be the captive? How about we exchange you for the prisoners?" He looked around the room and got nods of approval.

"Troy," Winston said sternly, and the man looked at him smugly, but didn't say any more.

"The problem with that plan is that my father cares more about his research than he does about me," Adrian said.

"We supposed to feel sorry for you?" Troy asked with a sneer.

"I'm just telling you that your plan won't work. If I could bring one of you in, it would only take me a few days, a week at the most, to get everything lined up. We could get everyone out safely. When my father returns to the lab, it will just be empty, his captives and his research gone."

"Even if we did that, he'd just keep coming for us," Winston said.

"But if his research were destroyed, he'd have to start from scratch," Adrian pointed out, "and it's too late for him to start over."

"You've already got one of my children locked up," Winston's dad said through gritted teeth. "You're not getting another one."

"I don't like his plan. I think he should let us all in at once, so we can take the place by storm," Troy added. Two of the men nodded, but most of them ignored Troy's attempt to rally them.

"There are locked doors here," Adrian said, pointing to the map, "here and here. I could probably get you through the outer doors, maybe even the second doors, but the lab would be on lockdown before we were able to get in. That would leave us trapped between locked doors."

"What else do you have?" Winston asked. "Because you're not taking another one of us captive."

Adrian looked at the sketch of the lab, tapping his pencil for a few moments. "I could try to do it alone. If I could speak with Arnold, he might help me release the others while I empty the lab. I just don't know if he'll be strong enough, or if he'll trust me. He has no reason to." Adrian looked up at the hard eyes that watched him. "I guess that would be the next best thing," he added.

"Just for the sake of argument, what would your father do to your captive?" Shaka asked.

"He'd probably do some minor testing, try out a couple of his standard drugs. He has one that forces the shift. I'd shield this person from him as much as I could, but he'd want to do a full physical at the very least."

'This person' could only be Shaka or myself," Winston said coldly, "and it's not going to be me. I won't speak for Shaka, but I think we need to start focusing on plan B."

"Okay," Adrian said. "We'll make it work."

"Hang on," Shaka said, stepping forward. "How much do our chances improve if I go in with you?"

Adrian looked at her nervously. "They would improve greatly. I don't want to pressure you, but we would have a plan before you went in, so I wouldn't need to have complicated conversations with the captives. Plus, I will be in my father's good graces if I bring him another 'patient.' That would help immensely. It will be easier to convince him to clear out the lab when the time comes to set the captives free. It just fills in a lot of blanks. But I'm not going to pressure you, Shaka. This is your call. I know you probably don't want to gamble on me."

"It's not gambling when you know you're going to lose," Winston said coolly. "Like I said, we need to focus on plan B."

"No. I'll go. We have a better chance that way," she said. "And I believe Adrian is telling us the truth."

The room was silent for a moment.

"Shaka," Winston spoke up, "you know that if he's lying, or even if he's mistaken about how easy this will be, we may not be able to get you out."

"I know," Shaka answered, looking at Winston sincerely as her eyes welled with tears. She quickly wiped them away.

"Come outside with me for a moment," he said softly to her.

She turned and followed him onto the porch. He held out his pack of cigarettes to her. She took one and lit it quickly.

"Just think about this before you jump. You're a young woman; you've got your whole life ahead of you," he said.

"So does Rachel," she answered.

"Just because Rachel is in there doesn't mean you have to be too. You have a life of your own. As much as I want to see my sister again, I don't think you should risk giving up your freedom and possibly your life to get her out."

Shaka nodded and took a drag from her cigarette, its red tip crackling and glowing. "I have to do this," she finally said. "We have one chance. We need to make it count."

"You're a brave girl, waabiska ma'iingan." Winston said. "No one will fault you for not doing this."

"I know. But it's not about that. If we're going to do this, I don't want to do it halfway."

Winston nodded.

"And why does every one keep calling me that?" she added.

"It means 'white wolf,'" he said, smiling.

She gave a little laugh. "Well, I'm actually a gray wolf."

"Technicality," he said with a grin.

She crushed out her cigarette and turned back to the door. Inside, the room was silent as the circle stared down at Adrian, who in turn stared down at the table.

Shaka looked at Winston, and he nodded to her. "I'll do it, Adrian. You can take me with you."

He looked up at her, regret on his face. "I'm sorry, Shaka."

"Don't be sorry, just make it work. I don't want to spend the rest of my life in a cage."

"I will. I won't leave you in there, I promise."

CHAPTER THIRTY

AFTER SHAKA AGREED TO ENTER THE LAB AS ADRIAN'S prisoner, she lost interest in the conversation. She let the rest of them devise the plan; her mind was elsewhere. She thought about seeing her grandfather again and felt a flicker of joy. Even if Adrian left her in there, at least she would be with him, though the thought did little to console her when she considered spending years—possibly the rest of her life—in a cage.

As the rest of them argued, Shaka quietly slipped out the door. She walked the length of the driveway, watching her feet as they crunched the gravel beneath them. When she reached the road, she turned and walked back to the house; when she reached the house, she again turned and walked to the road. She listened to the sounds of the forest. The birds were speaking all around her. How long since her grandfather had heard the birds sing, she wondered? His favorite had always been the red-winged blackbird. Because of him, she always knew their high, trilling song.

It occurred to her that maybe she could bring their song to him. When the idea came to her, she immediately started jogging toward the trail to the lake. She cut through the woods, her shoes padding on the soft soil. Navigating the forest was so much easier as a wolf, but she needed her hands for this. She reached the water and followed the shore to the eastern edge, where the lake turned to swamp, then she sat down and listened. The red-wings liked to perch on cattails, and she was looking at acres of cattails. One would come sooner or later. She lay back, shut her eyes, and listened. Her mind floated in a sort of meditation, where thoughts of cages and white-coated doctors couldn't reach her. There was only the rattle of the cattails, the lapping of the lake, the conversation of crows, the gulping sound of a frog...then the trill of a red-wing. Shaka hit the record button on her phone. She sat up and slowly rose to a crouch, looking for a splash of red in the reeds. When she found it, she carefully zoomed the video in on the bird. She smiled as she watched it on the screen. She felt almost as though her grandfather was with her. She hoped she would get to show it to him.

The bird sang for a couple minutes before it flew to the far end of the swamp and his song was drowned out by closer sounds. She stopped recording and stood up straight. She felt calm, centered for the first time all day. Whenever questions about tomorrow arose, she simply batted them away. She let her lungs fill with air to the count of four, then release to the count of four. She let her mind be still.

She had always been good at creating her own peace, but soon it was interrupted: Adrian was calling for her. She wanted to be alone. She didn't want to leave this quiet place she had created; she wasn't ready to start talking about her captivity yet. She didn't answer him.

He called her name several more times before he reached the lake. He was quiet then, and she knew that meant he had spotted her. She heard him approach, and when he reached her, he gently rested a hand on her shoulder. For the first time, when he touched her, she felt nothing—no affection, no rage.

"I'm sorry, Shaka," he whispered. "I don't want to ask you to do this. I don't want you to do it. You can say no. In fact, I *want* you to say no."

"What will they do to me?" she asked flatly.

He squeezed her shoulder softly. "First, they will examine you, then they'll inject you with a serum that will force you to change and examine you again. If you show any aggression while you're a wolf, they will sedate you and restrain you with chains. Blood draws, X-rays...it will be like being at a very long doctor's appointment. You won't be there long though—few days, a week at most, just long enough to get everything set. When the time comes, I'll show you how to free the others."

Shaka heard him, but she didn't respond. She was sending her mind to an unfeeling place where the fear of what was about to happen to her couldn't follow.

"Do you want to do this?" he asked nervously.

"No," she said.

"Okay." Adrian sighed. "I really didn't want to bring you there." He wrapped his arms around her shoulders and kissed her neck. "We'll find another way. That's all."

"I don't want to do it," she said.

"I know. And you don't have to. You'll stay here, where it's safe. I'll go to the lab and look for another way."

"But I *am* going to do it," she continued. "If this is our best chance, then I must. The odds are already against us. We need to go after them with everything we have, or risk all of this being for nothing."

He didn't say anything, but he kept his arms tight around her. She knew he wouldn't argue with the truth of that. They stood still for a moment before she turned and wrapped her arms around his waist. Behind them, the red-wing returned and called out for his mate.

CHAPTER THIRTY-ONE

LATER THAT DAY, SHAKA AND ADRIAN RETURNED TO DULUTH. They decided it would be best if he brought her in from her own apartment, so as not to alert any of his father's people to the coup they were planning from the reservation. She looked out the window as the glow from the setting sun reached eastward around them. Tomorrow at this time, she would be a test subject in a lab—no sunlight, no fresh air, no big lake.

She wanted to call Rena. She hadn't talked to her in days, not since she'd seen her at the bar. But what would she say? She couldn't tell her the truth, and she wasn't a good liar. Her best defense in concealing her secret had always been to avoid those she was in danger of telling. *Rena will have to wait,* she told herself.

When Adrian pulled up in front of her apartment, she saw the white van parked on a side street.

"Is that them?" she asked.

Adrian glanced at the van. "Yes. They won't do anything though. They don't want to break my cover. Listen," he said, turning to her, "I know that what I've asked you to do is huge, but I'm not going to let anything happen to you. I promise you that."

She looked at him across her shoulder. "You're not forcing me to do this. I want to do it this way," she said coolly.

"I know, but still." He looked at her pleadingly, long enough to irritate her.

"Okay. I suppose we'd better keep up appearances," she said and stepped out of his car. He did the same and followed her inside.

Once inside her apartment, she went straight to the fridge and got a beer. Adrian stood with his back against the door and watched her cautiously.

"So, how are we doing this?" she asked.

"I was thinking we could just try to relax for tonight, and maybe tomorrow we could go do something. We could drive out to the Boundary Waters, and you could run through the woods. We could camp out." He smiled at her. "Whatever you want to do. Then we could come back here, and eventually, when you're ready, I'll give you something that will put you to sleep."

"And then I'll wake up in the lab," she concluded.

"Yes."

"I don't want to prolong it; I just want to get it over with," she said harshly.

"Are you sure?" he asked without moving.

She nodded.

"I feel like such an asshole right now, Shaka," he said.

She looked at him, and a flame ignited in her eyes. "Let's get this straight: you're the inside man. You know what our chances are. If you don't think this will work, then we need to go back to the drawing board, but if you do, then let's begin. Now is not the time to grapple with your conscience!"

He watched her for a moment, but said nothing, then opened his black bag and pulled out a white bottle. He opened it and shook out two white pills and set the bottle on the counter.

"When this is over, I hope you won't hate me," he said as he pressed the pills into her hand.

"This isn't about you," she said as she popped the pills into her mouth and chased them down with beer.

Adrian pulled a chair out from the table. "You want to sit down? You'll probably start feeling funny in a few minutes."

"Not yet," she said, taking another drink. "Do you want a beer?"

He shook his head, watching her carefully.

She shrugged and took two long swallows of her beer, emptying the bottle. "Well, I'm going to have another one before the lights go out. Best to have a buzz in this situation."

"Party girl," Adrian said with a shy smile.

She set her empty bottle on the counter and grabbed another from the fridge. She opened it and drank about half of it in the first few gulps. She took a step away from the kitchen counter. Suddenly Adrian was beside her. She hadn't felt like she was staggering or even swaying. She rolled her eyes at him. "I can't even feel anything yet."

"You will," he said.

"You sound creepy when you say that," she said—and though the words were crisp in her mind, they came out slurred.

"Here, why don't you come lie down," he said as he put an arm around her back.

"Oh, wouldn't you love that—" she slurred, then stumbled, stepping on her right foot with her left, and fell forward. Adrian's arm wrapped tightly around her waist and caught her before she hit the floor.

"Easy now," he said. "Nice and slow."

"Oops. I guess they're kicking in. Man, they work fast!" she replied, and again the words in her mind were crisp and clear, but as she spoke them, they came out in a garbled string.

"Whatever you say, darling. Those work fast," he echoed.

She opened her mouth to respond but closed it again. She was feeling so exhausted. She leaned into him. He was warm and soft. When she reached her bed, he gently helped her lie down. The room was spinning, and she felt heavy. She tried to look over at him but found even that took an unimaginable amount of strength. She felt him sit down next to her. He leaned over her, and she looked up at his face.

"It's going to be okay, Shaka. I promise," he said.

His face was hazy and fuzzy; she didn't even hear what he said to her. She was losing track of her thoughts. It felt like she was in a dream. She knew she was with Adrian, and they were planning something together, but what? She felt his hand on her head, and she tried to reach an arm up to him, but her limbs were too heavy. He got up and grabbed a blanket from the couch and draped it over her, as if she had simply fallen asleep. Then he turned his back to her and pulled his phone from his pocket. She heard him talking.

"I need your help. I'm bringing one in... Yes, the girl, she's one of them... Right now. I sedated—... A wolf... I can answer your questions on the drive down, Amanda! ... Third floor." He hung up the phone and ran his hands through his hair, then turned back to Shaka. "No turning back now," he said.

Shaka barely heard him. She couldn't keep her eyes open any longer. The moment she shut them, darkness overtook her.

CHAPTER THIRTY-TWO

IN HER DREAMS, SHE WAS SITTING ON THE OLD BROWN COUCH at her grandfather's house. What little light that filtered through the thick growth of white pines around his small house fell in delicate beams through the picture window. There was noise in the kitchen, and her grandfather walked in with a mug in each hand. He handed her one—the purple one from Michigan. It was warm, and she held it up to her chest, just like she had done when she was a girl. She took a sip and smiled up at him, but he was already walking back to the kitchen. She got up and followed him.

In the kitchen, she found a grizzly sight. Blood pooled on the floor around the body of a man. His throat and belly had been ripped open. She didn't recognize him, but he wore a lab coat. As she stood in the doorway, immobilized in disbelief, her grandfather knelt down before the man and started carving into his abdominal cavity. Shaka stumbled backwards until she fell over and landed on her butt.

She suddenly found herself sitting on an empty beach of Lake Superior. Now it was winter, and soft snowflakes fell silently around her. The lake, frozen for many feet out from the shore, was finally quiet. She rested her head back into the snow and looked up at the millions of tiny white flakes floating down to cover her.

"I thought I'd find you here," she heard Rena's voice exclaim. She looked around until she saw her, but Rena's back was turned to her.

"I'm behind you," Shaka said, but Rena only gave a quick, angry glance over her shoulder. Shaka wondered who else she could be talking to. Then she saw Adrian walking up to Rena. He was healthy again, no bandaged arm or swollen face. His hair was combed, he was freshly shaven, and he wore a wool dress coat that came down to his boots. He was as handsome as he had been the first night they met.

"Did you stop her?" Rena asked him. Shaka noticed how nice she looked too. Her short hair was styled to curve around her chin, exposing a few inches of her soft neck above the black collar of her coat. Like his, the coat reached all the way to the fuzzy tops of her boots.

"Yes. She won't be getting out of that place."

"Who?" Shaka yelled from the snow. Now she was covered in a fine white layer. Rena looked over her shoulder with a glare again. Her lips were bright red; they stuck out against the snow like a candle in the dark. Then she turned back to Adrian.

"Good," Rena said. "I don't want to see her again."

"Don't worry, my dear," he said as he stepped closer to her and put his arms around her waist. "She's gone."

Shaka suddenly realized they were talking about her. She watched in anger as Adrian leaned in and kissed Rena. Her anger grew as she struggled to get up and confront them, but she found the thin layer of snow that covered her held her down. She pushed and twisted, but only managed to dig herself deeper into the snow. Soon she was completely covered, as if trapped by an avalanche. Their voices grew muffled. She heard Rena laugh to the murmur of Adrian's voice, and then she heard nothing. She was gone.

Then she found herself in a dark room. The floor was wet concrete. She stood and took a cautious step forward as a string brushed against her hair. She reached up and pulled it, and a dim bulb illuminated her.

She heard chains in a dark corner; they sounded heavy. Stepping toward the sound, she squinted into the dark. As she got closer, she could make out the outline of a man. He was thin and sat hunched over on the cement floor.

"Hello?" Shaka said.

"Shaka," came a weakened and cracked reply. "Get out of here." But she kept taking measured steps toward the gaunt figure in the corner.

"Winston!" she said when she was close enough to see him. Though his body was wasted down to skin and bones, his eyes remained fierce. "What happened?" she asked. H i s gaze remained hard as he leaned toward her. "GET OUT!" he suddenly screamed in a shrill screech that sent her stumbling backwards. "GET OUT!" he repeated, this time getting to his feet. His sunken abdomen, his wiry arms, his almost skeletal face and his wild eyes sent her scrambling for the stairs. She pushed through the door at the top and slammed it behind her.

Now she stood in a new room that was dark and quiet. The floor was soft and warm, like it was heated from within. She got on her hands and knees and crawled to the center, then she rolled onto her back and looked up. There was a skylight above her, and beyond it was the navy-black night sky dotted with millions of diamond stars. In her dream, she shut her eyes and fell into a deeper sleep.

CHAPTER THIRTY-THREE

SHE HEARD BEEPING, AND A MAN'S VOICE BUT NOT HIS WORDS. Her eyelids lightened as her mind traveled up from the depths of sleep. She cracked them open.

White walls. Suddenly she remembered: Adrian had brought her here. She looked around her room. It was a small space, big enough for only a cot and a latrine. Three walls were concrete, and one was glass. The glass wall looked out at an aisle of white computers. A man and a woman stood behind them. Their lips moved, but she couldn't hear them. Her legs ached, and she wanted to stand, but she was afraid. She didn't know what they had planned for her once they knew she was awake.

From behind the aisle of computers, the man looked up at her, and their eyes locked. He looked at her with indifference, his eyes traveling from her face to her body. His mouth moved as he looked, but she heard only murmuring. Then the woman too was looking at her. After a quick glance, she picked up a phone, spoke into it for only a second, and hung up.

The man grabbed a long wand, just like the one Shaka had seen in the woods, and pointed it at her. He looked at his computer monitor, and a smile came across his face.

A moment later, an old man with Adrian's blue eyes walked into the lab. He too looked at the monitor, and a faint smile touched his lips. He looked up at Shaka with eyes that feigned kindness, and then he said something to the man beside him, who set down his wand and grabbed something else. The two of them approached her cell together. As they neared, she recognized the long black cylinder in the younger man's hand as a cattle prod. She pulled her legs up and pressed herself against the wall.

The old man touched something on the outside of her cell, and the glass wall slid open. He stepped inside, but Shaka kept her eyes on the man with the cattle prod.

"Good morning," he said. "My name is Dr. Davidson. I'm Adrian's father. He told me about your unique ability, and I just had to meet you. I specialize in helping people like you learn about themselves. It may look a little sparse around here, but I promise, we will take excellent care of you." He smiled down at her, and she looked up at him with wide, fearful eyes.

"You've kidnapped me," she said quietly.

"That's not a good way to look at it. A more productive outlook is that you have a gift that could help others, and we're close to learning how to share it. Maybe you will be the one who gives us the first successful transition of a human to a multi-species individual like yourself. Shall we get started, Mitchell?" he said, turning to the man behind him.

As soon as he said it, the man stepped into the tiny cell, cattle prod still in hand. "Get up," he said to her sternly.

She did as she was told.

"Step out of the cell and turn right," he continued.

Again, she did as she was told. She could hear their footsteps behind her. She continued down a hall with concrete floors. Heavy doors opened to the left and the right as she went. She wondered if her grandfather was behind one of them. She wondered where the others were.

"Stop here," Mitchell said, and she halted in front of a door. He set his finger on a keypad beside it, and the door unlocked. Pulling it open, he motioned her inside. It was an open room with multiple showerheads coming out of the walls and a large drain in the center of the floor. It was something between a high school locker room and a gas chamber.

Mitchell typed something into a keypad on the wall, and one of the showerheads turned on. "Go on, strip," he said impatiently.

"No," she said, looking at him defiantly.

Mitchell immediately stepped up to her and pressed the cattle prod against her neck. A sharp shock ran through her body and a scream escaped her. She stumbled away from him.

"No need to be modest," he said. "Just do as you're told." He glared at her with the prod out and ready to shock her again. The doctor watched with a cool, studied look.

"One thing you will find," Dr. Davidson said to her, "is that it's just easier to be agreeable."

She looked at him with fire in her eyes. She thought maybe she could undress and shift, then rip out both their throats. Mitchell raised the cattle prod toward her again, and she quickly started unbuttoning her pants. She undressed hurriedly and stepped under the steaming water. She couldn't look at them, though she could tell from their silence that they were watching her. Rage burned through her. She vowed not to show them weakness, but to remember this moment and show them as much compassion as they had showed her when their time came. When she was done, she stepped out from under the water, and it shut off immediately.

"Now turn around," the doctor said calmly. She faced them, her body dripping, her eyes hard. "Adrian told us that you can change into a wolf. Would you please do that now?" It was more of a command than a question.

Shaka got down on the floor and felt her body tingle and stretch. When she opened her eyes she was looking at her gray paws.

She remembered she'd been captured, and these were evil men who had her trapped. Her lips pulled back into a snarl as they approached her, and her hackles stood up.

"Easy, now," the doctor said softly. "No need for that. I just want to have a look at you." As they neared her, he motioned to Mitchell with his head, and he shocked her again with the prod. She jumped and yelped, then turned toward Mitchell with a snarl. "Better use the sedative," he said to Mitchell, who took a black case out of his pocket, opened it, and removed a syringe with a long needle.

"Calm down, now," he said. "Make it easy on yourself."

His words meant nothing to her. She only knew that a dangerous man was backing her into a corner. He swung the prod toward her again, but this time she saw it coming and lunged at his arm mid-swing. She bit his hand savagely and heard the metal prod drop to the floor. He jerked his hand back, and she let go as she felt something hit her shoulder. An empty syringe stuck out of her skin.

Mitchell backed up, holding his bleeding hand as he watched her snarl in the corner. Her urge to lunge at him and sink her teeth into his neck was tempered only by her fear of being shot; for the first time, she noticed a man with a rifle standing near the door, the barrel of the gun pointed at her. She started pacing along the wall, always keeping one eye on the two men. The gun followed her as she moved. The room smelled strongly of fear, some of it theirs and some her own. The scent sickened her.

A moment later, the door opened, and a woman walked in.

"Kate," the doctor said to her, "take Mitchell back to the infirmary and bandage his hand."

"Oh no!" she said, looking wide-eyed from Shaka to Mitchell. "She got you!"

"Hurry up, now," the doctor said.

"What about her?" She pointed to Shaka.

"We'll leave her. She's had a sedative. It won't be long before she's down."

As they filed out of the room, Shaka kept pacing, her heart full of fear and hate, until she grew woozy and tired. When she started to stumble, she wandered to the far corner of the room, turned in three awkward circles, and lay down.

CHAPTER THIRTY-FOUR

BEFORE SHE OPENED HER EYES, NOW AS A WOMAN, SHE HEARD the steady beeping of a heart monitor. Her awareness grew, and she winced at the fluorescent lighting that seeped through her eyelids and made her head throb. For the second time that day, she found herself waking up into a nightmare.

"Easy, now," she heard a woman's voice say. "You're strapped down to the table."

Shaka tried to lift her hands and found it was true. She opened her eyes and saw leather straps around her wrists and ankles. She realized there was one around her neck too. She rolled her head from side to side, trying to loosen it, but it wouldn't budge.

Shaka looked around the room. There were two doors, one on each end, and each had a little keypad next to it that required a fingerprint. If she could knock the girl out, she could use her fingerprint to get out of there. But then what? There would be another door, and she couldn't just drag the girl's body around with her.

Shaka squeezed her eyes shut to stop her thoughts. She couldn't escape. She could hardly move on top of the table, but more importantly, she was supposed to be here. If she escaped, their plan would be ruined, and her grandfather would never get out. She just hoped that when the time to free the others came, she wouldn't be strapped to a gurney with electrodes attached to her. She swallowed her urge to change and attack the young woman who stood next to her. She felt her muscles relax a little. The beeping on the monitor, which had sped up after she awoke, slowed.

"Little poke here," the woman said as she plunged a needle into the crook of Shaka's arm. She watched as her velvety red blood ran through a tube and collected in a bag. "Just getting a little blood from you, doc's orders."

Shaka stopped watching. Her body was not her own anymore. It infuriated her. She took a deep inhale to the count of four, then let it out to the count of four. Her anger quieted as she focused on a spot on the ceiling and thought of cattails rustling in the breeze.

"Okay, we got it," the woman said. "Someone will be coming to bring you back to your room."

Shaka looked at the woman beside her for the first time. She looked like she was Shaka's age. She had curly brown hair that came to her shoulders and bright blue eyes. The name embroidered on her lab coat said KATE.

"Why do you do this?" Shaka asked her, wondering how someone so young could be part of something so evil.

"It's a long story," she answered kindly, but didn't say more. She seemed to quicken her pace as she labeled the blood, and in less than a minute, she had left the lab, and Shaka was alone with the steady beeping of the monitor. She twisted her wrists and found her right wrist had some give. If she could be left alone for a few more minutes, she could probably free herself, then tranquilize whoever came in next with the sedative that sat at the ready on the tray beside her gurney.

She stopped herself again. Escape was not the answer. She needed to be here. She looked around the room again: white cupboards, a fridge with glass doors that held tiny vials, another that held bags of blood, a cart full of IV tubing and bags of fluid.

The door behind her opened. She heard quiet footfalls approaching.

"I'm going to let you up now, but if you try anything, I *will* shock you." She recognized Adrian's voice immediately, and a tempered relief washed over her. He stepped into her view and stood beside her. As he unfastened the cuff around her left hand, he whispered, "This room has microphones everywhere."

She glared at him, remembering the part she was supposed to be playing. "How?" she said loudly. "How could you do this to me?" She had never known it before, but acting came naturally to her.

Adrian looked at her in shock, which was quickly replaced by nervous irritation. His acting was a little rough, but not bad enough to raise suspicion.

"I'm sorry I've hurt you, but this was always the plan." The words came out of his mouth a little forced.

"You'll get what's coming to you, I promise you that," she said coldly.

"We'll see, lover," he said as her left wrist was freed. He walked around to her right side and whispered, "We can talk tonight. Just don't attack anyone else, or they'll isolate you." She glared up at him as her right wrist came free. He then freed her ankles in silence. When he released her neck, he quickly slipped a wire noose over her head. She sat up and found the wire attached to a long pole, the kind she'd seen dogcatchers use.

"You," he said accusingly, "will be travelling by snare now."

She stood and felt the snare tighten a bit around her neck. The sensation flooded her with anger. How strange it felt to be treated like a stray dog.

"To the door on your right," he commanded, and she walked up to it. He leaned past her and pressed his finger on the screen, and the door opened. "To your right," he said, and she turned. Once they were in the hallway, he whispered a little louder, "I'm sorry."

"It's fine. I understand," she whispered back.

"Just do what you're told. No one is going to be kind to you here. I can't be kind to you either."

"I know," she said.

They passed a door on her right, then the wall turned to glass. Shaka looked into a room of cages that reminded her of a kennel. The cages held all types of animals. She saw foxes, turtles, sheep, parrots, monkeys, and on the end, a black wolf. Someone in a white jumpsuit was feeding them through little doors on the fronts of their cages. She could smell them from the hallway. These were not shifters; they were just animals. She wanted to ask Adrian what they did with them, but as her eyes locked on those of the black wolf, she figured she would find out soon enough.

Past the kennel, the hallway forked. To her right, a blue stripe was painted on the wall and continued all the way down to a blue door at the end.

"Keep straight," Adrian instructed from behind her.

They came to another door, and Adrian pressed his finger

to the pad again. She could smell him, sandalwood and soap, and his scent made her feel less alone. The door opened, and they were back in the lab. He walked slowly behind her, forcing her to move at his pace.

She saw a row of glass cell doors up ahead and knew he was going to walk her past the other captives. Her palms grew sweaty, and she felt her heartbeat quicken. As she neared the first cell, she could smell a familiar scent, like her own, but different; the scents of human and animal intertwined.

She peered into the first cell and found it empty. Beside the small cot was a stack of books, and on top was *The Singing Wilderness* by Sigurd Olson, a favorite of her grandfather. She reached out and touched the glass, feeling like the wind had been knocked out of her. This was where he had been since he'd gone missing—not running free in the wilderness, but reading about it from this cell. "Where is he?" she whispered, but Adrian only gave her a gentle push forward. She didn't know if she even wanted to know the answer anyway. She stepped forward, tears brimming in her eyes.

In the next cell, a woman with long dark hair lay on a cot staring up at the gray ceiling above her. She had Winston's dark skin and soft features.

"Rachel," Shaka said, and the woman looked up at her but didn't speak. Again, Adrian nudged her forward.

In the next cell, she saw a pale young man asleep on his tiny cot. He had dark bags under his eyes, and he hugged himself with long, thin arms. Suddenly his eyes shot open, and he looked at her. She jumped; he had the slatted pupils of a snake. He sat upright, and a forked tongue licked at the air to taste her scent as she walked by. She remembered Winston mentioning a man who could turn into a rattlesnake, but she had never seen anyone who could be both human and animal at the same time.

"How is that possible?" she asked, more to herself than anyone else.

"My father's been developing a drug that can make you both human and animal at once. Looks like it hasn't worn off yet. Keep moving though. Your room is next," Adrian said.

Then she stood before her own tiny concrete cage and waited for the door to open. When it did, she stepped inside and looked at the gray walls. She already felt them pressing in on her. She felt goose bumps rise on her skin when she thought of spending days on end confined to this tiny room, let alone months or years.

Adrian followed her in. He was removing the snare when she heard a familiar voice.

"Shaka?"

She spun around to find herself face-to-face with what

looked like the ghost of her grandfather. The young man she'd seen in the woods hunting for Winston walked beside him. When Arnold stopped, Adrian raised a hand, signaling to the man to give Arnold and Shaka a moment to speak.

Arnold had grown pale and thin since she'd seen him last. His eyes were deep-set and full of emptiness. When he came near, she saw only fear and anxiety on his face. He was not the man she remembered. "How did they find you?" he asked, his voice filled with sorrow.

"Grandpa," she whispered. She tried to take a step toward him, but Adrian slid the snare back around her neck and refused to let her move.

Arnold's eyes shot to Adrian's. "You have to let her go, Adrian," he said. "You have me. You don't need us both. You have to let her go."

Adrian quickly looked away.

"Come on," the young man said to Arnold, "let's go." But Arnold didn't move.

"Grandpa, we're going to get out of here," she said.

He gave her a sad smile.

"Come on," the young man said again, this time pushing Arnold forward, and they both disappeared from Shaka's view. She wrung her hands together and looked down at them as tears streamed down her face.

"Shaka," Adrian whispered sharply, "we'll fix this."

Her eyes shot up to his face, and she searched them cruelly. "You can't fix what's already been done."

"It's not over," he replied as he removed the snare again and stepped out of the cell. She heard a door open and voices entering the lab.

"Trust me," he whispered as the door slid shut between them, and he looked at her through the thick pane of glass.

The curly-haired woman, Kate, appeared before her door with a tray of food.

"Hi, Adrian," she said, looking up at him with a smile.

He didn't respond. He was still watching Shaka.

When her greeting wasn't returned, Kate opened a small trap door near the floor and slid the tray into Shaka's cell. Immediately Shaka thought of the animals in the kennel and realized that here, there was no difference between her and them. She looked at her tray. It held a turkey sandwich, a bag of chips, a cup of peaches and a cookie. It reminded her of grade school. She didn't want to obediently pick it up and eat, but she was hungry. She waited until both Adrian and Kate had left, then brought the tray to her cot and ate.

CHAPTER THIRTY-FIVE

RENA HAD BEEN CALLING SHAKA FOR THREE DAYS AND getting her voice mail. She was starting to worry. She knew Shaka could be bad about keeping her phone charged, but three days was a long time to go with no phone, even for Shaka. As she hung up on Shaka's message one more time, she decided she was going to have to look for her.

The night before, she had asked Salem to ask Adrian where she was, but Salem had laughed off her suggestion and told her to leave the new lovers alone. That could have been it, Shaka could have been hiding out at a resort up the shore with Adrian getting couple's massages and drinking red wine beside a cozy fireplace, but Rena knew that wasn't the case. She couldn't explain it, especially not to Salem; she just knew that something was wrong.

She pulled on her blue pea coat and smoothed her dark

hair. She was going to Shaka's work. If they didn't know where she was, at least they could tell her how long she'd been gone.

The wind was cold and brought tears to her eyes as she walked to her car. She put on her sunglasses, more to save her eyes from the wind than the sun, and walked with her head down. The people she passed did the same. When she reached her car, she found a paper under her wiper blade.

"Not again!" she said as she reached for it. She had accumulated several parking tickets over the last couple years and felt she had already given enough to the city to build a small park. But as she opened the paper to see how much she owed, she found that it wasn't a parking ticket at all; it was a note. She read it where she stood, forgetting about the wind.

Rena,

My name is Winston, and I'm a friend of Shaka's.

She remembered Shaka mentioning a friend named Winston in passing. Rena had been suspicious of him from the start. She didn't understand what Shaka could possibly have to gain from a friendship with this man. She looked back at the letter and read on, scowling.

I apologize for the frankness of this letter, but I'm afraid Shaka may be in trouble. I know you are her friend. I also know you are a friend of Adrian's. I respect that, but this is a delicate matter, and I don't want our conversation getting back to him. I would like to find out as much as I can about him. Shaka's well-being rests in his hands now, and if he has misguided intentions, we will have to do something bold. Please meet me at Shiloh's at 10:00 a.m.

Thank you,

W.

"Shiloh's," she said out loud. She had never heard of it. A quick Google search revealed that it was a hole-in-the-wall coffee shop on the west side of town. She looked at her watch. It was now 9:00 a.m. She still had time to stop by Shaka's work. She stuffed the letter in her pocket and looked around. She wondered who this man was who wanted her to not only trust him, but to keep secrets for him as well. She knew next to nothing about him. She figured he was jealous and wanted to sabotage Shaka's relationship with Adrian, but that didn't explain why Shaka had let him into her life in the first place. She was going to meet him, but she would do so guardedly. Luckily, if it was information about Adrian that he wanted, she knew very little about the man.

She hopped into her car and drove to the restaurant where Shaka worked. She pulled into the lot, where only a handful of cars were parked. It was early yet, and she supposed the breakfast crowd was small on weekdays. This calmed her nerves a little. She had worried that maybe Shaka's coworkers would be too busy to talk to her. She got out of her car and hustled through the howling wind and into the warm stillness of the restaurant. Inside it smelled like fried potatoes and sausage. The grease made her stomach turn, and she decided to make her visit quick to avoid the smell getting into her clothes. She walked up to the bar where two women were laughing and dunking celery sticks into their Bloody Marys.

"Morning," said a big man in a baseball cap as he approached her from the other end of the bar. "Do you want a menu?"

"No, thank you. I wanted to talk to someone about a friend of mine, Shaka Reed."

As soon as she said Shaka's name the man nodded. "Yeah, Shaka. She's left them in a bind back there."

"She hasn't been in? Did she say anything to anyone?" Rena asked as the anxiety she'd been pacifying started to swell.

"I'll see if Jim's back there. If she talked to anyone, it would have been him." The man turned sideways to slide out from behind the bar and slowly walked toward the kitchen.

Rena looked around the dining room, which hadn't been updated since before she was born. She could hear Shaka telling her how she liked to imagine couples coming in with big perms and shoulder pads thirty years before and sitting in the same chairs they were sitting in right now. Rena didn't want to picture that though. She wanted to update the place. In her mind, she was removing the old curtains and replacing them with automatic shades, and she was tearing up the carpet and putting down barn wood flooring, or maybe revealing hundred-year-old wood floors that were already there and just needed to be restored. She was taking out the old vinyl booths and replacing them with dark tables. The room was full of untapped potential, and she supposed it would stay that way.

"You a friend of Shaka's?" a man asked from behind her.

She turned around to face him. He had a graying beard and a small gut. He wore an apron high around his waist. She remembered Shaka talking about her boss, Jim. She knew from her stories that he was a good man, kind and conscientious.

"Yes, I'm Rena. I haven't been able to reach her for the last few days, and I'm trying to figure out where she went. Have you talked to her?"

"Not in the last few days," he said as he rubbed his brow. "Last week, she told me something had happened with her family, and she was going to need some time off. Didn't tell me what. What kind of trouble is she in?"

"I don't know. I'm trying to figure it out though."

"She wasn't herself before that either. She'd just been quiet, like her mind was somewhere else."

"Yes, withdrawn." Rena found the word for him. "She'd been that way with me too."

"You think it's a guy that's messing with her head, or something worse?"

"It could be a guy, but I don't know. I'm trying to piece it together. When did she stop coming in, exactly?"

"Would have been..." He paused and looked up at the ceiling, his mouth silently counting. "...last week Friday."

"Okay. Thanks. That's helpful."

"Hey, when you find her, have her call me. Nothing to do with work, I'm just worried about her," Jim added.

"Of course," Rena said absently and started towards the door. She was unable to look at the heavy expression of worry on his face any longer.

CHAPTER THIRTY-SIX

RENA FOUND SHILOH'S AFTER TAKING TWO WRONG TURNS. IT was easy to miss, having only a small blue sign above the door. Inside she found a lunch counter where four old men sat reading the newspaper, and five tables lined the back wall. Three of them were empty, a young couple occupied one, and at the other sat a tall Native American man who watched her with his hands wrapped around a steaming cup of coffee. She walked directly to his table without ordering and sat down.

"Winston?"

"Yes," he answered.

She waited for him to start talking. After all, he had summoned her here. But he seemed to be in no hurry. He took a careful sip of his coffee.

"Coffee's good here. You should get a cup."

"I'm fine. What is it you'd like to talk about?"

"I think we're pretty anonymous here, but still, if you order something, we won't arouse suspicion," he said.

Already she could tell that she wasn't going to like him. She always had a hard time listening to men who felt entitled to tell her what to do. Still, she got up from the table and went to the counter.

"Thank you. So, how long have you known her?" he asked as she sat back down.

"Since grade school. You?" she returned accusingly.

"Not long," he said with a sort of submissive smile. "But we have some things in common."

"Such as?"

"Did you ever feel like she was keeping a big secret from you?" he asked.

Rena felt her annoyance with this man come to a boil. Who was he to question her and Shaka's relationship? Shaka had only known this guy a few weeks, while she and Shaka went back decades. But it wasn't just that. She knew that Shaka did have a secret—one that she had never trusted her with. Rena didn't know the specifics, but she knew it made Shaka different; she knew it was why she was a loner. She also knew that her own tendency not to push or pry was the reason she and Shaka had been able to remain friends for so long. And now this man she barely knew was insinuating that she had shared her secret with *him*. What made him so trustworthy? Who the hell was he?

"I don't know. Maybe." she said coolly.

"Do you know where Shaka is right now?"

"Why? Do you?"

"Yes, and it isn't good. I don't know how much you know about Adrian, but his father runs a medical testing facility where he tests on human subjects. Shaka has volunteered herself as a test subject in hopes of freeing the others." He looked at Rena for a reaction. Her eyes remained hard, but a tiny smile appeared at the corners of her mouth. He continued anyway. "The problem is that her plan depends on Adrian. If he doesn't orchestrate everything to make the escape possible, she will be stuck in there for a long time—her and all the others."

"That's quite a predicament," Rena offered.

"That's why I wanted to meet you. Your partner has known Adrian for years. I was hoping you could tell me about him."

"I hate to disappoint you, but though my *partner* has known Adrian a long time, he has never known him well. I'd never even heard of Adrian until a couple weeks before he and Shaka met. You probably know him better than me, on account of your investigation." Her smile grew a little as she taunted him.

Winston sighed, then started again. "I know how this sounds. But please, just listen. I think we need a back-up plan," he began. "Adrian has implied that the government is paying for his father's research so it will do no good to go to the police. But if we involve the media, they will be forced to investigate." He paused and seemed to wait for a response. When he got none, he continued, "Would you be willing to call the news stations, both local and in Minneapolis, and tip them off when it's time?"

"Okay, that's about all I can take," she said. "I admit Shaka has been distant lately, and I also admit that I have no idea where she is right now—but a human testing lab? Are you trying to say Adrian's father is some kind of Dr. Frankenstein? And why would he want to test on her anyway? What makes her so special?" She looked at him accusingly, and he quickly grew uncomfortable and averted his eyes.

"It all revolves around her ability. I know she doesn't like to share it, so I'm not surprised that you don't know about it. If I told you what it is, you'd think I'm crazy."

"I'll take that chance," she said sharply.

Winston slowly stirred his coffee with a spoon but didn't speak.

"So...?"

He looked up at her and smiled politely. "She can turn into a wolf."

For the first time, Rena reacted to his words without constraint: she threw her head back and laughed, the sound shaking the quiet air of the café. "You must be off your meds," she said to him. "Thank you for wasting my morning though." She took one last sip of her coffee. "Horrible coffee," she muttered as she stood and turned toward the door without giving Winston another look.

CHAPTER THIRTY-SEVEN

RENA WALKED QUICKLY TO HER CAR, FEELING FOOLISH FOR having sat through that entire conversation. She couldn't help but wonder what Shaka had been doing with that man. As far as she could tell, he was delusional, maybe even schizophrenic. At least now she knew that she was on her own.

She started her car and let it idle as she tried to think of where else Shaka might have left a clue. Opening her glove box, she dug through the fast food napkins and oil change receipts until she found it: an extra key to Shaka's apartment. She put her car in drive and turned toward Shaka's neighborhood.

She never understood why Shaka didn't move out. Her building was old and neglected. Most of her neighbors looked strung out, or at the very least, down on their luck. Rena pulled up in front of the old brick building. The once grand staircase in front of it was crumbled and gaping with holes. A young mother, wearing pants so tight that Rena knew what style of underwear she had on, yelled at her son as she unlocked the front door. Rena looked away, disgust all over her face.

When the woman had gone into the building, Rena waited another five minutes before she got out of her car and walked up the stairs. She slid Shaka's extra key into the keyhole of the front door. The old lock clicked, and she pushed the heavy door open. Inside, the ceilings were high, and a chandelier hung above the entryway. She could tell it had once been an impressive room, but now the floor was covered in stained brown carpet, and half the bulbs in the chandelier were burned out. Rena ascended the stairs quickly and quietly and walked directly to Shaka's door. She put the key in the lock, but the door opened as soon as she pushed on it.

She stepped inside and flicked on the light switch. Shaka's bed was unmade, and there were beer bottles on the table, which wasn't out of the ordinary; she wasn't the tidiest person. Rena opened the fridge. There were three bottles of beer left and a carton of milk. Rena looked at the expiration date on the milk. It had expired ten days ago. That told her something was definitely wrong. Shaka might have needed to go grocery shopping and clean her house, but she wouldn't leave rotten food in her fridge. She remembered her friend being disgusted with her just a month before for eating yogurt that was one day past its due date. She knew this carton of milk meant Shaka had not been home in over ten days. She felt her pulse quicken as the gravity of the situation sank in.

She shut the fridge and looked around the kitchen, and then she saw it sitting on the counter: a bottle of Rohypnol. She almost jumped forward to grab it. She looked inside; it was nearly full. She screwed the lid on and put it in her purse. Immediately she began questioning whether kind, handsome Adrian was capable of drugging and kidnapping a woman. She couldn't imagine it. The pieces didn't seem to fit, but she had the proof in her purse. Even if it hadn't been him, it had been someone.

She went to Shaka's bed and lifted the blankets. As she shook them, she grew dizzy, and there was a wind in her ears. Around her, the air moved, the beer bottles rattled, a few papers blew off Shaka's table, and the blankets she held in her hands rippled. She closed her eyes, knowing she needed to remain calm, open.

She suddenly felt as though Shaka were standing behind her. Rena turned and saw her standing at the table, though she knew she was just an apparition. Shaka tossed two pills in her mouth and chased them with a beer. Her gaze was aggressive and directed behind Rena.

Rena turned around and saw Adrian sitting on the bed,

his eyes heavy with sorrow. Shaka was angry, but she quickly grew wobbly from the drugs. Adrian steadied her, walking her to the bed, and laid her down. Moments later, she was sound asleep, and Adrian tucked her into the blanket and kissed her forehead. He stood up, then seemed to steel himself as he pulled out his phone and made a call. When he hung up, he kept his back to Shaka, his expression hard.

A minute later, the door opened, and a man and a woman came in. They quickly loaded Shaka onto a stretcher. Adrian kept his back to them until they were out of the apartment, then a moment later, he followed.

Rena ran to the door and looked into the hallway, still clutching the blanket, but the hallway was empty; the vision was over.

She stepped back into the apartment and shut the door. Dropping the blanket, she ran to the bathroom to splash water on her face. When the visions came on their own, sometimes they were so strong that she felt dizzy. She took a gray hand towel off the rack behind her and dried her face.

As she rubbed the rough fabric that smelled like Shaka against her skin, she felt the space around her shift again. She looked at herself in the mirror, but saw Shaka's face. She could feel Shaka's feelings: fear and sadness and excitement all at once. She had to do something she didn't want to. She saw flashes of fluorescent lighting and sterile white walls. Closing her eyes, Rena allowed herself to see what Shaka saw...

She was in a cell. A man in a lab coat walked; it was Adrian, with his hair slicked back. As he passed Shaka's cell, he gave her a sympathetic smile and kept walking.

A man followed him with black hair and cruel eyes. "Bring the wolf girl down to room B in ten minutes," he yelled to Adrian, who turned and nodded to him. She felt the anxiety stir in the pit of Shaka's stomach. Shaka wondered what they would do to her this time. She wondered how much Adrian could protect her, if at all. She wanted this to be over with. How long would she have to stay here before they could make their move? Then her heart filled with quiet sadness for her grandfather and how he'd been caged with no hope of escape for longer than she could imagine. She vowed she would make them pay in the end.

The air in the small bathroom seemed to ripple around Rena. She dropped the towel and clutched the edges of the sink. Two visions were all she could handle in one day. When the room stopped spinning, she took a deep breath and stood up straight. Her hair was a mess, and she fixed it with her hands, afraid to touch Shaka's brush for fear of another vision. Then she left the apartment, this time making sure the door was locked behind her.

She walked quickly back to her car, got in, and drove straight to Salem's office. She marched right past reception and opened his door without asking. He was alone, working in front of his computer.

"Darling," he said. "What a surprise!"

"Yes, hello, Plumpy," she answered. It was one of her terms of endearment for him, though he gave her a disapproving look as he got up to close his office door.

"Please don't give them any ammunition," he said when the door was closed.

"I'm sorry. I just need to know about Adrian."

"What for?" he asked, giving her a bewildered look. "What does he have to do with anything?"

"I think Shaka is in trouble. She's missing—and I think Adrian might have something to do with it."

"Really? Adrian?" He looked at her skeptically. "And where did you get this idea?"

"She's missing, like I said. Have you talked to Adrian?"

"I talked to him last week. He said Shaka was giving him the cold shoulder."

"Well, I found this in her apartment." Rena pulled the bottle of Rohypnol out of her purse.

"I'm not a pharmacist, my dear."

"It's the date rape drug. They're roofies!"

"Hmm. Maybe you should call the police. Shaka is a sharp girl though. I don't think she'd let anything like that happen to her."

Rena threw her hands up, exasperated. "Bad things happen to sharp women too!"

"All right," he said. "Then I think you should go to the police. I don't think Adrian is involved though. He's not a predator."

"Maybe not when you knew him before."

"Do you want me to call him?"

"No," she said as she quickly thought through her options. "But could you give me his number, and his address, if you have it? Can you just give me everything you have on him?"

Salem reached for his phone and scrolled through his contacts. A few seconds later, she got a text with Adrian's phone number and two addresses: one in Duluth and one in Minneapolis.

"Thank you, Plumpy," she said as she leaned over his desk and kissed him.

"You're welcome. But if you think something has happened to her, call the cops. I don't want you getting mixed up in anything."

"I will. You don't have to worry about me, Plumps." She smiled at him and walked out of his office. She didn't like lying to him, but she wasn't going to call the police—not right away.

She knew as soon as she did that she would be sidelined. She had to find out everything she could on her own first.

As soon as she got in her car, she dialed Adrian's number. Being in Shaka's apartment had filled her with a sense of urgency.

"Hello?"

She recognized his voice. "Hello, Adrian. This is Rena."

"Hey, Rena. How are you?"

"Oh, you know. Just trying to figure out where my friend is."

"Shaka? I haven't seen her in about a week now. I don't know if she told you or not, but she broke it off with me. I must not have been her type."

"Well, I can see that. She tends to prefer men who don't drug and kidnap women."

There was a pause on his end of the line. "What are you talking about, Rena?"

"I think you know."

"Well, I don't know, so maybe you could fill me in."

"Shaka is missing. She's been gone for more than ten days. Someone gave her Rohypnol and took her somewhere. You say she dumped you a week ago? Well, she was already missing a week ago, so I'm looking at you—and so is her crazy-ass friend Winston, and so will the police when I call them, which I'm planning to do as soon as I hang up with you."

"Hold on. What did Winston tell you?"

"Winston is nuts. He thinks she can turn into a wolf. But the not-so-crazy part is he thinks you're a threat to her."

"He should know I'm not. Look, Rena, you're onto something, but you have no idea what. Don't call the police, at least not yet. It would ruin everything Shaka's trying to do. Just believe me when I say she's safe."

"Why should I?"

"Because I'm telling the truth. Just hold on, and I'll prove it to you."

The line was quiet for several minutes, then she heard Shaka's voice.

"Rena?"

"Shaka! Are you okay? What happened? Do you need help?"

"I'm okay. I can't explain it right now, but just trust me. Winston can fill you in."

"He's wacko. He thinks you can turn into a wolf."

"I can't talk now, but just trust him."

"But where are you? Do you need me to get you out?"

"Rena" Adrian had picked up again. "Find Winston. This will be over soon, and Shaka can explain it all to you then."

"When though?" she asked, but he had already hung up.

She stared at her phone. She felt she was out of moves already. Shaka didn't want her to interfere; calling the police would derail whatever it was they were trying to do. She knew just enough to leave her completely confused. She did have one option left though.

She apprehensively started her car and pulled back onto the street. She could go back to the west end of town and look for Winston. She felt his crazy ramblings were all she had to go on.

She pulled up to the café first and stepped inside. He was still there, sitting at the same table, drinking coffee and writing in a notebook. He looked up at her as she approached him cautiously. Admitting she had passed judgment too soon was not easy for her, she hoped they could skip over that part.

"That was quick," he said.

"I work fast," she replied as she pulled out the chair across from him.

CHAPTER THIRTY-EIGHT

RENA TRIED TO KEEP HER FACE NEUTRAL AS SHE LISTENED to his stories of shape-shifting wolves and birds and secret human testing facilities, though it wasn't easy. By the end of his explanation, she found it too difficult to try to distinguish truth from fiction. The part she believed was that Shaka was being held somewhere against her will, and Winston knew where. To her, that was the only part that mattered. She couldn't figure why Shaka would volunteer herself to the role of test subject. Maybe the part about her grandfather being there was true as well. That would explain his absence, and Shaka had always been willing to do anything for him.

She watched Winston suspiciously as he sipped coffee. Funny, she thought, he seemed sane enough. His expression was calm and controlled; his eyes were steady, even patient. His black hair was peppered with strands of gray, and only a thin scar below his right eye marked his caramel complexion. He was a handsome man, if she forgot everything he had just said to her. Experience had taught her that handsome men could rarely be relied upon.

"I know you don't believe me," he said, as if reading her mind.

"Would you believe you?" she asked coolly.

"No," he answered. "But if you believe that Shaka is being held captive, none of the rest should matter."

"That's true. But you're able to prove you're telling the truth." She leaned forward and whispered quietly so no one could hear her, "Why don't you just change into a bird for me? Then I won't say another word." A smile started at the corners of her mouth again. She always liked to see people squirm.

"I can't. They're probably watching."

"Oh," she said, leaning back into her chair again. "Of course."

"You can mock me if you like. I don't even blame you for it; in truth, it's what I expected from you. But even if half of it sounds like a joke to you, you came back because you believe the other half, and I need you to help me help her."

"You expected me to mock you? You already know me so well!" she said.

"I wouldn't say that, but I can see you've got a hard shell and like to push people away with games and sarcasm. I bet there aren't many people in your circle, and of them, how many have really seen you? Shaka is one of the few, and no one can take her place. She needs you now. You can't turn your back on her just because you don't like me."

Rena was stunned at his unexpected frankness. For a second, her mind reached for an argument. But what was the point? He was right.

"So, will you help her? Even if you don't believe everything I've told you?"

"Yes," she replied, for the first time seeing him as someone capable. "If we're going to break Shaka out, I have a question. I know you can't call the police, but how about enforcement from the other side? A biker gang, or something like that?" she said, getting the edge back in her voice.

"It's not muscle that we need. It doesn't matter who is on the outside of the building if they can't get in. What we need is to infiltrate. Right now, everything rests on Adrian, and I'm not comfortable with that."

They sat quietly for a moment, thinking. The waitress came by and topped off their cups. Winston smiled warmly at her while Rena looked out the window, deep in thought.

"How long would it take to get hired at the lab?"

"They know who you are. They wouldn't hire you."

"Not me, obviously. Someone they don't know."

"I don't know, but I suspect there's a lengthy vetting process. After all, what they're doing is kidnapping and torturing people."

"So, it would have to be someone they already know."

"I suppose. But if there was someone else who could help, Adrian would have thought to involve them."

"Don't bet on it. Didn't you say you know of another family of shape-shifters?" she asked, though saying the sentence out loud made her feel ridiculous.

"Yes. But they won't help us; they work for them. They're more likely to turn us in."

"Are you sure? Everyone has a soft spot. If we appeal to theirs, maybe they'll work with us."

"I don't think so. It's not a risk I want to take."

Rena looked at him squarely. She hoped he wasn't a coward. However they chose to free Shaka, it would involve risk. She looked at his hand on the table, his neatly trimmed nails and soft skin. She wondered what he did for a living.

"But if they agreed to help us, we'd have them working from the inside too. Isn't that a risk worth taking?"

"No. Because they will never help us."

"Couldn't we just talk to them?"

As she waited for his reply, it came to her: Adrian would know what kind of a deal his father had struck with this family. If she knew that, she would know how to talk to them.

"You don't even know their family name. And you could be risking everything by going to them."

"Do you have another idea?"

He looked at her as he tapped the side of his coffee cup. She watched him for a minute, waiting for a response, but got only the *tap, tap* of his nail against the cup.

She stood up and tied her jacket snuggly around her waist. "Call me if you ever figure it out," she said as she went for the blue door.

CHAPTER THIRTY-NINE

SHAKA WOKE UP IN THE GYMNASIUM. AGAIN, SHE WAS CHILLED by the sterility of the room: white walls, concrete floors, fluorescent lights, and nothing else. The room was big enough for her to hear the echo of a conversation between Dr. Davidson and Mitchell. They stood by two glass doors on the far end of the room, casually talking about a football game. She was lying in the middle of the floor in a hospital gown. Her grandfather was lying next to her, watching her with sad, sympathetic eyes.

"Hello, Shaka," he whispered to her.

"Grandpa, are you okay?" she asked.

"Yes."

"I've missed you so much," she said in a choked whisper.

"Me too, sweetheart," he replied.

"We won't be here for long. We're shutting this place down, Adrian and I. We have a plan."

He gave her a sad smile. "Honey, I'd be very surprised if Adrian turned on his own father."

"He will. He hates this place. He thinks what they do here is horrible. Him being here, it's all an act to gain his father's trust." She glanced toward the door. The doctor and Mitchell spoke theatrically about the outcome of the game, unaware that Shaka and Arnold were awake. "Just a few more days, and he's going to free us."

"I hope you're right, Shaka," he said, then hesitantly added, "but I have seen him do some horrible things too."

"You have?" Shaka asked, feeling a little stunned. "I thought he didn't have anything to do with this place until recently. He told me it disgusted him, and that he and his father never got along because of it."

"He's been here long enough for me to know that he is his father's son."

Shaka fell speechless as a tornado of thoughts whirled in her mind. Had it all been a trick she'd played into? Had Winston been right about him? She had no proof that what they had planned together was actually what he intended to do. What if it had all been a ruse to get her behind these walls?

"No," she said, more to herself than to her grandfather. "He'll do the right thing. He has to."

"Shaka, as much as I've missed you, I was hoping I wouldn't see you again."

"We'll be free again, together."

"You always were a warrior," he said to her kindly.

She looked into his eyes, then quickly looked away. So many feelings were dancing inside of her, and she was afraid they would show. One thing she knew for sure was that to survive inside these walls, she needed to remain hard. "What are we doing in here, anyway?" she asked.

"They'll want us to change, I'm sure. He likes to watch how we interact. Change on your own though. They have a drug that will force your body to shift, but it takes hours to wear off and will leave you exhausted for days afterwards."

She nodded. "Does he hurt you?"

"Not really. He takes a lot of blood, and he tests a lot of drugs on me, but he doesn't abuse me. Sometimes he'll show us old movies or bring us dinner from a steakhouse. He tries to make our lives bearable."

"It doesn't sound very bearable," she said. Her grandfather had been a wise and lively man when she'd seen him last; now he was reduced to a test subject. She wondered where his anger was.

"So, what have you been doing with your life?" he asked.

"Not much!" she said. "I shift a lot. I wish I could do it all the time. I thought that's where you went; I thought you shifted and decided not to come back—and I didn't blame you for it. I even envied you sometimes. Life just makes more sense out there. It's honest. Something this horrible would never happen out there."

"But life can be horrible out there too, honey," he said. "Starvation, hunters, predators.... Life can be harsh and indifferent in the wild. Cruelty and compassion exist in all worlds."

She had missed her grandfather's simple clarity. "I saw a red-winged blackbird last week. I made a video of him for you. I wish I could show you, but they took my phone."

"You remember the red-wings. What was he doing?

"He was perched on a cattail, calling for his mate."

"Then it must be springtime." He looked away from her, and she knew he was picturing the forest coming to life. She didn't interrupt him.

She noticed the room had gone quiet and glanced at the door. The doctor and Mitchell were both watching them. A chill ran down her spine. She feared what they had planned for them.

A moment later, the doors opened, and Adrian walked in. He was pushing a cage that held a large black wolf. Its scent reached her almost instantly, and she knew that it was an animal, not a shape-shifter. It cowered and snarled in its cage, angry and afraid. So, this was what they planned: she and her grandfather would be interacting with this wild, fearful creature.

The doctor said something to Adrian, and he nodded, then pulled two syringes from his pocket and started toward Shaka and her grandfather.

"Remember, Shaka," her grandfather said, "change on your own. Don't let them inject you if you can help it." She watched as he rolled to his side and the outline of his body contorted, and a moment later he stood up on four legs, an old, gray wolf. His face was white and his coat patchy, his spine stuck out like a ridge down his back, but his eyes were still keen, and now they looked at the wolf in the cage.

Shaka rolled on her side too, readying herself to change, when she felt Adrian's hand on her shoulder, and suddenly a needle poked into her arm.

"I appreciate your cooperation, Shaka, but we have to do it this way right now." Halfway through his sentence, she lost track of his words and felt her body changing without her effort. Her eyes were still on him as she became a wolf. She now knew only that he was the enemy, but not why. She snarled at him, hackles raised.

Her grandfather brushed his body against hers to break the tension and distract her. She turned and licked his chin.

It didn't matter how much time had passed; she knew he was her family.

Adrian retreated to the doors and opened the cage, letting the black wolf out. The three men then stepped behind the glass doors and watched the black wolf approach the two grays. He made a wide circle around them first, sniffing the air and quietly snarling at them. Shaka danced beside Arnold, who stood still watching the black wolf. He was smaller than Shaka, and younger. He appeared less and less fearful as he sized them up, and his circles tightened around them.

Shaka stepped out cautiously with her head lowered to show him she didn't want to fight. He approached her, and she licked his chin. His body loosened, and for a moment, it appeared he would join their small pack. But what happened next was so quick and unexpected that Shaka remembered only blood and pain. The black wolf launched himself at Arnold, teeth bared in a full snarl. Despite his age, Arnold was still quick and dodged the first attack. But when the black wolf came at him again, Arnold was not so lucky. The wolf caught the side of Arnold's neck with his teeth, and blood spilled from the wound, spraying as the two wolves spun.

Shaka attacked the black wolf from the side, and he let go of Arnold and turned on her, snagging her shoulder with his teeth, leaving a wide gash. She didn't even feel it, though her gray leg was quickly stained red. Arnold bit the black wolf's shoulder, and as he turned to snap at him, Shaka sank her teeth into his neck and tore. Weakness overtook him almost instantly, and he sank to the floor as a pool of blood grew beneath his neck. He whined softly, struggling to rise twice. Then he was still.

Shaka and Arnold stood quietly next to his body. Shaka turned to Arnold and licked his face, then the wound on his neck. He stepped away from her and shifted back into a man. She watched him as he yelled at the men behind the glass, the enemies. She growled at them as she paced beside her grandfather.

They opened the door and entered the gymnasium. One was pointing at her and saying something. Her grandfather yelled at them again and stepped in front of her. As they approached, he grew quiet and turned to her. He spoke to her soothingly until she stopped snarling. The men were right beside them. Shaka wanted to attack, but there were too many.

Another low growl sounded in her throat, and then a dart hit her. She yelped and jumped, then turned and snapped at the dart that hung from her shoulder. She couldn't reach it and spun in circles trying. She heard the bad men laughing, and her grandfather started yelling at them again. She turned back to the men and jumped at the closest one. Her teeth caught his pant leg, and he stumbled backwards. It was Dr. Davidson, whose laughter had ceased. She trotted up to where he'd fallen with teeth bared—but she was growing dizzy. She tripped over her own feet, and once down, she couldn't manage to stand up; she kept losing her balance and tipping over. Finally, even the attempt to stand was too much. Her body grew heavy, and darkness fell over the room like a curtain.

CHAPTER FORTY

RENA HAD BEEN WATCHING ADRIAN'S TWIN CITIES APARTMENT complex all afternoon. It was almost 6:00 p.m. when she finally saw his car pull into the parking garage. She waited another ten minutes, then followed a woman carrying groceries to the door. Rena timed her approached carefully, pulling the door open as soon as the woman unlocked it.

"Let me help you," Rena said, offering her a warm smile.

"Thank you," the woman replied and stepped through the door without giving Rena a second look.

Rena slipped inside and found the staircase. She took it to the second floor and walked quickly down the hall until she found unit 214. She took a deep breath, then knocked on the door.

"Who is it?" she heard Adrian's muffled voice ask from inside.

She didn't answer. A few minutes later, she heard footsteps nearing the door, then a pause. She was sure he was looking at her through the peephole. A moment later, the door opened.

"Rena," he said.

"Adrian," she answered. "Your breath tells me you've got whiskey in here. That's good." She pushed past him and made her way to his dining room, where she pulled out a chair and sat down. He shut the door and walked over to her.

"What can I do for you?" he asked.

"A glass of whiskey, neat, for starters."

"It's bourbon," he said, and she shrugged nonchalantly. He went back to the mini bar and poured her a glass, then sat down across from her and eyed her suspiciously.

"So, what is it that you want?"

"You know what I want."

"I've had kind of a long day, Rena, so I need you to be specific."

"I bet your day wasn't as bad as Shaka's," she responded sharply. He didn't reply, he just swirled the bourbon in his glass. She watched him for a moment before saying, "Trade me glasses, mine's chipped." He rolled his eyes with a quiet sigh and slid his glass across the table to her. She carefully wrapped her fingers around it, locking in the energy he'd just put there before it floated away.

Adrian sat up straight in his chair as a breeze blew through his apartment. A pile of bills blew off his kitchen counter, and the bottle of bourbon rattled in place on the mini bar.

"What the hell was that?" he asked, but she didn't reply. She was staring straight past him with a vacancy in her eyes. In her mind, she saw him inject Shaka with some kind of drug, then, right before her eyes, Shaka turned into a wolf.

"Holy shit," she mumbled from within her trance. She felt Adrian's fear and shame as he retreated and stood behind a set of glass doors with two other men as a black wolf was released from a cage. The other men made calm observations as they watched the behavior of the three wolves. Adrian couldn't speak. He feared for Shaka's safety; his hands shook. He stuffed them in the pockets of his lab coat.

Suddenly, the wolves were all fighting, and within seconds, Shaka had ripped open the black wolf's throat. Adrian was frozen with fear, both of Shaka and for Shaka. A hand slapped him on the shoulder, and someone said, "Your girl's a real killer!" Then he followed them back through the glass doors, and one of the gray wolves stretched and contorted grotesquely on the ground... and an old man stood up.

"Arnold," Rena mumbled in disbelief. He was yelling at Adrian and the others, asking how they could do this to them. They could have been killed! Blood ran down his neck as he yelled. Guilt swelled in Adrian as he watched a dart shot by a black-haired man pierce Shaka's skin. She felt Adrian work to act indifferent as Shaka lunged, stumbled, and went down.

"Rena, Rena!" She heard her name being yelled over and over again. The wind blew through his apartment again. "Rena!" he yelled as she came back to his dining room. The walls spun into place.

"What happened?" he asked.

"It's my party trick," she said as she gripped the table to steady her mind. "It gave me a look at your day," she continued. "You're literally throwing her to the wolves, aren't you? It must be nice to be protected by Daddy, while Shaka fights for her life."

"Are you psychic?" he asked, stunned.

"I'm not here to talk about me. I know what Shaka is now, and I know what you two are planning, but there's one thing I don't know: which side you're really on." She stared at him squarely as he nervously took another drink.

"I'm doing this for Shaka. We're going to free the captives. Couldn't you see that when you were looking into my memories?" he asked.

"I believe you started out with those intentions. I believe you don't like what your father does to humans or animals, but I can feel your reservations. I can feel your fear. It would be easier for you to just be a good boy and do what Daddy asks. I know you're tempted."

"That's not it. I just don't know how I'm going to do it. Security is so tight in that building, and they're instructed to kill, not wound, anyone who is breaking in or out. I'm never alone there. Even if I'm the only one in the main lab, someone is always watching everything in the camera room."

"Adrian, I don't blame you for not being smart enough to find a way around these things. That's God's fault. But I do blame you for bringing Shaka into this under the pretense that you have the intelligence and the nerve to carry it out."

"Well, what's your brilliant idea, Rena, if you're so smart?"

"Do the people in there trust you?"

"Yes, as much as they trust anybody... which isn't a whole lot."

"And does security trust you?"

"I guess so. I don't talk to them much, but they do work for my dad."

"You need to get chummy with them. They need to trust you—not enough to invite you to their weddings, but enough to accept food from you without being suspicious. One day, you're going to drug them."

"And where am I going to get the drugs? And don't say the lab; that will never happen."

"Not to worry, Adrian. I found your leftovers in Shaka's apartment this morning." She reached into her purse and pulled out the bottle of Rohypnol. "There should be enough in here to put everybody down for a short nap."

"I forgot about those," he said with a grimace. "And when they wake up? Then what? The captives will be long gone, but what's to stop my father from coming after them? We can't call the police. The federal government is buying my father's research. They won't bite the hand that feeds them."

"They probably don't want people to know that their tax dollars are funding involuntary human experiments either. They will have to act if they're in the spotlight. We'll alert the media to what's going on after the escape and see if they still have the police stand idly by."

"Are *you* going to tip off the media?" he asked.

"Yes. And I will be working on a backup plan too, because to be honest, I don't know if I trust you with even this two-step plan."

Adrian scoffed at her insult but didn't reply.

"I need you to tell me about the Fisher family," she continued.

"Why? They're not going to help you. They work for my father."

"That doesn't make sense to me. Why would a family of shifters work for a man whose sole purpose is to destroy the lives of shifters?"

"They have an arrangement. They search for other shifters and alert my father; in return, he doesn't touch them."

"How incredibly spineless of them. Not to mention, you'd think a whole family of shifters would be worth more to him than an occasional tip. Do they have something on him?"

"I don't know, but one of the Fisher children is of particular interest to him. Years ago, one of the kids shifted into a mountain lion and killed his sister. After that, the Fishers came to my father looking for something that would stop them from shifting. He gave them a drug in exchange for the chance to do some tests on the girl's body. He was able to recreate an embryo with almost identical DNA. The Fishers raised her from a baby. They bring her in every few weeks for him to monitor her growth. She's probably seven or eight years old by now. In fact, I'm pretty sure Shaka and I saw her in the woods. I didn't realize it then, but it had to be her. She looks like a girl, but watches you like an animal. There's something about her that just chills you. That's about all I know. I don't even know if she can shift."

"I'll work on that. You work on making friends at work."

"Rena, they're not going to work with you, and they're dangerous. They shift into cougars, for God's sake! If you get hurt out there, no one will come looking for you, and they're very aware of that."

"Noted. But have some faith in me, Adrian. I have skills of my own."

CHAPTER FORTY-ONE

RENA LEFT ADRIAN'S APARTMENT WONDERING WHAT SHAKA saw in him. One thing they had never shared was their taste in men. Adrian was handsome, and he had a way of looking at you that made you feel like he was an old friend. Rena thought it must have been an expression he'd been working on. Though he was handsome, she did not find him interesting, and she liked a man who could keep her attention. She also didn't trust that he had the ability to overthrow his father's lab, even if he intended to do so.

She rushed home wishing she could tell Salem about her day, but the less he knew, the better. It was hard enough for her to believe it all. Salem would laugh her out of the room if she told him Shaka could turn into a wolf—or worse, he might believe it and forbid her from going. She would have to keep Shaka's secret, a task she could have been performing since childhood if Shaka had trusted her with it.

She found Salem watching crime dramas on the couch, the empty wrapper from a store-bought sub in front of him.

"Hi, Plumpy," she greeted him.

"Hi, Weasel," he answered. He had called her Weasel once when she'd found and opened her birthday present early, and to her annoyance, the name stuck. She imagined he wouldn't refer to her as a rodent if she quit calling him Plumpy, but it was her term of endearment for him now, and she couldn't imagine changing it.

"How was your day?" she asked.

"Wonderful. Did you find Shaka?"

"Yes. She figured out where her grandfather is and ran off to find him." Rena knew the closer to the truth she kept her story, the easier it would be to believe. "She texted Adrian before she left."

"She should have texted you too."

"Maybe she did and I didn't get it. My phone sucks."

"See, Nancy Drew? Everything was fine," he said.

She threw off her jacket and jumped on the couch beside him. "Yes," she repeated. "Everything is fine."

The next morning, Rena woke up to her phone ringing. She squinted at the screen to see it was an unknown number. Normally, she would have assumed it was a sales call and declined it, but instead she answered. She glanced over her shoulder to find Salem's half of the bed empty. It was almost 9:00 a.m. He'd been at work for over an hour already.

"Hello," she said in a defensive voice.

"Hello. Coffee? Same place?" It was a man's voice, only vaguely familiar, but by the invitation to coffee she knew it had to be Winston.

"Okay. One hour," she said, and heard a click on the other end of the line. Winston wasn't a man to waste words, and she liked that about him.

An hour later, she saw him standing in front of the café they'd met in before. He had a to-go cup in each hand.

"I got it to go. Bea Fisher will be waiting for us."

"You already talked to her?" Rena asked, a little stunned.

"No, but my cousin sent her a message that we'd be coming." He handed her the warm cup of coffee and turned toward his old Buick.

Rena glanced back at her car and considered offering to drive; she would have been more comfortable in her Audi. But when she turned back to suggest it, Winston was already starting the Buick. She sighed and walked over to the passenger's side door and got in.

"What are we going to say to her?" Rena asked him when they were well on their way.

"That's your territory," he answered.

"I could have used a couple hours to figure it out," she muttered.

"We can stop at my cousin's house for a few minutes if you need to think it through, but we don't have long. Like I said, she's waiting for us. I don't know if you noticed, but time is not on our side."

"We can just go straight there. I'll wing it," she said, and the car returned to silence.

The roads got smaller and smaller until they were driving down what looked like a hunting trail. Rena hadn't been on the reservation since she was a child. After her grandfather died, she had no reason to go back. She didn't even recognize it now. The vast expanses of woods all looked the same to her. As the Buick dipped and bobbed on the rough, uneven road, she was relieved she hadn't offered to drive them in her car. She peered down a long driveway to see two trailers surrounded by scrap metal and looked away. It felt unpleasantly familiar. She wanted to forget her early childhood; she had blocked out the nights she'd spent hiding under the stairway while her parents fought. She could almost smell the cheap vodka that burned her nose and hear the sound of her mother being thrown to the ground.

"How much further?" she demanded.

"Just a few miles."

"Well, hurry up, please. I hate this place."

Winston shot her a glare.

"It just brings back bad memories," she explained.

"I'm sorry," he said, as if he expected her to continue, but she didn't say any more, and again the car fell into silence.

He pulled onto a long driveway. Curve after curve revealed only more woods, until finally there was a brown house with smoke coming out of the chimney. Broken-down cars lined the north side of the yard. In place of the windshield on an old Ford, there was a piece of plywood with the words No Trespassing painted in red. Four dogs ran out from the back of the house and barked at the Buick. Then the front door opened, and a big woman with graying hair and hard eyes filled the doorway. She stood up straight with her arms crossed and watched them.

"There she is," Winston said as he put the car in park.

"She looks like she's gonna chew us up and spit us out," Rena observed.

"She probably will," he answered as he opened his door and got out. Rena followed his lead, and they walked up to the house.

"Hello, Bea," Winston said guardedly.

She returned his greeting with a glare. "What do you want, Belleau?"

"I thought your name was Winston," Rena said to him accusingly.

"Winston Belleau."

"You brought an outsider with you too." Bea's glare turned to Rena. "You got darkness in you, girl," she said. "You're not bringing that in my house."

There was movement behind an upstairs window, and Rena saw two small faces watching her. Two children with shaggy black hair looked down on her cautiously.

"Bea," Winston began, "we're here about the doctor."

"I don't know any doctor," she snapped.

"What about Dr. Davidson?"

"Never heard of him!" she lied. "And I don't like you coming out here, Belleau. Feels like you're accusing me of something."

Bea took a step forward from the doorway. She looked as if she had been waiting for an excuse to yell at one of them, and Winston had just given it to her. Rena knew this was her chance, while Bea was distracted. She shut her eyes and let Bea's rising voice fade away. She felt herself swirling, and a gentle breeze blew past her. She saw glimpses from the past: a limp little girl with deep gashes on her chest and stomach lying in Bea's arms on the front step. Dr. Davidson sitting at the kitchen table with his hat in his hands, as a cougar prowled behind the house. Rena had enough pieces to see the picture.

She pulled herself out, and the wind blew around her again. She opened her eyes. Bea was still yelling at Winston, now a few steps closer to him and with a finger pointed.

"Your sister was a troublemaker her whole life!" she accused.

"I've got it," Rena said.

Bea turned on her, her eyes on fire. "You've got nothing, skinny little bird."

"I know about the girl. Killed by one of your own, right? Was she your daughter or your granddaughter? I know you held her on the porch, right where you're standing now. That's why you're hateful, because you lost her. Then the doctor came and promised to bring her back if you kept him informed. He took her away and came back in the winter with a new girl, a baby. You were so grateful, you told him everything. You didn't know he was going to take people, and by the time he did, it was too late to take it back. So instead, you tell yourself they had it coming, that they did something to deserve it. Besides, you are safe, for now...yet you know tampering with death has consequences. They just haven't arrived yet.

"The girl frightens you," Rena went on. "She is different from any child you've ever known. She may look like a girl, but she acts wild like an animal. You don't like the way she watches the other children. The girl who died would chatter on for hours, but this wild girl speaks only in single words, which she uses to demand things. You knew the girl died that day, even when the doctor promised to bring her back, but desperation can make a person believe crazy things. It's true that this new child has sworn allegiance to you, and you are her mother, whatever she is. But it's also true that in your bartering with the doctor, you caused another mother to lose her daughter, and this is eating a hole in you, even if you say she was 'always a troublemaker.'"

When Rena closed her mouth, quiet settled around them for the first time. She watched Bea try to understand everything she'd just said. Bea's eyes shifted around the yard nervously, then began to fill with tears.

"She was my granddaughter," she finally said. She wiped her eyes and looked up at Winston with a softer gaze. "Belleau, you didn't tell me you were bringing a seer along with you."

"I didn't know that was part of the plan," he said.

"Where is the child? Inside?" Rena asked.

"No," Bea said quickly. "Just like you say, I don't like her around the other children when I'm not there. She's in the woods. She spends most of her time out there. Crazy girl will kill deer with her bare hands." She choked out a laugh. "She comes back after dusk."

"Does she shape-shift?" Winston asked.

"Lord, no. Not yet, anyway. I hope she never does. She's wild enough the way it is."

"She won't shift," Rena said. "The doctor can't recreate a shape-shifter. She will always be as she is: part human, part animal, all the time."

"She's not a monster," Bea said in a choked voice. "She's not."

"We know that," Winston added. "She's family."

She looked up at him earnestly. "I never meant for any of this to happen, Belleau. I never meant for them to take Rachel. That doctor, he tricked me, and now if I don't do what he says, he'll take my Rosy away, and maybe my boys too." Rena glanced up at the window where the two small faces still watched them.

"We came here to see if you and Rosy would help us stop the doctor," Winston said quietly.

Bea was shaking her head before he'd even finished speaking. "No. I don't want to cross that man. You know what he'll do to us."

"Do you want to live in fear of him forever?" Rena asked.

"I'd rather live in fear of him than not at all."

"You would only have a small role. We already have two people on the inside, and they're going to do most of the work."

"You mean Rachel, and who else?"

"Not Rachel," Winston said. "She's still in there, but she's too weak to help. And really, the less you know, the less the doctor could press you for."

"What has he done to her?" she asked cautiously.

"Uses her as a guinea pig for drugs. Sometimes he forces her to shift and studies her behavior, but she isn't very active in either state now. He has others there now too. The number of people he has changes; new ones come in, old ones die. I just hope I can get Rachel out of there before it's too late."

Bea's eyes hardened again. "What would you want me to do?"

Rena explained their plan to get Rosy on the inside and have her help free the captives when the time came. Bea then said the doctor had her bring Rosy in once a month for a checkup, and she wasn't due for three weeks.

"You could request one, say she's been ill."

"I could, but how will I know she'll be safe?"

"Our plan to is get everyone out quickly and unharmed, but I won't tell you there are no risks," answered Winston.

"To her, the risk is small," Rena added. "When it's safe, someone will ask her to open cages, maybe lead people out of the building. Do you think she could do that?"

"Of course she could," Bea snapped.

"Okay, then do you think you could get her to understand that the doctor is a bad man?"

"Don't worry about that. She hates that place, and every person in a white coat."

"Bea, if you can help us, it would make a big difference," Winston said.

"I know you wouldn't come out here unless you had to, Belleau. I just don't know if I can help you."

"If you decide to try, we're going to move on Tuesday. Every day Rachel is in there is a day I've failed her."

Bea didn't reply. She just crossed her arms again and looked at him.

Sensing that the most important part of the conversation was over, Rena turned around and headed back to the car. Winston nodded to Bea and followed.

As they pulled out of the driveway, Rena saw a flash of white in the woods. "Look!" she exclaimed, "there she is!" A girl of about eight watched them from the brush with a flat expression and hunter's eyes. "Puts chills down your spine."

"Rosy," Winston whispered.

As they drove past, she stepped out of the woods and watched their car. She stood in the middle of the driveway, hunched forward as if waiting to pounce on something. Her hands were red with blood.

"First time I've seen anything like that," Rena said.

"Yes," Winston answered, "but it may not be the last."

CHAPTER FORTY-TWO

SHAKA WAS GETTING USED TO BEING DRUGGED. THEY GAVE her one shot to force her to shift and another to keep her from shifting. The latter made her drowsy and complacent. She often couldn't tell what was real and what was just a dream. In this state, she'd wake to find herself on the cool gurney in the lab, the outline of a young woman at her side. She'd feel the pinprick of a needle in her arm, but her limbs would be too heavy to move. When she looked around the lab, the colors blurred into a rainbow, and the fluorescent lights looked like cold white suns from another world. Then she'd wake up on the cot in her cell with a pounding headache and her arms bruised from blood draws.

She watched Adrian closely from her cell. If Winston was right about him, then he owned her now. He could do anything he wanted. She thought of Rachel—her tired dark eyes, her sunken cheeks and thin fingers. Once she had been full of life, but they had taken it from her piece by piece until she was just a shell. Shaka wondered if it was too late for her. She tried to avoid her when she could. Sometimes when she looked at her, she feared she was looking at her own future.

One day, she woke groggy in her cell to find Adrian staring through the glass door at her. He rubbed his chin as he watched her. He had stubble on his face. That usually meant it was late in the day. His eyes were narrowed as if he were deep in thought. She sat up, though her head ached and the lights hurt her eyes. She looked at him, and his expression softened into a smile.

"How are you feeling?" He only asked her clinical questions anymore; someone was always listening.

"Not great. Why?"

"Do you want some Tylenol?" he asked.

"Pass. I think my liver has been through enough."

He gave her a sympathetic smile that irritated her, then nodded, turned on his heels, and walked away.

Shaka heard Mitchell ask him if he'd had a lovers' quarrel and laugh. Adrian ignored him.

The hours spent in her cell were grueling, though it was the safest place for her in the building. When she saw one of them approaching, she prayed under her breath that they wouldn't pull her from her cell.

She watched the doctor as he stood behind a row of computer monitors, looking from one to another. The whole time he was sipping coffee from a green mug that said *Minnesota State Bird* and had a picture of a mosquito. She often liked to imagine taking that mug from him and throwing the scalding coffee in his face. Then one day as she imagined it, a smile crept across her lips, and he glanced up at her.

"Something amusing, Shaka?" he'd asked her, and she quickly turned away and faced the back corner of her cell. After that, she didn't kid herself. She was powerless, and any thoughts to the contrary would only get her in trouble.

She was quickly becoming conditioned to her captivity. She worried that she wouldn't be able to rise to the occasion should the day finally come when Adrian set them all free. In fact, she feared that day now. She feared the consequences if they failed and she were caught. Adrian would be fine, of course. The worst that his father would do to him was disown him. But what would he do to her? There was no end to the ways he could torture her.

If the light hit the dark windows behind the doctor just right, she could see the reflection of her grandfather's cell. She watched and watched, and so did he, and when this happened, they would wave to each other, and for a moment she didn't feel so horribly alone. She would hold onto that feeling as long as it lasted, which was usually until she was taken from her cell and brought to the lab.

That morning, when the light hit the windows and she saw him, he looked groggy, and his lip was swollen. Still, he gave her a crooked smile. She smiled back. The doctor looked up, and their faces fell flat. Then Kate appeared in front of her cell and tapped on the glass.

"Time for a blood draw," she said in a chipper voice.

Shaka looked back at the glass, but her grandfather's reflection was gone. She obediently followed Kate out of the cell.

In the lab, she didn't need to be told to get on the gurney; she knew the routine. She lay there waiting for the prick of the needle in her hand, and it came. She watched her crimson blood flow freely through the tubing and collect in a red vial, then a purple one, then a green one. When the needle was withdrawn from her hand, she felt a cool swab of rubbing alcohol on her arm, then the deep stab of another needle—the one that injected the sedative into her muscle.

Minutes passed, and her eyes were getting heavy. She heard the door open and struggled to see who it was. She heard voices echoing as if they were talking down a long hallway. It was a man's voice, one she knew: Mitchell.

"How's she doing?" he asked.

Shaka found that no matter how hard she tried, she couldn't open her eyes.

"Just out," Kate answered.

"Doc wants me to bring her to the arena," he said.

"Sounds good!" Kate said. "I'm going on break then."

There was no reply, but a moment later she heard the door close. It sounded like it was hundreds of feet away. She tried to move but couldn't. The urge to sleep was overwhelming, and she fought as hard as she could to keep her awareness.

Suddenly, she could feel Mitchell's breath on her face, and the sensation made her nauseous. She felt his hand smoothing back her hair, then it drifted down her body and caressed her breast through the thin hospital gown. She fought even harder than before to hold onto her consciousness. His touch filled her with dread and rage. If she could have shifted, she would have sunk her teeth into his throat. She could nearly feel his trachea crunching in her mouth. Her jaw twitched at the thought, but she remained otherwise motionless.

Then she heard the muffled sound of a door opening, and his hand jerked away from her body.

"Don't touch her," she heard Adrian demand in a cold voice.

"I'm just bringing her down to the arena, Adrian. Jesus, you'd think she really was your girlfriend!"

"You don't work with her anymore. I don't want you around her."

"You're kidding me! You really *do* have a thing for her.

That's messed up, Adrian. She's a freak, and she's a test subject. She belongs to the lab."

There was the sound of movement and quick struggle, then a thud.

"Ow! You broke my nose, man!" Mitchell yelled.

She knew Adrian was standing beside her, she could smell him. Then she felt another pinprick in her arm, and a moment later the fog in her head began to clear. She saw Mitchell sitting on the floor, watching them. Blood ran from his mouth and nose. She smiled at the sight of him. The urge to sleep was getting easier to resist. She tried to rise, then felt Adrian's hands on her back.

"Shaka," he said, "coming here was a mistake. I hate what they're doing to you. We need to leave. I gave you a reversal agent for the sedative, but it will wear off in a few minutes. We need to go—now."

"And him?" was all she could say as she nodded toward Mitchell.

"Let karma catch up with him," he said, then handed her Mitchell's cattle prod. "But in the meantime, here, just make it quick."

She swung it clumsily past Adrian and shocked him on the arm.

"Shit!" he yelled as he yanked his arm back.

Mitchell laughed as he got to his feet. "Serves you right, Adrian," he said, then turned to Shaka. "Come on, honey, let's see what ya got!"

Shaka slid off the gurney and stumbled toward Mitchell. Adrian had a hand at the small of her back and she tried to move away from it.

Mitchell laughed as she got closer to him, his teeth covered in blood.

If she could just wake up a little more, she could do it. She felt a little stronger with each passing second. Then finally, it was enough. She dropped the cattle prod, and in seconds, she was a wolf leaping through the air toward Mitchell. It happened so fast that his laughter turned to a scream in the same breath. Her teeth sunk into his neck, his carotid arteries and trachea cradled in her jaw. She squeezed until his screaming stopped.

She put her weight in her shoulders and was preparing to rip open his neck when she was shocked from behind. She spun around and snapped at Adrian. Mitchell lay still behind her. She snarled, but the drowsiness was already returning. She stumbled and fell, and once she was on the floor, she involuntarily shifted back to her human form.

"Why did you do that, Shaka?!" Adrian demanded. "Now they're going to kill you! We have to get out of here, now!"

"I don't trust karma," she said, her speech starting to slur.

She was drifting again, finding it hard to hold onto time. She felt a blanket wrap around her, and she was lifted up. She felt Adrian's body next to hers, his rapid heartbeat pounding against her. He was warm, and she was so cold.

They passed through a door. She was bouncing with his steps. It wasn't a soft bounce, but she sank into it. Another door opened, and the bouncing stopped. Suddenly, there were so many loud and incomprehensible voices. She felt like she had walked into a thunderstorm. Then Adrian yelled too; she felt the sound rise up from within him. As he shouted, his hands tightened around her, pinching her. Then they released her completely, and she was free for a moment before she cracked against the floor. Something else fell beside her—something heavy. It slowly dawned on her that it was Adrian. She reached her fingers out until she touched him. He was warm and quiet. She tried to pull herself next to him, but her body ached with each tiny movement. As soon as she stopped trying to move, her thoughts floated away from the noise, the hard, cold floor, and Adrian. Soon she was surrounded by a quiet darkness, from which she did not return until morning.

CHAPTER FORTY-THREE

BEA HATED DRIVING ON THE FREEWAY. SHE TOOK HIGHWAY 61 South as far as she could whenever she had to see the doctor, but after she passed through the outer suburban ring of the Twin Cities, every road she drove on made her nervous. Everyone moved so fast, and she worried that her old Pontiac couldn't keep up. She was not good at merging and usually received a honk from the car behind her, sometimes a middle finger. When she drove in big cities, she became fearful, and she hated to feel that way.

Once the car was parked, she felt only slightly more comfortable. The next obstacle was keeping Rosy safe as they walked the suburban streets. Passersby looked at Rosy with open curiosity, sometimes even disgust. Bea pulled the girl in close to her to shield her from their cruel looks.

"Forget them," she said. "They aren't anybody."

But then, Rosy never seemed to care much about other people. She was preoccupied with the motion of the traffic and the neighborhood dogs. Just like the strangers on the streets, dogs never liked Rosy either. But unlike the strangers, Rosy did notice them. She growled in her throat when she saw them. Bea worried that one day Rosy would break away from her and kill one of them. Then it would be all over— locked up in an institution for sure.

Bea watched the streets closely for approaching dogs. A jogger and his goldendoodle passed them, and Rosy said, "Bad dog" in what sounded like both a question and a growl.

"No, honey, good dog," Bea answered. That was enough for Rosy. She always listened to Bea. The other Rosy had been that way too: a good listener. It helped Bea to remember that this strange child was still her granddaughter.

Bea had lost sleep the night Winston and the girl had visited her. Everything the girl said was true. As much as Bea told herself she'd done what she'd needed to do to save Rosy, she also hated herself for betraying Rachel, one of her own people. When she woke up the next morning, she knew she had to go. She woke Rosy and explained everything to her. She worried that Rosy wouldn't understand, but she'd smiled when Bea got to the part about freeing everyone the doctor held captive.

"I will do it," Rosy said before Bea had even gotten around to asking her.

As they turned onto the clinic's street, Bea let out a sigh of relief that only slightly loosened the knot in her stomach.

"Now, remember, why are we here?" she coached Rosy as they approached the building.

"I'm sick," she said.

"Sick how?"

"Seizures."

"Good girl," Bea said and smiled, though she felt sick herself and her hands trembled slightly.

Once in the vestibule, they needed to be buzzed inside.

"May I help you?" a man asked over the speaker. Bea turned to it and spoke.

"Bea Fisher here. I need the doc to take a look at Rosy."

"Do you have an appointment with him?" the man asked.

"No, but she's sick. She needs to be seen."

There was a moment of silence, then the door buzzed open. She pulled Rosy into the lobby, where a tall, blond security guard sat behind the desk.

"You can have a seat, ma'am," he ordered.

She took Rosy to the stiff gray couch that sat next to the window. She clutched her hand the whole time. Rosy watched a seagull jumping across the parking lot and seemed oblivious to all else. A TV on the wall flashed news headlines, and as the seconds became minutes, Bea felt her heart rate increase.

What if he turned them away? She hadn't thought of that. Honestly, part of her hoped that he would. She could just put Rosy back in the car and leave. She would tell Winston she'd tried. But just as she was getting comfortable with that idea, the doctor walked into the lobby.

"Ms. Fisher. How are you doing?" he asked.

"Not great, Doc. Rosy's got me worried. I think she had a seizure yesterday."

"Is that so?" he asked. "Rosy," he said, turning to her.

She looked away from the gulls in the parking lot.

"How are you feeling?"

"Sick," she answered.

"That's not like you," he said, and Bea started to panic again. Perhaps he already suspected that they were lying.

"I'd better take you back and have a look," he added.

Bea stood and pulled Rosy to her feet beside her. They followed the doctor out of the lobby and through the locked doors. As they walked down the corridor, she paid close attention to the locks on every door, the cameras in the ceiling. Each door required a fingerprint to open it. She wondered if Winston knew what he was getting into. She half expected him to screw the whole thing up and end up a captive himself. If that happened, she might never get Rosy back. She quickly pushed the thought out of her head. There was no turning back now, anyway.

They rounded a corner to find a young woman in a lab coat mopping up a bloodstain on the floor.

"Sorry for the mess. We had an incident this afternoon," he said as they walked past her. Bea pulled Rosy closer to her.

They went through another set of locked doors and passed the laboratory where Rosy usually had her blood drawn. Bea glanced inside. It was a mess, and there was a big pool of blood on the floor, but what caught Bea's attention was the man on the gurney. Three people hovered over him, as if working to save him, but he looked gray, like someone waiting for death. She recognized him; he was one of the doctor's assistants.

"Geez, Doc, did somebody go crazy and attack you guys?" she ventured.

"Yes. It's a risk we know we're taking in this line of work, but it's still hard when it happens. Right this way," he added, directing them out of the hall. "But don't worry. Everything is under control now." He opened the door to a sterile, fluorescent-lit exam room with a cot in it. "Rosy can stay in here tonight. I won't be able to examine her for another hour or so. If she's having seizures, I'd like to observe her for a day or two. I'll have security come and help you out shortly, Bea. Do you have a place to stay down here?"

"Yeah, I can stay with my sister." As soon as she said it, she regretted it. He hadn't known she had a sister. Would he look for her now too? She wasn't a shifter, but Bea feared he might want to check for himself.

"Okay. If you run into trouble, come back, and we can get you a voucher for a hotel."

"Thanks," she said. "Actually, Doc, maybe I'll do that. Now that I think about it, my sister is in Milwaukee right now." Bea didn't think her sister had ever been to Milwaukee, but she didn't want to lead anybody to her house.

"All right, I'll have security bring you a voucher." And then he turned his back to them and left the room.

Bea waited ten seconds, then walked to the door and turned the knob. It opened. She gave a sigh of relief.

"At least he didn't lock us in here!" she said to Rosy, who sat on the cot and looked at the floor. Bea felt her heart sink when she looked at her. She went to the cot and sat down beside her.

"You are a hero," she whispered in Rosy's ear and wrapped her arms around her.

A few minutes later, a security guard opened the door. Bea kissed Rosy on the cheek and stood up.

"This way, ma'am," he said, holding the door open.

"See you soon, my girl," she said and forced herself to turn around and walk out of the room.

CHAPTER FORTY-FOUR

SHAKA WOKE UP WITH ANOTHER POUNDING HEADACHE, this one worse than usual. Her whole body hurt. She remembered bits of the night before but couldn't remember what had been a dream and what had really happened. Perhaps it was all a dream. Had she really killed Mitchell? Had Adrian tried to carry her out of the building? It all seemed too extraordinary. She sat up, wincing as a sharp pain shot from the small of her back up to the top of her pounding head. She felt dizzy.

As the spinning slowed, she opened her eyes. She saw a dark lump on the floor of her cell. As her eyes came into focus, she realized it was a man: Adrian. She gritted her teeth, slid off of her cot, and crawled over to where he lay.

"Hey," she whispered. "Adrian. Wake up."

His bloodshot eyes cracked open. She wondered if he had

been drugged too. Then she noticed an ugly gash on the top of his head and a small pool of dried blood on the floor beneath his face. She remembered him falling beside her. He must have been struck over the head and dragged to her cell. "Are you okay?" she asked.

He slowly and stiffly reached his hand to the gash on his head, touching it lightly with his fingertips. Then he sat up and leaned against the wall.

"I ruined it," he whispered.

Shaka didn't reply. She didn't blame him, but it was true, their plan was ruined.

The sun had started shooting warm rays through the windows. When Shaka noticed, she stood up and looked at the tinted glass behind the computers. If she stood in the right spot, this was one of the times of day when she could see her grandfather. She watched intently until inch by inch she could see into his cell. He was waiting for her to appear as well. She smiled and waved to him, and he returned the gesture, but his expression abruptly changed to puzzlement.

"Adrian," she said slowly and deliberately, and Adrian looked up. Her back was to him. He followed her eyes to see the reflection of Arnold in the glass. He waved to him, and Arnold waved back, still looking confused. Then the doors to the lab opened, and they quickly backed away from the glass.

Adrian's sister Amanda walked in and went right to the computer. She didn't look up.

"Hey," Adrian said as he struggled to his feet. "Hey, Amanda. Let me out of here. Please."

She quickly glanced at him out of the corner of her eye, but didn't respond.

"Please, Amanda, I don't belong in here. This is all a big mistake."

She finished typing with her head down and ran out the way she came in, passing her father as she left.

"Now, now, Amanda," he said as she pushed past him. The doctor watched her leave, then turned toward the lab, his green coffee cup in hand. "And on my birthday, no less," he muttered to himself.

"Happy birthday," Arnold said from his cell.

The doctor looked up at him and smiled. "Thank you, Arnold." He made his way to the computer and started clicking through screens.

"Dad," Adrian pleaded from Shaka's cell. "This isn't what it looks like. You're making a big mistake."

Dr. Davidson didn't look up right away; he spent a few more seconds clicking before he looked over to Shaka's cell. "I want to believe you, Adrian. You are my son. But I'm not a fool. I know you've never completely agreed with what I do, and it's hard for you to turn off your sympathy for these creatures. I imagine it's especially difficult for you to turn your heart off to this one." He nodded toward Shaka. "We all know that she's your favorite. Of course you would want to protect her. You were always such a sensitive boy. Perhaps bringing you here was a mistake."

"Is Mitchell dead?" he asked.

"After having his throat ripped open by a wolf? Yes. And that makes your girlfriend the most dangerous animal in the building."

"Other than you," Shaka said as she approached the glass.

"I haven't murdered anyone with my bare hands."

"But you have murdered."

"There have been casualties in the name of progress, yes. But 'murder' is hardly the appropriate term."

"Mitchell's death was also in the name of progress." Shaka said. "But you don't seem very upset about that."

"Mitchell is a great loss to this place and to my work. He was always the first to help, but at the end of the day, he is replaceable. He was an associate, that's all. He wasn't family. Truth be told, I didn't like his personality all that much. He was a bit too loud."

"So, what now?" Adrian interjected.

The doctor didn't reply right away, and the hum of the lab grew deafening. Finally, he said, "Your girlfriend will need extra security from now on. The cattle prod will be replaced with a rifle, and she will wear a muzzle and shackles whenever she leaves her cell."

"And me?" he asked.

"I don't know yet, Adrian. You betrayed me."

When the doctor said nothing more, Adrian moved away from the window and let his father work. The lab was quiet but for the humming of the computer system and the clicking of the mouse. Shaka and Adrian sat on the floor of her cell in hopeless silence.

The door to the lab slid open, and Kate walked in. "Happy birthday, Doc," she said. She had a doughnut in one hand and a Starbucks cup in the other.

"Thank you, Kate. Did you make a Starbucks run?" he asked. "Because I could use a refill."

"No, but there's a stand in the lobby. It must be a birthday present. Do you think Mitchell ordered it?"

"He did love doughnuts, God rest his soul," the doctor said with a quiet chuckle.

"I don't want to dishonor him by letting it get cold." And he headed out of the lab.

Once he was gone, Kate looked into Shaka's cell curiously. Inside, Adrian and Shaka sat beside one another on the floor, both looking dejected.

"I just don't understand, Adrian," she finally said.

"Wouldn't expect you to, Kate," he replied.

"Hey. Where's ours?" someone asked from another cell. Shaka could tell by his voice that it was Caleb, the young man who could turn into a rattlesnake. Kate looked up at him briefly, then back at the computer without replying.

"A coffee cart for someone's birthday?" Shaka reflected. "That doesn't sound very Mitchell."

"It's not," Adrian answered in a whisper. "I did it. It's all drugged. In an hour or two, everyone here will be asleep. Kate might be dead if she keeps chugging it like that."

"Adrian, that's great! Does anyone else know your plan? Maybe they'll come looking for us when we don't come out."

"I wouldn't count on that. I'm supposed to call Rena when everyone is passed out. It'll be kind of hard to do that from in here."

"Maybe she'll figure it out on her own. She's smart, you know."

"Maybe," Adrian answered absently. He just wrapped his arm around her shoulder and squeezed her against him.

The clock ticked, and every person that walked into the lab seemed to be in good spirits, despite Mitchell having been killed less than twenty-four hours earlier. They all had a Starbucks cup in their hand.

As the sun got higher, they started to notice less commotion in the lab. It was only the doctor at his computer, and he seemed to be struggling to keep his eyes open. Then there was a crash as his coffee mug fell to the floor and shattered. A few seconds later, the doctor, who had slumped over on the desk, slid to the floor with a thud.

"They're all out," Shaka said.

"Yep. And we're in here."

"Do you think we could break this glass?" she asked.

"It's bulletproof."

She stood up and walked over to the glass. She could see into Rachel's cell through the glass behind the desk. She was sleeping on her cot. She always seemed to be sleeping. When she walked along the glass, her perspective shifted, and she could see inside Caleb's cell. He was also sleeping.

"Grandpa?" she yelled. "Are you there?"

"Of course, Shaka." She heard his voice muffled through the glass.

"Everyone has been drugged. Adrian was going to let us all out, but now he's locked in here with me."

"I'm sorry, honey." he replied.

"Can you think of any other way we can get out of these cages?" she asked.

"If I knew that, we would have been out of here a long time ago."

An hour had passed since the doctor had gone down. In a couple more hours, he would be awake again, and Shaka feared they would still be sitting in her cell, except he would know he had been drugged, and Adrian would be the obvious suspect. It might mean the difference between disowning him and killing him. Fearing for Adrian, she wrapped her arms around his waist. If they were going to die in here, she wanted to be near him for as long as she could.

"We tried," she finally said.

"Yes," he answered despondently, and quiet fell around them again.

Another half hour passed. The sun was reaching its late morning height. Shaka's stomach growled, though she found it easy to ignore the feeling of hunger. She shut her eyes and rested her head on Adrian's shoulder.

"Shaka." She heard the muffled voice of her grandfather. She opened her eyes and walked up to the glass. "Shaka," she heard again.

"Yes, Grandpa? What is it?"

"Someone's coming to see you," he said happily. She waited for someone to appear, but no one came.

"Shaka," Adrian said from behind her. "Look down."

She did—and saw a brown rabbit hop in front of her cell door. It stopped in the center and sniffed the floor.

"Hey!" Adrian said to the rabbit. "Hey! Shift back. Shift back and let us out of here!"

The rabbit didn't even look at him. He got up and banged on the glass, but the rabbit just jumped and ran away. "Hey!" he yelled after it. "Come back! We can all get out of here!"

"It's just a rabbit, Adrian," Shaka said. "It can't shift."

Adrian hit the glass with his fist.

"Shaka," her grandfather called again, "he has company."

Shaka looked through the door again. There were two raccoons on the desk by the computer, and a black dog trotted past the cell doors as he followed the scent of the rabbit.

"Where are they coming from?" she asked.

"I don't know. Someone must have passed out with the cages open in the kennel," Adrian answered.

Then a rhythmic click-clack sound grew louder and louder, and a horse trotted into the lab, following the same path the dog had taken. She trotted right past the cell doors, so close that if there hadn't been glass between them, Shaka could have reached out and touched her.

"How did *she* get out?" Adrian said more to himself than anyone else.

"Hello, there." Shaka heard the muffled words of her grandfather.

"Are you talking to me?" Shaka called back, but got no reply. She walked along the glass door of her cell, looking out at the windows behind the computers until she could see a reflection. She saw into Rachel's cell. She was awake and standing at the glass. Shaka had never seen her stand up in her cell before. She was looking at something. Her mouth was moving but Shaka couldn't hear what she said. Then a dark-haired girl stepped up to the glass of her cage.

"Adrian!" Shaka gasped. "There's a girl out there! She must have freed the animals!"

Adrian jumped to the glass and looked at the reflection. "That's the girl from the woods!" he said.

They watched as Rachel put her hand to the glass, and the girl did the same. Rachel mouthed words, but they were too soft to hear. Suddenly the girl turned from the glass and ran to the desk. Shaka remembered the way she ran, with her shoulders forward, like she wanted to drop to all fours. They watched as she disappeared behind the desk, then reappeared a moment later, dragging the doctor facedown by his right arm. She pulled him to Rachel's cell and lifted his hand to the keypad, kicking his body closer to the glass as she worked to press his thumbprint against the pad.

Suddenly the door to Rachel's cell slid open. Rachel cautiously took a step outside of her cell and looked around as if she'd never been in the room before. Then she looked down at the child and placed her hand on the side of her face. The girl took Rachel's hand and pulled her toward the door.

"Rachel!" Shaka heard her grandfather's voice again and the sound of banging on glass. "Rachel, please, don't leave us here!"

Rachel paused, then turned around and grabbed the doctor by his hands. She tried to pull him over to Arnold's cell, but she was too weak. Rosy grabbed his arms and pulled too, and his body slid across the tile. Rachel lifted his hand and pressed his thumb to the keypad outside of Arnold's cell while Rosy lifted his shoulders off the ground. Arnold's door slid open. He stepped out, and he and Rachel stood before each other for a moment. They regarded one another as if they were seeing each other for the first time. Then a smile crept across Rachel's face, and Arnold embraced her. When he released her, she took the girl's hand, and they ran in the direction the animals had gone.

Arnold grabbed the doctor by the hands and pulled him across the floor. The doctor let out a moan, and his eyes fluttered.

"Not yet, Doc," he said. He stopped at the door of Caleb's cell and pressed his thumb to the keypad. The door slid open, and Caleb stepped out. He stood over the doctor for a moment, then Shaka watched in astonishment as his skin grew scales and his face grew long, and his clothing fell in what looked like an empty pile. There was the sound of a rattle, then she saw the head of a rattlesnake rise out of the clothing and strike the doctor three times, twice in the leg and once in the stomach.

"Did he *bite* him?" Adrian asked in astonishment.

Shaka didn't answer him. Adrian had seen what happened. He couldn't expect mercy for his father now that the tables were turned.

Caleb quickly shifted back and grabbed the doctor's hand. He dragged him twice as fast as Arnold had over to Shaka's cell—but when he saw Adrian inside, he stopped. Adrian knew enough to keep his mouth shut.

"Please," Shaka cried, "let us out!"

They heard glass breaking down the hall but couldn't see what was happening. Arnold and Caleb looked behind them, then quickly back. Caleb dropped the doctor and ran for the door. Arnold grabbed the doctor's hand and pressed it to the keypad, rolling his thumb from side to side. Finally, the door slid open. Shaka jumped out into her grandfather's arms. She squeezed her eyes shut, but tears spouted from them anyway.

"Guys," Adrian said as he too stepped out of the cell. "Guys, we need to go."

Shaka and Arnold released each other and followed Adrian's gaze to the end of the lab. A grizzly bear was making its way into the room. It walked with a swagger, stopping to sniff here and there.

"Is it a shifter?" Adrian asked with fear in his voice.

"Nope," Arnold answered. "It's just a bear."

"Can we get out of here, then?" he asked.

"Just go slow, don't run, and don't turn your back on her."

"What about him?" Adrian asked as he motioned to his dad. "The bear will probably eat him."

"Hopefully," Shaka muttered.

"He's my father," Adrian said. He looked down at him. He was starting to move a little more. The drugs were starting to wear off, and the rattlesnake venom hadn't taken ahold yet.

"Just lock him in a cell, then," Shaka said as she watched Adrian struggle with the decision.

"He'll die," he said. "The venom will kill him if he doesn't get an antidote."

"He'll be fine so long as he gets it in the next few hours. We can put him in a cell for now, then come back with the antidote once the bear is gone," Arnold explained in a calm tone.

Adrian thought about it for moment, then nodded. The two of them quickly pushed the doctor inside Shaka's cell, and Adrian rolled his thumb over the keypad. His thumbprint still worked.

"Now let's go before the bear sees us," Shaka said.

"You two go on," Arnold said. "I'll be close behind."

"We should stick together," Shaka said.

"There's something I have to do first. It won't take long, dear. You two go outside, count to twenty, and I'll be there."

"Shaka, come on," Adrian said as he grabbed her hand. "Arnold can take care of himself!"

"Be careful!" she called to her grandfather and turned toward Adrian. They slowly walked to the door, keeping a close eye on the bear.

When they got through the first set of doors, they turned around and ran. The second set was propped open. A deer ran ahead of them and made a sharp right where a shaft of light spilled into the hall. The light was like an arrow pointing them toward the way out. An overwhelming determination fueled Shaka as she raced for it. When the light hit her skin, she realized they had done it; they had won.

CHAPTER FORTY-FIVE

THE PARKING LOT WAS PACKED. THERE WERE FOUR NEWS stations there. Shaka squinted into the sun and saw a woman with a microphone interviewing Caleb. Shaka scanned the parking lot and saw Winston. His father and all the others who had interrogated Adrian at Terry's house were circled around something, or someone. Shaka realized that somewhere at their center was Rachel.

"Shaka!" she heard Rena's voice calling her. She looked across the lot and saw Rena running toward her. "I'm so fricking glad you're safe!" she said. "I was so worried!"

"I was too. How long have you known?"

"Not long. Winston just told me about it, but when I heard you were in trouble, I knew I couldn't trust those two losers to save you. It's just so good to see you!" Rena said as she leaned in and hugged Shaka, flinging Adrian's arm off her shoulder in the process.

As they embraced, an old man walked out of the building and stood in the sun.

"Is that your grandfather?" Rena asked in disbelief.

Shaka looked behind her and saw Arnold facing the sun with his eyes closed.

"Yes," she answered. "That's him."

Rena started walking toward him, while Shaka and Adrian followed. Halfway there, Adrian grabbed her by the hand and pulled her back. He pulled her against him, and she threw her arms over his shoulders.

"Come here," he said as he squeezed her.

She felt a growing warmth for him in her belly, and a tingling at the back of her neck. She pulled away from him and looked into his eyes. She felt foolish for having ever doubted him.

"Shaka," he said as if he were trying out her name. "You are radiant, even in that hospital gown."

"Thanks?" she replied, then added "Come on. Let me give you a proper introduction to my grandfather."

"Right now?" he asked. "Don't you think we should wait a bit for that?"

"Why would we?"

"Maybe he wants some time away from the Davidson family."

"What are you talking about? You are the reason he's free!"

"It's not really that black and white. Remember how you wanted to kill me when you found out I was connected to this place? He probably still sees me that way."

"You've already proven yourself."

"It's not just that. Maybe I'm not quite ready. I mean, he was in there for a long time, and I did nothing."

"You couldn't free them all by yourself. Just trust me, he forgives you. He's my only family, so it's important that you know him."

Adrian nodded and reluctantly followed her over to Arnold.

Shaka threw her arms around her grandfather for the second time that day. Hugging him felt so good! She'd forgotten what it was like, how he smelled like woodchips, somehow even now. "Grandpa, I missed you so much."

"I missed you too, darling. I should have known if someone was going to get me out of that place it would be you."

"It wasn't just me though. It was Rachel's brother, Winston, and Adrian too."

Arnold's gaze moved over to Adrian. "Thank you, Adrian. I imagine it wasn't easy for you to go against your father."

"No, sir," he stammered, "but I guess better late than never."

"Timing can be the most important thing," Arnold replied.

"I'm sorry for what he did to you," Adrian said.

"You don't need to apologize for another man's crimes, or to carry them on your back, son. You're not your father."

"No, sir," Adrian replied, visibly relieved.

"Do you smell that?" Rena asked.

"Smoke," Shaka said.

They all turned around and looked at the building. There was smoke curling up from the roof.

"It's on fire, and my father's still in there!" Adrian said with alarm in his voice.

"Adrian," Shaka said quietly, "your father is a monster. Let the world be rid of him."

He looked at her with anger in his eyes. "Killing him wasn't part of the plan, Shaka. Neither was burning down the lab," he added as he turned to Arnold.

"Adrian, try to understand," Arnold said, "we won't be safe as long as this place stands, or your father lives."

Adrian wasn't listening for his reply though. He ran his hands through his hair as his eyes darted over the building. Pacing in two quick circles, he stopped and looked at Shaka. "Monster or not, I can't just leave him in there!" he said, then he spun around and ran into the burning building.

"Adrian," Arnold yelled after him, "don't go back in there!" But it was no use; Adrian had already disappeared.

Shaka stood in a stunned silence for a moment. She anxiously watched the door as smoke seeped out of it, hoping he would turn around and come back out.

"Why would he do that?" Rena asked.

"The doctor is his father, and blood runs thick, Rena," Arnold said while in the distance, the first sirens pierced the air.

"He'll never make it out!" Shaka said as she took a step forward. She felt a hand land on her shoulder. She looked behind her to see Arnold smiling gently at her.

"We don't know that," he said. "I know you care about him, Shaka, but this is his choice. We'll wait here for him."

She searched her grandfather's face for a moment, all the while willing herself to stay put. Her legs ached to run after Adrian.

"We'll wait here for him," Arnold repeated. Shaka felt his hand tighten ever so slightly on her shoulder. She looked back at him and reluctantly nodded, feeling helpless as she watched the smoke roll from the door before them.

CHAPTER FORTY-SIX

SHAKA AND HER GRANDFATHER DIDN'T LEAVE MINNEAPOLIS right away. They spent the first few days going back and forth between the hospital and their hotel room. She was haunted by the image of the firemen pulling Adrian's unconscious body from the burning building. She had feared he was dead. She stood beside Rena and Arnold and nervously watched as they put an oxygen mask over his mouth and loaded him into an ambulance. Rena then drove them to the hospital, where they found him in the ICU with lines and tubes coming out of him. He was so still; his only movement was the rise and fall of his chest with the mechanical breath of the ventilator. Shaka sat down beside him and held his hand. He was somewhere else. She cried beside him as she whispered "wake up" into his ear, but he didn't stir.

On the third day, the doctor came in and explained to her

that his chance of recovery was guarded. She didn't understand exactly what that meant, but his expression told her it wasn't good.

When there were no changes by the fifth day, she decided to say goodbye to him. Her goodbye was simple: a kiss on the forehead, a squeeze of his right hand, and the words, "I'll see you again." She didn't linger. When she left that day, she knew she wouldn't be back unless he woke, and she started building walls in her heart to keep the image of him in the hospital bed from taking over.

She needed to get her grandfather out of the city anyway. Though he never mentioned it, she knew the crowds made him nervous, and he longed to finally return to his cabin in the woods. He spent his time at the hotel watching local news with the curtains drawn. He was still consumed by the world he'd just escaped from, and it saddened Shaka to see it.

On the day she said goodbye to Adrian, the news channels released their final report on the fire at the lab. The police had declared it an electrical accident. They referred to the laboratory as a pharmaceutical development agency, and to the deaths of Dr. Miles Davidson and his assistant Katelyn Winter as "tragic and untimely." They were not seeking comments from family or witnesses. The case was closed before it was even opened. The media, which began by reporting on the story of a deranged scientist who had been performing involuntary experiments on his captives, quickly changed its angle. At that time, all they had to go on was Rena's anonymous tip and an interview they'd done with Caleb after he broke out of the facility. After the police statement was released, they threw out Caleb's interview, writing it off as the ravings of a mentally unstable patient.

It was over. Shaka and Arnold watched the news report in silence. When Arnold clicked off the TV, Shaka said, "He won after all."

"No one won," Arnold responded. "But for what it's worth, we are free, and he's dead." He smiled at her.

She tried to smile back, but couldn't.

"I'm ready to go home," she said.

"Are you sure?" he asked carefully.

"I think so. I mean, we can't stay in this hotel forever. Are you ready, Grandpa?"

"I've been ready for years," he answered.

Shaka made a call, and Rena picked them up that afternoon. By nightfall, Shaka was back in her apartment. It was still a mess from the night she had been taken, but she straightened it up quickly and made a bed for her grandfather on the couch.

She was exhausted, but more than anything, she wanted

to shift in the lake and run through the night. As the sky grew darker, the urge grew stronger. It had been so long since she'd asked her grandfather to run with her, she had trouble finding the words. She went to the window and opened it up. The breeze and the cool scent of the night invigorated her; it gave her the courage she was looking for.

"I know a place we could go to run," she said.

"Not yet, Shaka," he answered. "It's too soon. We don't know if we're safe yet."

She sighed and sat down on the couch.

"Tomorrow we can go to the cabin," he said. "We'll be safe there, kiddo."

Shaka felt better as soon as he mentioned the cabin. She hadn't been there in years. It had been her favorite place as a child—the knotty pine walls that still smelled like sap and the little woodstove that crackled and popped, keeping the cabin toasty in the winter while the snow piled up on the motionless pines outside. It had been vacant for so long now, she hoped it was still livable.

Early the next morning, she called Rena and begged her for a ride. Shaka imagined that cleaning out a cabin that had been abandoned for years was not how Rena wanted to spend her day, so she was grateful, though not surprised, when Rena told her she could instead borrow her car while they fixed up Arnold's cabin.

They drove up the shore until they reached Two Harbors, then turned north and wound into the woods for another half hour. The houses fell away, and soon they were alone for miles in every direction.

The driveway was long, almost half a mile, and trees had fallen across it in the years of Arnold's absence. They drove the car as far as they could and walked the rest of the way. When they reached the cabin, it was better off than either of them expected. Other than a broken picture window and a mess left behind by a family of squirrels, it was in good shape. Shaka and Arnold got to work right away, clearing the driveway, cleaning the cabin, and repairing the window. In the afternoon, they drove into Two Harbors for supplies and to have the electricity and phone line reconnected. To see the place put back together with her grandfather cooking in the kitchen made Shaka feel like a child again, happy and safe.

Finally, come twilight, it was time to run. Shaka walked through the woods on an overgrown trail to the lake behind the cabin. When she reached it, she held her hand out in front of her; she was a silhouette. She stripped and dove in quickly before the bugs could find her. In the chill water, she reveled in the stretching and twisting of her body. Bit by bit she felt her attachment to one world fade and her urge to be part of another one grow. She jumped out onto the opposite shore and shook the water from her fur, then she threw her head back and howled.

That was Arnold's cue. He came down the trail a moment later, dove into the lake, and popped up on the opposite shore near Shaka. He glanced at her and trotted past. She fell into place behind him.

When they were human, they spoke as equals, considering each other's points of view before making decisions. But when they were wolves, her grandfather always made the decisions. It had always been that way, and she took comfort in it.

She followed him into the woods. They trotted for a couple of miles before they reached a clearing. From the edge, they stood and sniffed the air, then Arnold leaped out into the grass, and Shaka tore out after him and passed him. She ran fast, smooth circles around the clearing, leaning as she turned, digging her feet in as she changed direction. She zipped past her grandfather, taunting him. He nipped at her the first time. The second, he tripped her, and she tumbled to the ground, coming to a stop and letting out a happy yip as she lay panting before him. He threw his head back and howled. She followed suit, first as she lay on the ground, then standing beside him.

Their chorus rang out through the clearing and echoed into the woods. Deep in the forest, animals stopped grazing and moving to listen to their calls. Miles beyond them, their howls were answered by others; apparently, a new pack had moved in during Arnold's absence. The pack was saying hello, but also sending a warning to them to stay on their side. Shaka and Arnold would have to take care not to travel into their territory. It was a clear expectation though, unlike those Shaka felt were put on her in the human world. Out here, in the heart of the wilderness, she felt whole, free in a way she'd never felt as a human, and with her grandfather by her side and the threat of capture gone, she felt like it was all beginning anew.

CHAPTER FORTY-SEVEN

SHAKA KNEW SHE NEEDED TO RETURN TO WORK, BUT SHE JUST wasn't ready to leave the woods yet. She had been at her grandfather's cabin for a week, and it was starting to feel like her home too. It was true that it was a small space for two people, and she missed having unquestioned control of the TV remote, but those things were small sacrifices compared to the elation she felt at being able to go outside and shift at any moment. She did it often, at least daily. She ran every night, and sometimes in the morning too.

Her grandfather preferred to trot, or to sit and listen to the sounds of the woods. Though he didn't have her energy, he noticed more: the smaller animals that hid in the ground, the songs of the birds, the scents of familiar plants. After she ran, she would sit beside him and listen for the quiet story of the forest.

It was a sunny morning, and the cool and fog hadn't quite lifted from the lake. She'd had a good run, and her legs felt happy and tired. She emerged from the lake shivering as she slipped back into her clothing, then she walked to the cabin feeling calm. Her days always went better when she began them with a run. When she rounded the bend, she found her grandfather sitting on the porch, waiting for her. The look on his face stopped her in her tracks, and her feeling of calm stalled as she waited for him to speak.

"The Hennepin County Medical Center just called for you. Adrian woke up this morning."

She had been trying to keep Adrian out of her mind since she'd left the hospital, and it had started to work, but in an instant, it all flooded back. She was overcome with memories of him: the sight of him in the hospital bed, the sound of his voice, his bright blue eyes, his surprising sense of loyalty.

"He's awake?" she stammered. "Did they say anything else?"

"No. Just that he woke up and asked for you."

"Okay," she said as she tried to pull her thoughts together. "Okay. I need my purse, and Rena's keys."

"Way ahead of you," Arnold said as he handed them to her, along with a bottle of water and a granola bar.

"Okay," she said again as she turned to the car.

"Shaka," Arnold yelled after her. She turned around

abruptly. "He's not going anywhere. Drive safe and get there in one piece!"

"I will, Grandpa."

"Okay," he echoed. "Love you."

"Love you too!" she said and ran to the car.

She did get there in one piece, but narrowly. She was speeding the entire way, and once she got into the city, she was cutting people off almost every time she changed lanes. She was oblivious to all of this; her mind was already in the hospital room with Adrian.

When she finally reached the hospital, she was so full of hope and fear as she walked in that her hands shook, and she had to stuff them in her pockets to keep them still. She walked quickly down the long hallways, avoiding the eyes of those she passed. She wouldn't be slowed by having to stop and return someone's greeting.

When she saw the door to his room, her pace quickened, but when she reached his doorway, she froze. She stood silently just outside of his room for a moment and looked at him. She had been afraid to let herself imagine this moment, but if she had, it would have looked exactly like this. He was sitting up and looking out the window, unaware of her presence. There was no ventilator in the room, there was no beeping of a heart monitor. There was just the voice of Richard Dreyfuss coming from the TV where *Jaws* was playing, and then Adrian released a soft, familiar sigh, and Shaka knew he was really okay. She stepped into his room, and he looked at her for the first time.

"Shaka," he said in what sounded like disbelief.

She embraced him, and they held on to each other as if the moment might be snatched away from them.

"You knew I wouldn't leave you, right?" Adrian said.

"I know now," she said. "And I won't doubt you again." She rested her head on his chest, his whiskers softly scratching her skin. Shaka shut her eyes and let herself feel his warmth, the weight of his arms as they wrapped around her, as she listened to the steady drumming of his heart. He knew what she was, and he was unafraid. She realized that her story was changing.

CHAPTER FORTY-EIGHT

FOUR MONTHS LATER

RENA WAS BECOMING A WELL-KNOWN CONTRIBUTOR TO the Duluth art scene. She had completed a new series and was displaying it in a gallery downtown. Shaka had promised to come to her opening, and Adrian had been ordered to attend by Salem, his new boss. The opening was on a Saturday afternoon, and the air was crisp with the scents of fall.

After returning from the hospital with Adrian, Shaka had found that her urge to shift and run through the woods never really diminished. She also missed her grandfather when she was at home in Duluth. He rarely came south of Two Harbors. One month after Adrian came home from the hospital, she moved out of her apartment and into her grandfather's cabin. He welcomed her decision, but quickly got to work building an addition; the one-bedroom cabin now needed two bedrooms. He worked quietly and steadily. Shaka helped him whenever she could, though he never asked. She could tell it gave him purpose and focus. After his years in captivity, he needed something to do to remind himself that he was still a capable person.

Though he did a good job of hiding it, Shaka could see that the experience had left him shaken, more fearful than the man she'd known as a child. On a good day, he'd accompany her to Two Harbors, and his good days were growing in frequency, but he didn't like to leave the woods. Shaka wondered if he would ever come to a city the size of Duluth again. That's why she wasn't surprised when on the day of Rena's art opening, he'd told her to give her his apologies, but he would not be making it.

"I will," she said, though she knew Rena wasn't really expecting him to come anyway.

Shaka had cashed out the last of her savings and bought a little pickup truck. She needed her own transportation now that she was living so far from civilization, and more importantly, she needed to get to work. She hated to do it, but she had left her job at the grille and started a new one cooking at a café in Two Harbors. It paid less, but she got to run the little kitchen, and the owner had mentioned retiring in a couple years. From her first paycheck, she started saving money with the hopes that one day she could buy the café and have a place of her own.

In a small black dress she thought fitting for an art show, she drove the rough roads into Two Harbors. When she got into town, she pulled in the driveway of a small white house that looked out on the Great Lake. The wind was always blowing, but the view was beautiful. She honked her horn in the driveway, and Adrian came out. He was dressed in black slacks and a white dress shirt with the sleeves rolled up. He had a leather messenger bag slung over his shoulder. She hoped that didn't mean he was planning to work during the art show.

He smiled at her, then looked out at the lake. As he squinted with the wind blowing his hair out of his face and his shirt against his chest, Shaka felt a thrill run through her. They hadn't spent much time apart after they'd left Minneapolis. After she decided to move in with her grandfather, Adrian decided if she was going to live up the shore, so was he. He'd bought the little house from a coworker who had wanted to use it as a getaway cabin, but rarely left the city. It was half an hour from both Adrian's work and Shaka's cabin, so when his coworker mentioned wanting to sell, Adrian had seized the opportunity quickly.

Adrian slid into her truck and leaned over to kiss her. As

always, he smelled like soap and sandalwood. Shaka wanted to pull him in for a deeper, longer kiss, but they were already running late. It was her fault. She found it harder and harder to be punctual.

"Are you sure," he whispered in her ear, "that this thing will make it to Duluth?"

"That's not for you to worry about, boyfriend," she teased as she pulled out on to the highway and turned toward the city.

Rena had been busy these last few months. Her new paintings were different from the others, and they left most people puzzled as to where she had gotten her inspiration. The first painting Shaka saw was of an Ojibwe man who held out his arm for an owl to perch on. It was night in the painting, and the man was lit with moonlight. It was clearly Winston, but younger and with longer hair that trailed down his back. He was beautiful. Shaka had thought Rena hated Winston, yet this painting suggested admiration. It was titled *The Lucky Strike*. Shaka smiled when she read it.

Beside that painting was one of Shaka's grandfather. At first glance, he was just an old man with a gray ponytail, but there was something arresting about him. His pant legs were rolled up to his shins, and he stood ankle-deep in the rushing water of a stream. He looked straight out at the viewer with piercing eyes, as if both welcoming and challenging whoever looked upon him. The painting had power. She felt it captured his spirit perfectly.

"Shaka!" Rena called as she walked over to her with a wine glass in her hand. "I'm so glad you came! I mean, you had to come, or I'd have killed you...but still."

"I wouldn't miss it!" Shaka replied. "This is amazing," she said as she motioned to the painting of her grandfather.

"Yes, thank you. I'm just glad he isn't here. I have a feeling he would hate it."

"Yeah, well, his idea of art is a wood carving of a duck."

"Did you see yours yet?" she asked.

"No. You made one for me?"

"Obviously. I want to watch your reaction when you see it for the first time," she said. "It's this way."

Shaka followed her to the center of the room. Three people stood in front of a large painting, blocking their view. When they stepped out of the way, Shaka's jaw dropped.

"Adrian already offered to buy it, but I told him to forget it."

The painting was almost eight feet high. It was a picture so true to her features that she almost felt like she was looking at a photo of herself. Her body faced the viewer, but her face looked over her bare shoulder to the dark woods. She wore a white dress that was torn and tattered. From the bottom of the dress, her thighs began as her own, but faded into black fur near the knees and grew slender, ending in wide, wolf paws. An oily black tail wrapped out from behind her, growing wider and fuller until it tapered to an end a few inches from the ground. Wolves circled her, some lying down, some howling. The title was *Diana of the Forest.*

"Wow, Rena! I feel like you're in love with me or something," Shaka said with a grin.

"Does that mean you like it?" she asked.

"Yes. It's amazing."

"Okay. Good. I was worried that it would be too much. Other people seem to like it though."

"Thank you," Shaka said and hugged Rena. "For seeing me like this."

When she let her go, she glanced over at Adrian. He was standing beside Salem, who was talking to him, though Adrian was looking at her. He nodded toward the painting and smiled. Shaka grinned at him, then she noticed someone walking in behind them. It was Winston and Michal. They both looked nervous. Shaka hadn't expected to see them; she had lost touch with Winston soon after they escaped. With her living in the woods north of Two Harbors, their paths hadn't crossed.

Winston was wearing a brown tweed suit coat with leather lapels, a white shirt, and jeans. Michal wore jeans with a tucked-in basketball jersey. Shaka thought they were the most authentic people there. She walked over to Winston and hugged him without even saying hello.

"Shaka," he said. "You look great."

"So do you."

"Where's the picture of my dad?" Michal asked her.

"Right this way," she said and led them both to *The Lucky Strike.*

"Whoa," said Michal. "Is that what you used to look like?"

"Something like that," Winston answered. "Who knows, that might be you in a few years, buddy!"

"How is she?" Shaka asked.

"Better," he said.

Shaka hadn't seen Rachel since they'd broken out of the lab, but she thought about her often.

"Progress is slow, but it's still progress," he added. "She isn't sleeping all day anymore. Yesterday she even went outside. Baby steps, I suppose."

"It's different for everyone. It will just take time, Winston. She'll come back though."

"Yes, just not all the way, I'm afraid."

"We're all different now," Shaka reflected.

"And how's he?" he asked as he pointed to the painting of Arnold.

"He's well. He's happy, as long as he doesn't have to leave

his cabin. But I bet he would come to see Rachel, if you think it might help her."

"Yes, I think she'd like that. She says he was the only kindness she knew in there."

A woman walked up to them with a serving tray of champagne flutes and offered them both one.

"Will you say hello to Adrian?" she asked.

"I suppose an apology is probably overdue. I was awful to him, and then I heard he was almost killed on the day of the escape."

"Yes, it was bad. He's better now though." She turned to face Adrian and found him watching the two of them. He raised his glass in cheers and they raised theirs in reply, then walked toward him.

"Hello, Winston," he said as he offered his hand.

Winston took it. "Hello Adrian. I've been meaning to thank you...for being who you said you were. I'm sorry I didn't trust you."

"You're welcome and forgiven, Winston. I think you reacted better than I would have if the tables had been turned. And if you hadn't gotten the Fishers involved, we'd still be in there, so thank you too."

"All right, now who's got the shots?" Salem said.

"Easy, Plumpy," Rena said as she snuck in beside him. "It's an art opening, not a frat party."

"It could be though!" Salem said as he threw his head back and laughed. "Now you must be Mr. Lucky Strike," he said, turning to Winston. "I don't think we've met, but it seems my girlfriend is in love with you." He laughed again, the sound filling the room.

"Winston," Winston said as he offered Salem his hand.

v"Winston, welcome," he said, shaking it.

Shaka looked from face to face in the circle she stood in. Everyone looked happy. Michal laughed at everything Salem said, and this seemed to make Winston warm to him a little. Rena was shining. Patrons stopped by to tell her how much they loved her work. One painting after another sold as the night went on, until almost all of them were spoken for. Two women had bid the price of *The Lucky Strike* up to $2,500 before it sold. A young man had bought the picture of Arnold. Shaka thought it would give him something to aspire to.

When the night ended, every painting had sold except for Shaka's. As the guests filtered out, Shaka found Rena and stood beside her.

"You sold all but one. That's incredible, Rena!"

"Thanks. But to be more accurate, I sold them all. I wanted to tell Adrian to forget about it when has asked to buy yours, but money talks. Yours was the first to sell."

Shaka looked at Adrian. He was talking to Winston. She could hear just enough to decipher what they were talking about. "The champagne must be getting to him," she said with a giggle. "He's digressed to talking about cars."

"Then he needs food," Rena answered. "Everyone who's still here, dinner is on me!" she announced.

"See, I knew you were going to do that," Salem said as she grabbed Rena by her waist and kissed her.

They filed out of the gallery and walked down the street in a perfectly mismatched group. For the first time since she could remember, Shaka wasn't preoccupied with guarding her secret, and she'd never felt so free. Different as they were, these were her people, and nothing felt better than to be among them.

THE END

EPILOGUE

THE WOODS WERE LISTENING TO HER. SHAKA felt the air stall around her as the wild sounds were swallowed up in a great paralyzed silence. They didn't know that she was only playing at being a wolf, but to be fair, she had become quite convincing. She looked like a wolf, she smelled like a wolf, and she behaved like a wolf. She just didn't eat like one—at least, not until recently. After she'd killed her first deer in the woods outside of Duluth, she'd sworn off that kind of pointless killing. She'd changed back just to have her stomach do flips until her body finally ejected the meat. A waste of a life, she'd thought. But she'd changed since then, since she'd met the others in the Wyoming wilderness. They had found her while she and Adrian were on vacation, and they had taught her how to be a wolf, not a woman who becomes a wolf. She stopped thinking of death in philosophical terms rather quickly. Killing was just what wolves did.

When she and Adrian returned home, she found it impossible to explain how she felt to people who didn't share her gift. Sometimes she would return to her grandfather's cabin after a run, covered in dirt and blood, and find Adrian sitting with her grandfather by the fireplace. The anxiety in his eyes never escaped her when he saw her in this state.

"Did you have a good run?" her grandfather would ask.

"It was wonderful!" she'd say and watch as Adrian forced a nervous smile. He wouldn't relax until she showered and looked like a normal woman again. She suspected he had hoped that after she moved into the woods with her grandfather, she would settle down a bit, maybe reserving her ability to shape-shift for full moons or other celestial events. But it was the opposite: she found herself shape-shifting every day. She loved Adrian; there was no denying that. But whenever he looked at her that way, she felt something she'd hoped was in her past: shame.

Now Adrian was hundreds of miles away, and she felt no shame, only the fearless power of a predator as she and the others found their positions around their next kill. She lowered herself to the ground and crept toward the small elk in front of her. When he froze, so did she. He stood like a statue, his big ears flicking from side to side. Shaka glanced to her left and caught the eye of the wolf beside her. They spoke without sound or movement. She held her position. Then, when the elk turned his head back to the pine boughs he was eating, four wolves leapt from the woods, and in seconds they were on top of him, pulling him kicking and bleating to the ground. The alpha sank his long teeth into the elk's neck and held him by the throat as he struggled. The elk thrashed, but soon weakened, and within minutes, he was still, and his eyes grew glassy. The alpha ate the best parts. If anyone else wanted them, they had better be ready for a fight.

Shaka and the others bit and ripped at the back legs, snarling at one another if they got too close. The warm blood felt good on her snout, and the scent invigorated her. She was filled with a primal joy, a feeling of absolute belonging. She threw her head back and howled. Her companions raised their heads and joined her. The song of the night belonged to them, and as she sang, the human buried deep inside of her recognized that there was a distinct difference between being accepted and being understood.